THE MAN
MADE OF
SMOKE

THE MAN MADE OF SMOKE

A NOVEL

ALEX NORTH

CELADON
BOOKS

NEW YORK

THE MAN MADE OF SMOKE. Copyright © 2025 by Alex North. All rights reserved. Printed in the United States of America. For information, address Celadon Books, a division of Macmillan Publishers, 120 Broadway, New York, NY 10271.

Designed by Michelle McMillian

ISBN 9781250757890

For Lynn and Zack

THE MAN MADE OF SMOKE

It could be anywhere, this place.

A rest area in the countryside, just off the motorway. There's a low-budget hotel on one side of the car park, gas pumps on the other. Inside the single-story building at the far end, there is a food counter, a shabby amusement arcade, and a shop with snacks and newspapers and a selection of bestselling books. Outside the entrance, a van is selling flowers. The bunches rest in battered metal buckets, wilting in the afternoon heat.

After parking, the man sits in the darkness of his van for a time.

Then he gets out and walks slowly toward the main building.

The first witness to see him is a teenager dressed in creased kitchen whites, who is leaning against the wall of the hotel, smoking a cigarette. Hours later, he will give the police the same vague description as others who are present here this afternoon. The man is tall. Long green coat; dirty jeans; work boots thick with dried mud. The teenager will mention brown tufty hair, and a sun-weathered face. But the main thing he will remember is a sense of threat that he can't quite put into words.

"He was someone you don't want to look at," he tells the police.

The man stops briefly at the flower van. A young woman is working inside. From behind the counter, she can really see only the man's upper body, and so she wouldn't be able to describe his face even if, like the young man outside the hotel, she had been prepared to look at him for long enough.

She will be clear about the words, at least.

"Nobody sees," the man says. "And nobody cares."

Inside the main building, the man approaches the food counter and stands there for a moment without ordering. Another teenager is working there, but he's too busy and distracted to pay the man much attention.

He's scanning the racks of burgers and hot dogs wrapped in greasy paper, making a mental count. A smart kid, this one. He's only been there for two weeks, but he knows what sells and when, and has been trying to get the guy working the grills in the back up to speed.

"Nobody sees," the man says. "And nobody cares."

The middle-aged man in charge of the arcade catches only a glimpse of him, because he's concentrating on a boy who wants to come in and play on the machines. It's gambling, so adults only. If you ask him, it's stupid to have an amusement arcade when you know there are going to be families coming in and kids running loose, but nobody asks him. He seems to spend half his life telling children that they can't come in. That's something he'll think about a lot after today.

The man enters the shop next, loitering in the aisles for a minute before leaving. The teenage boy behind the counter barely notices him; he's keeping an eye on a kid he suspects of being a potential shoplifter. At home, this teenager is obsessed with true crime, and spends a lot of his time reading lurid accounts of serial killers, the more violent the better. In the years to come, this afternoon will loom large in his memory.

"Nobody sees," the man says. "And nobody cares."

It's not really true. After today, a great many people will care. They will watch the television coverage, read the newspaper reports, and scan the websites. A few years from now, they will buy copies of *The Man Made of Smoke* by Terrence O'Hare, billed as the definitive account of the Pied Piper killer and the children he took away.

But right now, I suppose, the man is correct.

Finally, he walks down the concourse toward the back of the rest area, where the crowd is sparse and the lights are flickering.

And he waits.

"Why are we stopping?" my mother said as the car slowed.

"Snack situation evaluation."

My father craned his neck to look back at us.

"Plus, I feel like stretching my legs a little. That okay with the troops?"

"Fine by me," I called.

"Me too," Sarah said.

Sarah was sitting beside me on the back seat of the car. We were both twelve, and my dad and hers had been friends once, before he left the island for somewhere better. While my family didn't have much money, Sarah's mother had next to nothing, and my parents often brought her with us on days out like this. We had been friends for a long time. When we were eight or nine, I remembered she'd knock excitedly on the door every morning in the summer holidays.

Want to go on an adventure, Dan?

Which I always did. Sarah was pretty cool for a girl, I thought. We both liked the same superhero comics and TV shows, and exploring the woods on the island, and we insulted each other horribly, even though we'd never let anyone else get away with it. But in the last six months or so, I'd started to feel a little awkward around her. I wasn't sure how to describe it. It was as though the two of us had spent years playing a game for fun, whereas it was beginning to feel like it was developing new rules I didn't understand. That there were things I wanted to say that I didn't have the words for yet.

My father took the turnoff for the rest area.

My mother said nothing. Which meant that she didn't approve. She probably figured we were only an hour away from the island, so why not keep going? My mother was a woman who was always impatient to be somewhere else, even when she'd just arrived. When I think back to those times, it felt like she never knew what to make of me, as though a family had formed around her by accident. When she was frustrated with me, she'd tell me that I was *just like my father*, and I wouldn't know how to take that. It wasn't true, for one thing. But it also seemed like it should have been a good thing if it was, and yet she never seemed to mean it that way.

We parked.

"Careful getting out your side, Daniel," my father said.

"Yeah."

I glanced to my right.

The spaces here were narrow, and my father had parked close to the vehicle beside us. It was an old camper van. The sides were streaked with dirt, as though it had spent its long life being driven back and forth through fields without ever once being cleaned. There was a rusted metal grille screwed over the black window in the side. Staring at the glass behind it was like looking into a night sky: a kind of fathomless darkness dotted with pale, misty constellations of mold.

I edged carefully out of the car.

The space was so tight that my elbow almost touched the grimy side of the van, which made my skin crawl slightly. The vehicle seemed to tower over me, and the shadow it cast felt colder than it should. As I moved to the front, I noticed there were patterns in the dirt along the bottom of the van that looked like children's handprints.

The metal was ticking slightly in the heat.

The four of us walked across the tarmac and into the rest area. My father bought us sandwiches from the shop and then we sat in the small area next to the arcade, Sarah and I side by side across from my mother and my father.

"Did you enjoy the zoo, Sarah?" he said.

She nodded as she ate.

"Really did, Mr. Garvie. Thank you so much."

"Not at all. A pleasure to have you along. Right, my son?"

He looked at me. I had a mouthful of sandwich and used it as an excuse not to answer for a second.

I was thinking about what Sarah just said. Just as I had begun to think about her differently recently, I'd also started to look at her more: secretly and sideways, when she didn't realize. Maybe I was trying to catch sight of whatever it was that was changing between us. Regardless, my gaze had kept finding her today. Sarah loved animals more than anything; she could name all the birds on the island and even identify most of the tracks we found in the woods. So I'd imagined she would love the zoo. All those exotic creatures we never dreamed we'd get to see in real life.

But while she *had* seemed to be enjoying it at times, there were also moments when I'd seen her frowning a bit, a hint of sadness pinching her face as she stared into the enclosures. I wondered now if it hadn't been the animals she was looking at right then, but the cages.

Our friendship dictated that I should answer my father's question by saying something sarcastic and awful about her, but instead I found myself wanting to tell her something else.

I see you, maybe.

I care.

I swallowed the food.

"Honestly?" I said. "I thought the plan was to *leave* her there."

My mother looked shocked. "Daniel!"

"What?" I raised my hands. "We all agreed. No?"

Sarah kicked me under the table.

"At least the zoo would take me," she said. "I don't remember them having an enclosure for *rats*."

My mother shook her head.

Ten minutes later, we were done and it was time to leave. As my father took our rubbish to the bin, I thought of the journey ahead. An hour to the coast, then the ferry back to the island, and the small, ordinary world awaiting us there. It made my heart sink a little. As we walked toward the exit, I found myself dawdling behind the other three, reluctant to leave.

Ahead of me, my father looked so broad and strong. It was the opposite of how I thought of myself, but it felt like I might become that too if I tried. My mother: perhaps she would settle and stop searching for a place that could never be better, only different. And Sarah ... if the words I wanted to say to her were out of reach right now, perhaps it would only be a matter of time before I found them.

For a moment, it felt like all of that was possible.

I didn't know the term *liminal spaces* back then, but a part of me was already drawn to them: places that weren't starting points or destinations, but stopgaps a step sideways from reality, like the crossing points between worlds in a fairy tale. And a part of me recognized that I was in one right then. A place where magic could happen.

I didn't know that my mother was going to leave us before the end of the year. Or how badly my relationship with my father was about to fracture and shatter. Or that I would never tell Sarah how I felt. All I knew right then was that I didn't want to leave here and for this moment to end.

My father turned back.

"You okay, Daniel?"

"Yeah," I said.

I glanced behind me, back up the concourse. To where the crowds were sparse and the lights were flickering.

"I think I might just go to the toilet first," I said.

Coins clattering in the arcade; shouts from behind the food counter; mingled conversations. All that noise disappeared as I closed the door to the men's toilets and started down the corridor beyond. There was only the unsettling hum of the bulbs flickering overhead.

Old trails left by a dirty mop had dried on the tiled floor like swirls of faint, ghostly hair, and the air smelled stale. The hum from above me grew louder as I walked, and my heart started beating a little harder. It felt like I was entering a place in which I didn't belong yet, and I had to fight the urge to turn around and head back out. But that was stupid; I wasn't a little boy anymore. There was nothing here to be frightened of.

And then I heard someone whistling.

I faltered. The sound was coming from ahead of me, around the corner. It was neither casual nor mindless, clearly a deliberate and purposeful tune, and I recognized it from somewhere without being able to name it. It was familiar in an odd, unnerving way, as though I'd heard it in a dream, or a nightmare, or in some different life altogether.

Everything is fine, I told myself.

There's nothing to be scared of.

I reached the end of the corridor and turned to the right. The toilets were long and narrow, with four cubicles on the right-hand side, a urinal along the wall opposite, and a sink and mirror on the far wall. The door of the cubicle farthest from me was closed. The whistling was coming from whoever was in there, and a little boy was standing outside it.

The atmosphere had already put me on edge, but the sight of the boy made my breath catch in my throat. Because I felt it immediately: something wrong was happening here. The boy was small and skinny, wearing old clothes that were at least a couple of sizes too large, and which hung loosely off his thin frame. One of his cheeks was streaked with dirt. As he turned his head to look at me now, it seemed to move in slow motion. Along with the otherworldly whistling and the flickering light, I was suddenly convinced I was looking at a ghost.

Then I registered the expression on his face.

Terrified. Desperate.

His eyes begging: *please help me.*

The two of us stared at each other for what felt like an age, that whistled music continuing from behind the closed door. I held the boy's gaze, unable to break it. But I had no idea how to react. What to do or what to say. Nothing in my life so far had prepared me for the strangeness of this encounter.

I could see the fear on the boy's face.

Please help me.

And I wanted to. The boy was small and emaciated, and his expression reminded me of how I felt facing the bullies in the schoolyard, desperate for someone to come and help me, rescue me, make it stop. I had the uncanny sensation that I was looking into a fairground mirror, in which the reflection was only very slightly distorted. And I felt an immediate, deep connection to the boy. I knew that I had to help him.

But then the whistling stopped.

The silence lent an instant charge to the air. The urge to help shifted inside me, like an animal that had been frozen in headlights jerking back to life. All I knew for certain right then was that there was something dangerous on the other side of that closed door. That a monster was about to emerge, and I needed to get away from it as quickly as I could.

It was blind panic. I reacted without thinking, stepping into the nearest cubicle and pulling the door closed quickly. I clicked the lock down just as I heard the door at the far end of the toilets creaking open on its old hinges.

Then nothing aside from the hum of the lights.

I sat down as quietly as I could on the toilet seat, then lifted my feet off the floor, brought my knees up to my chest, and wrapped my arms around them. It was dark in the cubicle, but the door didn't go all the way to the ground. At the bottom, there was a letterbox of pale green light flickering weakly on the tiles.

I waited, my heart beating hard.

For a few seconds, there was nothing. But then I heard slow, purposeful footsteps, and I held my breath. A shadow broke the light beneath the cubicle door and stopped there. I stared down at the muddy tips of a pair of enormous, weathered work boots.

I heard slow breathing from the other side of the thin wood.

And then what sounded like fingernails tracing lazy circles on it.

"Nobody sees," a man's voice said.

I wanted to squeeze my eyes shut but I didn't dare. Instead, I looked down at the tips of his boots, not blinking. My vision began to sparkle.

Please, I thought.

Little dots of light danced in front of my eyes.

Please.

"And nobody cares."

The boots moved away.

I kept staring down at the gap. A few seconds later, a weaker shadow passed across the tiles: the boy, presumably, following silently and obediently behind. I waited until I heard the distant sound of the door back to the concourse opening and closing. Until all that remained was the pounding of my heart and the hum of the lights above.

Finally, I opened the door to the cubicle.

The toilets were empty now. But whoever had been outside the door had left something behind. There was a small square of white paper on the tiles of the floor, and without understanding how or why, I was sure that it had been placed there for me.

I reached down carefully, my hands shaking.

It was heavier than paper. Some kind of thin card. The back was perfectly white, but when I turned it over I realized it was a photograph.

It took me a second to make sense of what I was seeing.

And when I did, I began to scream.

PART ONE
DENIAL

One

Richard Barber's basement was cold and dimly lit. The redbrick walls were lined with old cobwebs, the air was filled with the slow, constant *plink* of dripping water from somewhere in the shadows, and rusty pipes ran down one wall from the ceiling to the floor. Between those pipes, set into the stone, was a wooden door with a metal handle.

He was staring at that now.

"I want you to know that you're safe, Richard," I said.

"I know."

"Nothing here can harm you. It's all in the past."

"I know," he said. "I trust you."

Richard was one of my patients. An average man in many ways, the type you would walk past on the street without giving a second glance to. The two of us were in the room at the hospital that I used for my one-to-one therapy sessions. Budgets were tight, but I had done my best to make this particular room as reassuring as possible. The walls were painted a calming shade of blue. The carpet was softer than the ones out in the halls. Years earlier, I had struggled into work with a plant pot balanced under each arm. Those now rested in the corners of the room, the plants having grown in the time since until they almost reached the ceiling.

There were two leather chairs, both of which reclined. As usual, I was sitting upright, with my notes on a clipboard on my knee, and Richard was practically horizontal. He was in a hypnogogic state right now, halfway between sleep and waking, with his eyes closed and his hands resting protectively over his stomach. It was important for him to be as relaxed as possible. Because whatever I'd achieved with the real life surroundings, I knew the room he was seeing in his mind right now was far from comfortable.

At the beginning of our therapy, I had asked him to imagine his mind was a house. In the months since, we had walked through many of its rooms together, discussing the memories he found there.

I was conscious that he would only open the easy doors at first: the ones that led into rooms that felt safe for him to be in, and to show to a guest. But like most people, Richard had much darker memories: ones his mind kept locked away out of sight. As we gradually established trust over time, he had allowed me deeper into his house, into rooms filled with abuse and trauma.

And finally, today, all the way down to the basement.

"Can you picture the door?" I said.

He nodded.

I glanced at the clock on the wall, the second hand moving silently. There were only ten minutes of our scheduled hour left, which left me with a dilemma: push forward or pull back? It had taken eight careful months to bring us this far, and if it took the same again for a breakthrough then that was fine. We both had all the time in the world.

But I wanted to know what was on the other side of the door.

"I'd like you to take hold of the handle," I said. "Do you think that you can do that, Richard?"

"Yes."

"How does it feel?"

"Scary." He grimaced, his eyes still closed. *"Sharp."*

"I know. You don't have to turn it if you don't want to."

"But it's safe?"

"Yes," I said. "There's nothing in there that can hurt you anymore."

"It feels like there is."

"Because it's like a splinter underneath your skin," I said. "Eventually you get so used to it that you forget that it shouldn't hurt. And even if removing the splinter is painful at the time, it might help eventually. It's the only way to heal."

I set the hypocrisy I felt to one side. This wasn't about my own splinters or doors. I had to concentrate on my patient, especially given what might happen next. The things Richard had already described to me were terrible enough. It was difficult to imagine how much worse the deeply buried memory waiting for him here might be.

"I understand," he said. "I'm turning the handle now."

"That's good, Richard. I'm here."

A few seconds of silence. Then he frowned.

I said, "Where are you, Richard?"

"I'm on a pier."

"At the seaside somewhere?"

He nodded slowly, but he was still frowning to himself, as though he couldn't make sense of what he was seeing. Whatever it was, it didn't appear to be obviously traumatic, and that seemed to have taken him aback a little.

"I'm on the promenade," he said. "I think that's what it's called. It's wooden, anyway. There are amusement arcades on the other side of the road. And on this one, there's some bollards. There's steps down to the beach and the sea."

Knowing his history, I considered my next question carefully.

"Are you on holiday with your family?"

"No," he said. "Just my mother."

I made a note in my file. As a child, Richard had been the victim of violence at the hands of various men who had drifted in and out of his mother's life. As far as I knew, she herself had never hurt him. It was interesting to me that, even after everything he'd been through, he still thought of *family* as requiring one of those abusive men to be present.

"Can you see anything else?" I said.

His demeanor changed suddenly. His face contorted.

"It's the ice-cream van," he said.

"Nothing here can hurt you, Richard."

"I'm not scared of it." He shook his head. "It makes me *angry*."

I looked down at his hands. His fists were clenched now.

"That was how it made you feel at the time," I said. "But it's important to remember that you're not there anymore. You're looking at this from the outside now, and you don't need to feel anything at all about what you're seeing. You are calm. You are detached."

His expression settled a little.

"What is it about the van that made you angry?" I said.

"It's not the van. There's a big queue for it, and I know we don't have the money anyway. I asked my mother earlier and she said no."

"Why are you angry then?"

"There's a girl standing beside it. I don't like her."

"What does she look like?"

"She's only little. Maybe five or six. She has a white T-shirt on, and these jeans with suspenders that go over her shoulders. Red shoes."

I made a note in my file, and then asked a question to which I wondered if I already knew the answer.

"What about her hair?"

"Long," he said. "Black. Curly."

"Why don't you like her?"

"She's looking at me." His fists clenched harder. "She's with her mum and dad. Her dad has *his fucking hand* on her shoulder. Just resting gently there. And she's eating an ice cream. She's looking at me, and when she sees me looking back, she *smirks* at me."

I wondered if that was true.

Perhaps the little girl had simply smiled. It was even possible that she hadn't noticed him at all, and that the sight of a happy child with an ice cream and a loving family had been enough to embed itself into Richard's mind. But in a sense it wasn't important whether it was actually true. What mattered was that it was true to him.

"I want you to relax," I said.

He frowned.

"I don't know what it means though."

I glanced at the file on my knee. It would be facile—ludicrous—to imagine that this brief encounter with a little girl as a child had led Richard, decades later, to commit murder, even if all three of his victims had been women with black, curly hair. And yet this memory had been here all these years, locked away behind a door in the basement of his mind.

The hour was nearly up; it was time to bring Richard out of his mild trance and call for the orderly to escort him back to his cell.

I don't know what it means though.

"Neither do I," I said. "But perhaps we can find out together."

Back in my office, I sat down at my desk and typed up my notes on that morning's session. When I was finished, I opened a separate document on the computer to record my personal thoughts. That was a habit I'd fallen into over the years. I found it helpful to work through my feelings and impressions in a more abstract and unguarded fashion. The knowledge that nobody else would ever read them freed me to speculate and get my thoughts into some kind of order.

> It is interesting to note how an event that becomes formative for a patient might appear utterly inconsequential to an observer. We can never know the importance of our actions, however small and innocent they might seem. An interaction that, for us, is gone in a heartbeat might be something that another person finds impossible to forget.

I leaned back in my chair.

The incident Richard had described to me was utterly trivial. Brief eye contact with a stranger. Perhaps a smile of some kind. It was something that happened millions of times every day, and which most people would barely register. Assuming the little girl was real, I doubted she would have any recollection of what happened that day, or any idea of the influence it might have had. Equally, I might have expected Richard, as an adult, to take his anger out on men who resembled the ones who had abused him. And yet it was the random image of this girl that had lodged in his mind.

I don't know what it means though.

And that was the rub.

Richard Barber's childhood contained a number of markers that were familiar to me from the offenders I saw. Poverty. Neglect. Abuse. Addiction. Those factors were so disproportionately represented in the prison population as a whole as to be unremarkable.

But they were not, of course, predictive in reverse. While people who went through extremely traumatic experiences in childhood would almost certainly carry issues into adulthood, the vast majority became decent, well-adjusted adults.

We are shaped by our pasts, not defined by them.

It was important to remember that.

I leaned forward again, about to continue typing, but then the phone on my desk rang. I looked away from the screen, irritated by the distraction. The light for reception was blinking on the handset.

I picked it up.

"Dr. Daniel Garvie," I said.

"Hi Dan—Myra here. I have a call for you. Gentleman on the line who says it's urgent. He's been trying your mobile but hasn't been able to reach you."

"Thanks, Myra," I said. "Can you put him through?"

"No problem."

She disappeared from the line.

"Dr. Daniel Garvie?"

The man's voice was gruff but familiar.

"Yes." I switched hands with the phone. "Who is this, please?"

"It's Detective Liam Fleming."

For a brief moment, the lights seemed to flicker.

"I'm afraid I have some bad news about your father," he said.

Two

I stood outside on the passenger deck of the ferry.

The sea ahead was gray, the water ridged like mud, the ferry was churning white froth steadily out to the sides, as though plowing a field. The wind was as cold as ice, but I leaned on the railing and forced myself to endure it. The enormous hum of the engines vibrated in the air, a sound and a feeling all at once.

You are detached, I thought.

You are calm.

Ever since the phone call yesterday, while I made the necessary arrangements, I'd been trying to keep my thoughts and emotions under control. But it was harder now. The half-hour ferry trip back to the island offered far too much empty time in which to think.

The coastline appeared at the horizon, and I leaned back from the railing, as though by doing so I could stop it approaching. The stretch of land was as thin as hair at first, but quickly grew larger, the island like a monster crawling through an ever-widening crack.

The main village was postcard-perfect in the afternoon sun. But most ports look pretty from the sea, and as the ferry juddered inexorably toward the terminal, my gaze found the peeling paint on the walls of the shopfronts. The closed stores and boarded-up windows. The day drinkers gathered together by the war memorial in the square. If the island looked nice from a distance, it was only because that was the best place to see it from.

There was always a sense of dread when I came back here. Any good memories of this place were tainted by bad ones, and at this point on the journey it always felt like I was returning not just to a place but also a time.

And today, that feeling was much worse than usual.

I have some bad news about your father.

As we arrived, I headed inside into the cheap lounge and queued up for the rickety metal stairs. The stone ground beneath the body of the ferry was stained with oil and strewn with coils of dirty rope. The air stank of petrol, but that smell faded as I stepped out into the cold afternoon air and followed the other passengers through the maze of railings. Gulls wheeled overhead and the water lapped insistently against the mossy wooden posts lining the dock.

A short walk through the cobbled streets to the police station.

I stopped outside, momentarily reluctant to open the door. That would be when all this became real. Instead, I took a few seconds to stare at the building. The sandstone walls; the peaked roof; the old blue lantern by the door. It was all exactly as I remembered. Easy to imagine that, if I were to turn and look at the low wall across the road behind me, I might see a shade of my younger self sitting there, kicking his heels after school and waiting for his father to leave work.

I pushed the heavy door open.

The layout of the foyer had barely changed. There was a seating area to the right, basic, a little grubby, and—because crime on the island was scarce—as empty right now as I remembered it usually being. Some of the informational flyers on the wall looked so old that they might have been relics from back then.

I rang the buzzer at the desk.

A man emerged from the back half a minute later. He was about my age, which meant we had probably grown up here at roughly the same time. But I didn't recognize his face or the name on his badge.

"Daniel Garvie," I told him. "I have an appointment to see Liam Fleming."

Which was a name I had recognized.

Fleming was a couple of years older than me, and the two of us had had plenty of encounters, in and out of the playground, when we were younger. It hadn't surprised me when I'd learned he'd gone into the police. Some men—and my father had been one—were drawn to the job because they wanted to do good and make a difference, but the power of the job inevitably attracted its share of bullies too. People could change, of course. But my father had worked with Fleming, and I knew well enough that he hadn't.

The desk sergeant buzzed me through and then walked me to Fleming's office. It was a small, cluttered room, with filing cabinets lining the walls and piles of paperwork scattered everywhere. Fleming stood up as I entered. He was much as I recalled him from our teenage altercations: tall and broad, albeit with a bit of a paunch now. He had the kind of build that suggested a visit to the gym every so often, but probably not regularly. His hair was shaved all the way down to the skull. I wondered if it was meant to give him an image of authority or it was simply because it was beginning to desert him.

"Daniel."

He held out a hand and I took it. Even though his tone of voice was professional and formal, I braced for an overly tight grip—a show of strength— but it didn't quite come.

"Liam," I said.

"I'm sorry you're back here in these circumstances."

"Yes," I said. "I am too."

He gestured. "Please sit down."

My work had ingrained in me the habit of analyzing people, and so I considered his tone of voice and choice of language. *Please sit down.* It had been slightly more of an order than a suggestion, and a part of me bristled. But the playground was a long way behind us. I took the seat across the desk from him.

"Not as grand as you're used to, I'm sure," Fleming said.

"I'm sorry?"

"The office." He waved at the mess around us. "I imagine yours must be pretty impressive."

I pictured the psychiatric ward, with its heavy doors, and the single plexiglass window in my office that faced down one of the three corridors. My office was smaller than this, and not much tidier. It smelled of cleaning product. When I arrived in from the fresh air each morning, it always felt like passing through an air lock between the outside world and the very different worlds of the men confined in the rooms around me.

"I work in a prison," I said.

"Really?" He looked surprised. "I thought you were a *profiler*, or whatever they call it these days. Catching killers with your mind, all that stuff? I imagined there'd be couches. Books everywhere."

"Not really," I said. "Most of my job involves looking after my patients. By the time I meet them, they've already been caught."

"Patients?" He gave me a pointed look. "These are killers, right?"

"Some of them."

"Rapists. Guys who've hurt kids."

"Some of them."

He whistled to himself.

"It must be hard talking to people who've done things like that. Especially after what happened to you all those years ago."

I held his gaze.

"Not really. And right now, I want to talk about what's happening here."

He stiffened a little at that. Then he seemed to shrug to himself, as though he'd attempted to be friendly and just been rebuffed, but it didn't matter to him much either way.

"The coastguard is still searching," he said. "The boats are probably out there as we speak. But it's been two days now. I don't want to be brutal, but you probably remember what the tide is like around the island."

"You don't need to worry about being brutal," I said.

"I just want to be sensitive."

"I understand," I said. "You don't need to do that either. What I want is for you to talk me through the timeline."

More of an order than a suggestion.

Fleming stared at me for a second.

"Yeah," he said slowly. "Sure. We found his car at the Reach."

The island rose steeply to the northeast, like a shoe turned at an angle. At the heel, it was over a hundred meters down to the sharp rocks and angry sea below, and one section of the cliff there jutted out farther than the rest. That was what gave the Reach its name, even if you would never see it called that in tourist pamphlets.

When we were kids, we used to dare each other to get as close to the edge as possible and, as Fleming spoke, I remembered standing out there.

Shivering.

Scared.

The height making me dizzy.

"It was Craig Aspinall who saw your father," Fleming told me. "You remember Craig?"

"Vaguely."

Aspinall was the same age as my father. I knew that he walked the trails a lot, an unofficial caretaker for the island's beauty spots. Picking up litter. Fixing signs and fences.

"Craig was out there a couple of days ago," Fleming said. "He recognized your father's car parked, and then came across him standing out there, close to the edge."

The two of them had exchanged pleasantries, Fleming told me. The conversation had been casual and Aspinall had had no reason to suspect anything might be wrong. But my father's car had still been there when Aspinall returned the next day. He had checked the door and found the vehicle unlocked. There was a folded piece of paper in the glove compartment, on which my father had written three words, along with my name and contact details.

Fleming passed me a piece of paper across the desk.

"Is this your father's handwriting?"

I read the words there—*Notify my son*—and then handed the paper back.

"Yes."

Fleming looked off to one side for a second. I knew what was coming.

"Do you have any idea why your father might—?"

"Kill himself?" I said. "No."

"Any health problems? Money worries?"

"Not that he ever mentioned to me."

Fleming waited. I matched his silence. The truth was that I wouldn't have been inclined to answer his questions even if I had been able to. I knew my father had felt isolated and aimless after retiring from the police last year, because it had been his life—as little as he might have felt that amounted to, stuck out here on the island. But that information seemed too personal to share with Fleming; my father would not have wanted me to. And in reality, it was no explanation at all. My father had seemed happy enough. Life had dealt him far harder blows than retirement in the past, and he had always rolled with them before.

"Well," Fleming said finally. "Like I told you, the coastguard is still searching. As I said, you know what the sea is like round here. His body could wash up on the rocks in the next few days. But it's also possible he'll never be found at all."

"Yes," I said. "I know that."

"Where will you be staying? In case we have news."

I thought about it.

"My father's house," I said.

Fleming insisted on walking me back to reception.

"So anyway," he said. "How's life working out for you? Married? Kids?"

I pictured my sparse one-bedroom flat. I had been alone there for a year, give or take, ever since Laura left. My last relationship had followed a predictable pattern. I never seemed to have much trouble meeting women, but offering them enough reasons to stay was a different matter.

"No," I said. "You?"

"No kids—not yet anyway. Partnered up, though. You remember Sarah from your year?"

I made sure not to miss a step.

The mention of her name was like a bruise I'd forgotten about: not pressed on for years now, and any real pain long dulled, but still surprisingly tender to the touch. After Sarah and I left for separate universities, we'd drifted apart, the way that people do, and I hadn't thought about her in a while. The last I remembered hearing, she'd been working on the mainland, having escaped from the island the way I knew she'd always dreamed of. But obviously something must have fallen through and she'd found herself back here.

It occurred to me that my father must have known that, and yet for some reason, he'd never mentioned it.

"I remember," I said. "Congratulations."

"Yeah, it's a good life. Nice job. Respect. Steady as she goes."

We reached the door to the reception.

"Seriously, though," Fleming said. "How do you do it?"

I waited.

"Those people you have locked up," he said. "Your *patients*, if you want to call them that. They've done the worst things a person can do."

"Yes."

"How can you bring yourself to talk to them like they're human beings?"

I thought about that.

It was a question that people asked me a lot, and I had sympathy with it. Richard Barber, for example, was a man who would never be released from prison, and I was sure many people thought he deserved to spend the rest of his days suffering for the damage he'd done. And it was difficult to argue with that. There were times when the details of my patients' crimes made me want to cry. Days when it felt like they crept home with me at night, and I could imagine them standing at the end of my bed in the darkness, whistling to themselves.

But however horrific their crimes might be, they *were* only human beings. It was important to remember that.

I pushed open the door.

"Because there's no such thing as monsters," I said.

Three

After leaving the police station, I followed the seafront around awhile, and then headed up the steep cobbled hill and along the country lanes that led farther inland. The smell of wild garlic hung in the air above the hedgerows, and the quiet was interrupted only occasionally by one of the few cars that traveled this back road.

Eventually I reached a cul-de-sac that ran a short distance into the woods. There were seven detached properties spread out along it. Three on one side; three on the other. The property at the far end was a wide, two-story log cabin, facing down the road with its back to the woods behind.

My father's house.

I stopped at the end of the driveway and looked up at the peaked roof of the converted attic. That had been my bedroom as a child, and I still slept there on my occasional trips to the island. The last time had been a few months ago, in May, because however much I hated returning here, I always made an effort to see my father on his birthday.

As usual, I had bought him a book as a present. In his older age, my father had become an avid reader. Mysteries and crime thrillers; he loved those. Not because they reminded him of his career in the police, but because they deviated from it. The stories were exciting and full of incident, the bad guy got caught at the end and justice was served. Real life was rarely that eventful. When it was, almost never so simple and satisfying.

The first thing I did when I was inside was make my way up to the attic, turning a few lights on as I went. I put my bag down on the single bed and looked around. The room had clearly been made up since my last visit, presumably in expectation of my return at some point.

Which forced the question:

How long had you been planning to do it, Dad?

Not a useful question right now, I decided.

Back down one floor, I let myself into his room.

After my mother left, my father spent the next summer knocking through three rooms on one side here, converting them into a single space that stretched the entire length of the property. At one end were his bed, wardrobes, and drawers. At the opposite end, his desk and shelves. In between was a rudimentary exercise area, with weights racked by one wall and a heavy leather bag hanging down on a chain from the ceiling.

When I was a teenager, he would spend whole evenings locked away in here, and the sounds I heard from behind the closed door had seemed to define the parameters of his life back then. Typing awkwardly on the computer. A monotonous thudding. And silence.

I walked over to the bag now and gave it a gentle push.

The chain creaked softly.

Finally, I moved over to my father's desk. The built-in shelves on the wall above housed his records: years of paperwork stored away in weathered ring binders and box files. Everyday police work on the island was dull, and at some point after I left for university, my father had channeled his energy into researching unsolved cases he found online.

Exciting, high-profile crimes.

I had no idea what he expected to achieve. A few years ago, on one of my visits back to the island, I'd asked him what he imagined he could find that all the more experienced investigators involved at the time had missed.

What did *he* bring to the table?

Brute force, he told me.

I'd rolled my eyes at that, and made some flippant comment about how he just wanted to be like the characters in the books he read. I didn't mean it badly—just a casual joke—but I remembered him looking at me strangely for a moment, and that I had regretted saying it. Then he'd laughed gently, and everything had been fine. But he'd never brought it up again after that.

There was a desktop computer and printer on the desk.

There was also a single sheet of paper. I picked it up and turned it over: a printed photograph. The resolution was poor, but decent enough for me to see that it was an image of my father, standing on a footpath in the woods with something in the undergrowth at his feet. The quality made it impossible to see what that was, but my attention focused naturally on my father. He was looking toward the camera, the expression on his face lost to blur. As I stared at the image, it was hard not to imagine that he was dissolving before me. That the photograph was developing in reverse before my eyes, becoming ever more faded and indistinct, until soon nothing would remain.

I blinked.

Then I headed downstairs.

The living room appeared undisturbed. My father had always been fastidiously tidy. He used to tell me that everything had a place in which it lived and, as far as I could tell, everything was living there now. The rows of books; the paperwork stored neatly on the shelf beneath the glass coffee table; the remote control in its place beside the television.

I knelt down and rubbed the carpet. It was freshly vacuumed.

The coffee table had been wiped clean recently.

I walked through to the kitchen. Again, everything was spotless. One by one, I opened the cabinets and drawers, finding plates and cups and cutlery that had been stored away carefully. A full jar of coffee sat next to the kettle on the counter. Beside it, there was a rack of herbs and spices, the bottles all turned so that their labels faced out.

The fridge was humming gently. I opened it and found it half full. My father cooked all his meals from scratch and shopped weekly. There was enough food here for at least three or four meals. He wouldn't have bought anything he wasn't planning to use, which suggested that, even just a few days ago, he had been anticipating that he would be here, standing where I was right now.

And then something had changed.

But what?

The question made me feel helpless. I wasn't sure what I'd been expecting, beyond that there should have been *something* here to help make sense of what had happened. Some clue as to his state of mind. And yet I could see no obvious indication of disorder or distress. Quite the opposite, in fact. The house had the feeling of a home whose owner had simply stepped out for a time.

I unlocked the back door and stepped out onto the decking.

Night had fallen now, and the long garden ahead of me was black, the hedge at the far end lost in darkness. To my right, two lounge chairs and a table were set out on the patio. During my last visit, on his birthday, the two of us had sat there drinking. It was always nice out back on an evening, especially in spring. Everything was quiet, and the air smelled of the woods beyond the hedge.

I had got through more bottles of beer than he had that night, but I remembered him chuckling, and there being a little sparkle in his eyes. He had been at least a little bit drunk. What had we talked about? I wasn't sure. Probably nothing much. Our relationship had become easier over the years, and the silences between us more comfortable. It was as though we'd both accepted that some of the doors between us were always going to stay closed, but that we could work well enough with the open spaces that we did share.

He'd seemed *content*.

I was sure of that much.

And yet, a couple of days ago, he had left this house, locked the door behind him, and then driven out to the Reach and done the unthinkable.

What had been going through his mind? It was a question that occupied me in my work, and I was usually good at explaining and predicting behavior. Making *sense* of things. But there was no case file to work with here, and no longer any patient to talk to.

I tried to picture my father alone in the car on that final journey. Had

he been scared? Was he crying? Did he doubt himself in those last few moments or did he act swiftly—decision made—and step easily off the edge?

I would never know.

Why didn't you talk to me, Dad?

The question tightened my throat.

Regardless of the difficulties we'd had in the past, I had imagined
our relationship had settled into one in which he would have felt able to
share whatever pain he was facing. It broke my heart to realize that had
not been true. For some reason, the weight he always prided himself on
bearing had become too heavy for him, and he had kept that from me.

In his final moments, my father must have felt utterly alone.

Ever since the phone call yesterday, I'd been keeping my emotions
shut away. I had been *detached*; I had been *calm*. They had become watchwords for me over the years, because I knew that emotions could be
dangerous, and that it was safer to keep the world at arm's length. But
now—alone in the dark and silent garden—I finally allowed a door inside me to open. Just a crack. But still enough for the feelings I kept so
carefully under control to come flooding out.

And with nobody around to see, I knelt down on the decking and
sobbed.

There was food in the fridge, but it felt too soon to use the kitchen, as
though the house itself should be allowed a period of mourning. After
I'd pulled myself together and washed my face, I walked back down to
the seafront.

I sat down on a bench by the water with a carton of fish and chips.
The night was cool and the food steamed in the air as I ate. The lights of
a few boats were scattered out in the dark water, but none of them would
be coastguard vessels. Assuming they were even still out at this hour, they
would be combing the coastline to the north. If my father's body was going
to wash up anywhere, it would be there. But the island's tides were capri-
cious; the sea here kept hold of things. The reality was that my father's
body might never be found, and I knew that I had to prepare myself
for that.

I wiped my hands with a napkin and put the rubbish in a nearby bin.

The silence that I knew would be waiting back at the house for me felt forbidding, and so I walked along the seafront for a time. There were pubs here, but the laughter from behind the clouded glass windows pushed me away. These weren't places to drink alone; if you went in by yourself, you wouldn't stay that way for long. I had no desire to encounter someone I half remembered from my childhood here. What I wanted, I realized, was more of a *liminal* space. Somewhere I could exist out of time and space for a while, and in which everyone else there had made a silent pact to do the same.

I headed round into an even more run-down stretch of the village. Most of the buildings were long boarded up, but eventually I heard the sound of music, and then saw soft light falling out of the open doorway of a bar ahead. The front was painted a dull blue color, with two dirty windows occluded behind metal grilles. Old cigarette ends lay scattered beneath a broken bin hanging half off the wall. The music coming from inside was karaoke: a woman singing a surprisingly respectable rendition of "Raspberry Beret."

I walked in.

The bar looked rough from the street, but while it had clearly seen better days, there was no underlying sense of threat. It was a long, narrow room, with a bar running the length of one wall and small tables with weathered stools crammed in against the other. There were maybe ten people inside, all elderly and sitting alone. I glanced to my right. The woman with the microphone was facing away from me, but the wording on the back of her shirt suggested she was one of the barmaids, keeping herself amused while the place was quiet.

Another woman was serving behind the bar. I bought a beer and sat down at one of the rickety stools there, swallowing the first mouthful of cheap lager quickly. And then the second. Because suddenly, the thought of getting a little bit drunk tonight was very far from the worst idea in the world.

The song finished, and there was a smattering of applause from the bar's patrons. I joined in, for what it was worth. The woman might not have been the best singer in the world, but at least she'd given it her all, and that always counted for something.

She punched the air happily.

"Thank you, Cleveland!"

Then she turned around.

And I felt my heart drop.

She was older than the image I had of her in my head. Of course she was. But even after all these years, I recognized her.

And she recognized me right back.

Sarah stared at me for a long moment. Then she blinked quickly and looked away. She lifted the gate on the bar and approached the woman serving there.

"Fiona," she said. "Can you cover for me for a bit?"

Four

We sat at a table all the way at the back of the bar.

"I'm sorry about your dad," Sarah said. "So sorry."

"Thank you."

"He was a good man. He was always very kind to me."

I nodded. I remembered the way he had made a point of including her. And also all the good times we'd had together as kids. She had been my best friend back then. Looking at her now, there was a little gray in her hair, and some crow's-feet emerging at the corners of her eyes, but she hadn't changed all that much. She was still beautiful, and it was easy to see the excited girl she had been back then.

Want to go on an adventure?

Before everything went to shit.

"He was," I said quickly. "He was a good man."

Which made me frown to myself. It was odd to be talking about my father in the past tense. But those were probably not words I would ever have spoken out loud in the present. I wasn't sure if the alcohol was hitting me more quickly than usual, but that air of calm and detachment I prided myself on felt a little looser around me right now.

"Maybe I should have told him that," I said.

"I'm sure he knew what you felt."

"I didn't see him enough. I didn't call as often as I should have done."
Sarah smiled sadly at me.

"Oh, Dan. You can't think like that."

"I can," I said. "I'm doing it right now."

"Yeah, okay. It really doesn't help, though. Believe me."

I nodded again. I'd repeated that same sentiment—*it doesn't help to blame yourself*—to clients outside the prison system countless times, or even just attempted to steer them toward recognizing the truth of it for themselves. But it was easy to offer advice from the outside. Right now, I found it difficult to take any comfort in the tentative relationship my father and I had built up in recent years. My mind kept returning to times when we were both younger and angrier, and letting each other down every day. When every disagreement between us had to be someone's fault.

I took another sip of my drink.

"Anyway," I said quietly. "What about you. Your mother?"

"She passed away last year. Cancer."

"I'm—"

"Sorry?" Sarah smiled sadly again. "You know what? Maybe we should both stop saying that and just take it for granted?"

"That might be an idea."

"And honestly, there's no need for you to be sorry." She looked down at her bottle, a thoughtful expression on her face. "She was sick for a long time. That's why I came back to the island: to look after her. Maybe I didn't come back soon enough, which is what I meant about blaming yourself. But I didn't know how sick she was. And obviously, who wants to come back here, right?"

"Right."

Sarah told me that she'd worked her way through various jobs after finishing university, but for the last few years had been settled at a charity for animals. I wanted to smile at that, remembering how she'd been able to identify tracks in the woods as a kid. She'd always had a passion for wildlife. It felt right.

"But when Mum got sick, I took compassionate leave," she said. "And they were good people there, honestly. There was an expectation that my position would be waiting for me, as and when I could go back. But then some things went south for them, financially, and they had to make a few difficult decisions, and one of them was me. Things were tight for me by then too. My mother had a lot of debt. And so here I am."

She took a mouthful of her own drink. The expression on her face suggested it tasted bitter.

"Here I am," she said again quietly. "Back where I fucking started."

I was about to reply, but a memory hit me: the last time I had seen her in person before now. Here on the island, the night before we both left for different universities. The gathering was a traditional one that happened every year: kids heading to a spot on the beach far away from the tourist areas, the police turning a blind eye as we all drank, played music, and danced around a bonfire so bright that it made everything around it seem pitch black and invisible, a small spot of light in the infinite dark.

Most people brought something to put on that fire. Notes they'd taken in hated classes; old school uniforms too worn to be passed down; report cards and detention slips. The symbolism was clear. We were all about to move forward into the various futures that awaited us, and so that night we would leave some of our past behind in ash on one of the island's beaches.

I had brought a book with me. It was called *The Man Made of Smoke*, the definitive account of the Pied Piper murders, and I had read it so many times that the pages were worn and feathery. I remembered sitting on the rocks, away from the others, turning it around in my hands. And at one point, I looked up and saw Sarah.

It was a cold evening, but she was wearing a bikini top and jeans, dancing barefoot at the side of the fire with a few other people. She was drunk and carefree, and she seemed so *happy*. The sight of her unraveled me. Everyone looks beautiful by firelight, of course, but she transcended that, and in that moment I knew that I loved her.

The loss ached inside me. There were so many things I could have said and done over the last few years. But my feelings for her were bound up in the horror of my encounter with the Pied Piper at the rest area. It had become impossible to look at her without reliving the fear and shame and guilt I'd felt that day. Safer not to look at all.

But it meant I'd missed so much.

So stand up, I thought.

I looked down at the book in my hands.

Put this stupid fucking thing on the fire and go and talk to her.

But I didn't. I just watched her dance, throwing her head back and laughing, the warm light of the fire playing across her face. The book had gone home with me at the end of the night, a weight in my coat pocket that it seemed I wasn't yet ready to leave behind. And as I lay in bed, I told myself that it was enough to know she was escaping from the island. That her life would be a good one, and better for not having someone like me in it.

Here I am.

Back where I fucking started.

"Not forever," I said.

"Yeah, we'll see."

I turned my bottle slowly on the table. Considering.

"I saw Liam earlier. He said you two are together now."

She grimaced.

"He told you that?"

"It's not true?"

"It's complicated." She put her drink down. "I mean, honestly. *Complicated.* If I was on Facebook, that would have been my relationship status for the last twenty years. But yeah, Liam and I were together for a while."

"Okay."

"Don't judge me, Dan." She gave me a pointed look. "Your options are pretty limited here on the island. And he does have some good qualities."

"I'm not judging you at all."

"But things are a little more . . . shall we say *nebulous* these days?" She sighed. "Look: can we leave it at that? I don't want to talk about it right now."

"Of course."

And I had no intention of probing further. But I couldn't help my mind going back to the conversation I'd had with Fleming earlier. He'd made a point of mentioning his relationship with Sarah to me, and he hadn't made it sound *complicated* or *nebulous* at all.

I wondered why. Did he see me as some kind of threat? That seemed ridiculous, given the reason I was back here, but I was also aware that he was the kind of man who viewed life in terms of dominance and territory. And in my experience, the weaker that type of man had a grip on what they thought was theirs, the more they felt a need to tighten it.

"I—"

But whatever I might have been about to say was interrupted by a sudden commotion by the door. I looked down the bar to see a large group of young men stumbling in, arms around each other. Already drunk; already rowdy.

Sarah slapped the table decisively.

"Ah," she said. "The evening begins. I'd better get back to the bar."

"Of course."

My drink was nearly finished, and things were clearly about to get lively, so I figured it was probably time for me to leave too. But as Sarah stood up, I found myself thinking about the questions that had bothered me back at my father's house.

"You told me he was good to you," I said quickly.

Sarah turned back.

"My father, I mean."

"Oh," she said. "Yes. Always."

"Did you see much of him recently? I was just wondering . . ."

I trailed off, unable to say it out loud.

Sarah knew what I was asking.

"I didn't see him all that much recently," she said. "But I did from time to time. And he seemed *fine*, Dan. His usual self. So if you're beating yourself up for not noticing that something was wrong, then trust me. I was here, and I saw him, and I didn't realize either."

"Okay," I said, relieved despite myself. "Thank you."

"And if what your father found bothered him . . . he didn't show it."

I started to say *thank you* again, ending the conversation on autopilot, but then caught what she'd just said.

"What he found," I repeated. "What do you mean?"

"Well, I imagine it shook him up a little." She hesitated. "And I think it was pretty bad, from what I understand. But your dad was police for a long time. Even here on the island, he'd seen worse—he told me that himself. He even said it was a good job that it was him who found her, rather than a tourist or someone."

I shook my head. I had no idea what Sarah was talking about.

"Found who?" I said.

She looked down at me for a second, confused, as though my question made as little sense to her as what she was saying did to me.

"The dead woman in the woods," she said.

Five

John looks up into the trees at the side of the trail.

"What do you want?"

The crow perched in the branches above him stares back, its head tilted to one side curiously. The bird is out of reach, but still close enough for him to see the petrol-purple sheen on its black wings and—just about—the glint of the early morning sun reflected in its eye.

What does it want? He knows the old stories about birds carrying the souls of the dead to the underworld. But while he'd like to believe in an afterlife, he doesn't. It's only wildlife doing what it does. Probably just waiting for its chance. As a younger man, he might have thrown something to startle it away, but he's worked hard to be less angry over the years. And who knows: maybe those old stories are true. In which case, he doesn't want to be making enemies he might be meeting again before too long.

"Don't get any ideas," he tells it.

Then he slides the phone into his pocket and takes a deep breath. Nothing to do now but wait. The scene is a mile from the nearest road, and it will probably be half an hour or more before backup arrives.

Not backup, he reminds himself.

It is still difficult to accept that he's no longer police. When he called in the scene just now, he used a phone number he still knows by heart, and for a second had almost given his rank as well as his name. But he's just plain John Garvie now. And while the sergeant he'd spoken to had been a colleague for years, he had spoken to John the way he would have any other civilian. That's all he is now.

He looks up and down the trail.

Empty in both directions. But the sun has barely risen and the tourists will still be in their beds.

Nobody out here but you, old man.

Except that isn't quite true.

He looks down into the grass at the side of the trail.

He spotted the remains from a distance, although at that point they were partially concealed in the undergrowth, the dirty black and brown of them barely visible in the bright green between the trees. As he drew closer, he mistook them for a pile of charred wood. But then he realized what was lying here: a body, burned beyond recognition. None of the facial features remain. Any clothing has melded with the blackened skin. One arm pokes up in the air a little, and the exposed bone has the cracked, mottled texture of a stick in the ashes of a cold bonfire.

There is something small and pitiful about the remains. Fire diminishes a body, like a hand clenching slowly into a fist. But these remains seem tinier than most. Once upon a time, this was a living, breathing human being: someone full of motion and movement, love and laughter. But the remains in the undergrowth are so empty and still that it's hard to square them with that idea, and the sight of them stirs familiar emotions inside him. The sadness at this loss of life. The frustration of wanting to protect someone, and it being far too late. The anger.

I will find who did this to you, he thinks.

It's no longer his job, but it's there anyway: the need for justice. The feeling that the scales have to be tilted back to right, or else his own world will always be askew.

Keeping a careful distance from the remains, he examines them as best he can from the path. There is no damage to the surrounding under-growth, and so it's obvious that the woman—and he's sure the remains are female—did not die here. Her body must have been burned elsewhere before being brought out into the woods.

John looks around again. He knows these trails well, and works through a mental map of them now, trying to work out how she might have been delivered here. There are only a handful of possible routes, and even the most remote of them would take daring. The most likely sce-nario is that she was brought here under cover of darkness. And it would have to have been during the night just gone. If she had been here longer than that, someone would have found her already.

Or something would, he thinks.

He looks up.

The crow is perched in the branches above, its head tilted to the side.

"Why bring her out here?" he asks it.

The crow just watches him.

It's a good question though. And having gone to all that effort, why leave her so poorly concealed? The island offers a thousand isolated spots in which a body could be more effectively disposed of than this. Even here, if the remains had been carried just a few meters farther into the undergrowth, they might have remained undiscovered a while longer.

Assuming it happened under cover of darkness, he supposes it's pos-sible that whoever did it imagined they'd done a better job than they had. Or perhaps they'd got spooked and just wanted to get the whole thing over with as quickly as possible. Except the kind of man who would burn a woman's body and carry it into the woods in the middle of the night doesn't strike him as the type to get spooked easily.

He checks up and down the trail again.

A part of him wishes the culprit *was* walking toward him right now. That way he might have a chance to let out some of the anger he's feel-ing. But there is nobody is in sight. The woods are empty and silent. And another part of him is glad about that.

He looks back down at the remains.

I will find who did this to you, he thinks again.

And then he takes out his bottle of water and waits.

It is close to forty minutes before the police arrive.

He's beginning to worry that another walker will chance upon the scene first, but then he spots them in the distance. The two officers are ambling along casually. Not a care in the word.

Liam Fleming and David Watson.

Watson raises a tentative hand as they approach, and John nods in return. Fleming doesn't acknowledge him, of course. He has his hands in his pockets and is studying the trail, little tufts of dust at his feet like he's looking for a rock to kick into the undergrowth. Fleming never took John seriously as an officer, he knows. Now he no longer even has to pretend to.

"David." John nods again as the officers reach him. "Liam."

Fleming still doesn't look at him. Instead, he walks past—a little too close, as always—and then, his hands still in his pockets, he rocks up on his tiptoes and peers down into the undergrowth. His expression is blank; he might be looking at fly-tipped rubbish.

"I walked north from Garrett Rocks," John tells them. "Didn't see a soul along the way. It was seven twenty-three when I found her and called it in. My guess is that she was left here sometime last night."

"Her?" Fleming is still looking down at the remains. "She?"

"Just a hunch."

Fleming nods, as though he hadn't been expecting anything stronger.

"She wasn't killed here," John says.

"Obviously not." Fleming leans back up and looks at Watson. "We need to cordon off the path. North and south end of the trail. South is the priority, but there might be a few campers closer to the Reach, and we don't want anyone else stumbling into this."

"Yes, sir."

John fights to keep his patience.

"There's the Brady path too," he says.

"What about it?"

"It connects to the road a mile or so that way." John nods to the east, even though Fleming still isn't looking at him. "Not that many people use it. Quiet place to park, I reckon. It would still be a risk for whoever brought her out here, but I think it's the most likely route they'd have taken. Less chance of being noticed."

Finally, Fleming turns to him, angling his body slightly. Fleming is a big man, used to his physical presence holding center stage and pushing others away to the wings. *Once a bully, always a bully*, John thinks. The old red mist begins to rise, and he forces himself to keep his fists unclenched.

"That should be cordoned off too," he says. "It's crucial to preserve evidence."

"Yes," Fleming says. "I know that."

"Because this is a *wrongful* death."

"I know that too."

They stare at each other for a couple of seconds.

Then Fleming looks away and breathes out, so long and hard that John can smell a hint of last night's drink on the man's breath.

"We'll need you to make a statement, Mr. Garvie."

"I know that," John says.

"A sergeant will talk you through the process. We'll want a record of exactly what happened. The route you took and anything you saw along the way. However inconsequential it might seem to you, it might be important to our investigation. And your whereabouts over the last twenty-four hours, for what that's worth."

"Yes," John says. "I know that too."

"But the first thing I need you to do is remove yourself from my crime scene immediately."

Fleming looks back at him.

John makes a point of staring back. The humiliation stings, and there's a moment when he wants to swing for Fleming. But there's nothing he can do. As much as it burns him, he isn't police anymore. He has no authority here. And if Fleming is the kind of man to rub his face in that fact, there's nothing much he can do about that either.

Nothing much he can do about anything these days.

So he turns and walks away down the trail. But he feels that sense of duty pulling at him, like a rope tethered to his chest, and he glances back. Watson is on the radio, following his orders. Fleming is squatting down on his haunches, peering at the dead woman in the undergrowth.

Both men appear to have forgotten him already.

John looks up. A small black arc flits across the sky above the trees: the crow, flying away now. Taking its cargo off to the underworld, if that's what you believe. And although John doesn't, it's difficult to shake the sensation that the bird had been perched there the whole time waiting, wanting to watch the encounter that was about to unfold below.

To see who this man was that had found the woman's body.

What he was going to do.

And if so, he wonders what it thought of the little it saw.

Times passes.

That's what it does, if you're lucky. Which is exactly the kind of homespun aphorism that John has always despised and yet has found himself deploying more and more recently. *I've gotten so old*, he'll think, and then a voice in his head will answer back, *Better than the alternative.* But is it? As though that's some kind of comfort. It's like he's trying to find something positive in a life that increasingly feels lived for the sake of it. There's no real consolation to those phrases. Ultimately, they all mean the same thing.

What—you expected something more than this?

Maybe.

He supposes it's natural in old age to look back on your life and take stock. When you're young, there's so much time left ahead of you. You can still achieve something. But then suddenly you realize that time is mostly behind you now, and there's only the fact that you didn't.

Daniel doesn't call.

It's tempting to phone his son himself, but his self-respect won't let him. It's not that he wants to talk to Daniel so much as for his son to want to talk to him, and making the call himself won't make that happen.

In terms of *looking back and taking stock*, he knows that Daniel has turned out well, but it never feels like he can take any pride in that. He remembers how badly he floundered as a single father, winging the whole thing and crashing constantly. All the missed conversations and closed doors. Whatever his son has achieved in his life is as much despite of John as because of him. And even though things are better between them these days, it's no real surprise that his son doesn't call.

In his bleakest moments, he thinks:

Who is even here for him to talk to?

Times passes.

Yes, that is indeed what it does if you're lucky. John fills it as best he can. He reads voraciously; he watches television; and there are his files to attend to—all the unsolved cases that have caught his attention over the years, and which the internet allows him to pursue from a distance. He prepares his evening meals carefully, and then sits alone at the kitchen table with a glass of wine from his growing cellar. He works the heavy bag, but not as hard as he used to, no longer quite sure what he's imagining himself hitting, or why.

He takes his morning walks.

For a week, he chooses a different route. But then he returns to his normal routine. The place where he found the woman's body is already indistinguishable from the rest of the undergrowth, but it still seems quieter when he reaches that part of the trail. There's a residual sadness to the air, and he carries it away with him afterward, as though he's walked through a cobweb.

At first, the murder is covered heavily in the local news, so much so that he comes to resent the sight of Fleming in front of the cameras. Then he begins to resent the obvious lack of progress. He can't help thinking that he would solve the case if he was in charge, even though he knows deep down that he wouldn't. It's just a feeling of emptiness and worthlessness, along with that sense of duty, weighing him down. Whoever the murdered woman is, the crime doesn't make the national news, and a fortnight later, there is as little trace of her on the airwaves as there is in the undergrowth.

Times passes.

One evening, he is sitting on a bench at the seafront. The sky is a canopy of smeared yellows and purples, streaked in places with threads of vivid-blue cloud, as though the world has been dappled by a child's finger paints and then smeared and swirled. The island is a small and shabby place in many ways, but there is still beauty to be found here. It's just beauty that makes him feel even more small and irrelevant.

After a while, he becomes aware that one of the runners on the promenade has changed paths and is approaching him. Sarah Ross. The front of her pink top is damp with sweat, and a few strands of hair are sticking out from under a blue baseball cap.

She's breathless. "Hey there, Mr. Garvie."

"It's *John*, Sarah." He smiles. "Surely you know that by now?"

"Old habits die hard."

"Yes," he says. "Tell me about it."

She sits with him for a time, chugging water out of a bottle as they talk.

How's Daniel doing? she asks. He's doing fine, John tells her. Not heard from him for a while, but he's okay. He's busy.

How are you keeping?

I'm keeping busy too, he says.

He doesn't ask about her home life. It still baffles him that she's ended up with a man like Liam Fleming—but he has a nose for these things, and she doesn't strike him as being settled here on the island. There's a part of her that still wants *something more*, and he hopes to God she ends up following that instinct. He still remembers the girl who would show up for Daniel on the doorstep, wide-eyed and excited. *Do you want to go on an adventure?* There aren't many of those to be found on the island. His life is one long testament to that.

"I'm sorry about what happened," she says after a while.

He raises an eyebrow as a question.

"The woman's body," she says. "It must have been horrible."

"Oh." He shifts slightly. "Yes, it was. But I'm glad it was me who found her. Better me than a tourist. At least I've seen things like that before."

He hesitates.

"What's happening there?" he asks. "Do you know?"

A little, she says. She tells him that the woman still hasn't been identified, but it doesn't seem like she was anyone from the island, and so the
police are looking at missing persons from the mainland. Apparently
the woman had been dead for some time, and they can tell she was still
alive when someone set fire to her.

"But she'd been hurt before that," she says.

"How so?"

"There were knife marks on the bones."

John closes his eyes at that.

What he told her was true: he *has* seen things like that body before.
But only in the most mundane and everyday sense. Accidents; tragedies.
As far as he knows, he has been in the vicinity of actual evil only once
in his life, at the rest area all those years ago, and it remains impossible
for him to comprehend such gratuitous cruelty. He knows what Daniel
would say to that, of course. It's never gratuitous for the perpetrator;
there's always a reason; they're human beings, not monsters. But John
can't bring himself to go there. He can't get far enough past the suffering
the victim must have endured in order to visualize the man behind it.

"I shouldn't be telling you this," Sarah says.

"I don't think Liam should be telling you it either," he says.

Time passes.

He does what he does, continuing to wear his path into the landscape
of the world like an animal pacing back and forth in its cage. He tries
to cling to the small moments of beauty in the world. A sunrise here; a
well-cooked meal there. But it feels like wearing a heavy mask that he's
only putting on for himself now, and the question keeps occurring to
him. Why make the effort?

One afternoon, he drives to the Reach.

He parks and walks close to the edge. The sea stretches out far ahead
and he can hear the water crashing against the rocks far below. The wind
is cold enough to sting his face. He kicks a pebble off the edge and imagines it disappearing into the maelstrom below.

What would the world be like without you?

Not so very different, he thinks.

He spends a while standing there, hoping for a different answer to arrive, but none does. There have been moments over the years when he's come here and asked himself the same question. On those occasions, he was driven by the feelings of worthlessness and self-hatred that have flowed inside him his whole life, erupting uncontrollably from time to time. Days and weeks when the air he breathed was nothing but red mist. His inner land feels so much calmer right now, and yet for some reason the answer remains the same. It makes him wonder what he was ever expecting.

It wouldn't be so difficult, would it? Just a few steps farther and then nothing at all.

It's something to think about.

He drives home again. As he's closing the front door, he notices the envelope lying on the mat. The post arrives first thing here and today's delivery has already been, so this must have been put through the letterbox afterward by hand.

He picks it up.

There is no writing on the envelope. It hasn't even been sealed. He slides the contents out and finds a single sheet of paper. When he unfolds it, he sees that it's a photograph that someone has printed out. But while he recognizes what he is looking at, it makes no sense. How can this be? And then, as the image settles, a shiver runs through him.

There he is, standing in the woods that day.

With the dead woman in the undergrowth at his feet.

Six

Please help me.

I woke up suddenly. The room was dark, and it took a moment for me to remember where I was—that I was back on the island in the attic of my father's house—and then a moment longer for me to realize that a little boy was standing at the side of my bed, leaning over me and peering down from a bright white face.

Please help me.

I sat up quickly. As I did, he skittered away backward across the room, disappearing into the shadows by the door. I watched him fade away like mist, and sat there for a few seconds, my heart pounding hard.

Fuck.

I attempted to rub some life into my face, then checked the clock on the bedside table. Just after four in the morning. But the anxiety told me there was little point in lying down and trying to go back to sleep. It felt like I'd forgotten to lock a door downstairs and something dangerous had crept into the house without me knowing. So after gathering myself together, I got up, showered and dressed, then made myself breakfast and sat with coffee in the kitchen for a time.

Keeping the blinds on the window closed against the darkness.

The dead woman in the woods.

Sarah's words from last night, coming back to me now.

My father had been the one to find her. The body still hadn't been identified, Sarah said, but it didn't appear to be anyone from the island. Whoever the woman was, she had been murdered elsewhere, and then her remains brought here to the woods. The police still had no idea as to the killer's identity, or what the motive might have been for him to kill her.

And if what your father found bothered him . . . he didn't show it.

After my second cup of coffee, I headed upstairs to his office.

It felt strange, walking in, to find it the same as yesterday. How could it be otherwise, of course? Nobody had been in here since. And yet a part of me still expected to find some evidence of activity, because it was equally difficult to believe that he was gone.

I walked over to the desk and picked up the photograph I'd found.

My father. Standing out in woodland.

As I'd thought yesterday, the expression on his face was difficult to make out, but it was recognizably him. He was wearing his long green coat, which had been a birthday present to himself this year. I remembered that when we'd sat outside together on the deck during my last visit, he'd put it on when it got colder.

I peered more closely at the image.

What was that, lying at his feet?

There was something in the undergrowth there, but the poor resolution of the image made it impossible to see clearly. All I could really make out were unnatural patches of brown and black and red among the blurry swirls of grass. But even if I couldn't be certain of what I was seeing, it disturbed me.

I put the photograph on the desk and leaned down on either side of it.

The resolution of the photograph was evidence in itself. No camera was this bad at close range. The quality suggested to me that the picture had been taken from a distance, and then zoomed in on and cropped. And while my father was looking vaguely in the direction of the camera it didn't seem like he was conscious of it. That made me think that it had been taken surreptitiously, catching him in this particular moment without him being aware of a photograph being taken.

Which disturbed me more.

Detached, I reminded myself.

Calm.

My work had taught me that it was important to keep to the facts and not go off on wild flights of fancy. Even so, assuming that I was looking at what I thought I might be—my father in the moment he had found the woman's body—I couldn't think of any other explanation than that the photographer had been the person responsible for leaving it there.

I rubbed my jaw.

There was a sense of threat to the image now. Despite the fact my father was ostensibly alone in the shot, he seemed vulnerable, like prey targeted in a scope, and I wanted to reach into the photograph to protect him.

Where had the photo come from?

I was so used to storing my pictures digitally that it was strange to see one printed out on paper. As far as I knew, my father had not been in the habit of doing so, but it was possible that he had. Perhaps the picture had been emailed to him. If so, the image file might be on his computer somewhere, and there might be some clue in the metadata as to who sent it.

I clicked the power button on the desktop.

The screen flickered into life. My father's screensaver was a generic image of countryside, and there was a password prompt. My fingers hovered over the keys, but I had no idea what his password might be and couldn't even begin to guess. I felt frustrated, but put the emotion away; it wouldn't help right now.

I powered the device down again.

Regardless of how my father had received the image, how would he have reacted when he saw it? Sarah had told me he hadn't been affected by finding the body, but I was sure he would have felt a responsibility toward the murdered woman, even if he had hidden it. That was the kind of man he had always been.

This photograph was a clue to getting justice to her, but it didn't seem like he had reported it to the police. He must have had a reason for that, even if I couldn't fathom what it might be. But equally, he would not have ignored it. He would have felt a burning need to do *something*.

I tried to put myself in my father's place, based on everything I knew about him. A dogged and determined man. Beaten down by life but never allowing himself to buckle. A man who felt things deeply. Even if he hadn't pursued this through official channels, he would definitely have chased it somehow.

I studied the photograph again.

It had been a long time since I'd walked the trails myself, but Sarah and I had been out there all the time as kids, and the maps we made in our heads were often surprisingly strong. One of the branches of a birch tree on the edge of the photograph looked familiar. It poked out at an angle and then stretched down into the undergrowth, like a pale, skeletal leg that the tree had stuck out in an attempt to trip you. I thought I recognized that.

Or at least, that I would if I was there.

And I realized there was one question more important right now than what my father had done when he looked at this photograph and saw what it showed and suggested.

The question was what I was going to do.

Seven

It was too early in the day for tourists to be out on the trails.

Which was a shame for them, I thought, as I walked. Beads of dew clung to every blade of glass, and I could hear the quiet clicks of the undergrowth as the world stretched itself slowly awake. Sunlight cut through the surrounding trees, and the path was scattered with pine needles, the warm air filled with the sweet smell of the woodland. The area was at its most beautiful first thing.

This was the time of day when my father had always gone out walking. He had liked sunrises. He had liked seeing hares flitting across the trail far ahead of him. He told me once that he'd spotted a deer a distance away in the trees, and I remembered smiling at the quiet excitement in his voice, which had seemed such a contrast from the intense man in my memories. Maybe that happens to all of us in time, I'd thought. We slow down a little. We loosen our knots. We learn to find pleasure in the smaller, softer moments.

But then he had found something else.

As I walked, I turned the obvious questions over in my mind.

Who had sent my father that photograph?

Who was the murdered woman?

And nagging beneath those, a different one: *did whatever my father had done next play some part in his decision to take his own life?*

I headed north along the trail, moving at a slow pace and scanning the trees and the undergrowth as I went. The route was familiar enough. But I'd always thought of it as peaceful and calming here, and knowing what I did gave it a sense of threat instead. The world was almost silent, and as far as I could tell I was alone, but there was the sensation of being watched. Despite telling myself it was ridiculous, I found myself listening carefully and keeping an eye on my surroundings, and I made sure to walk in the middle of the path, well away from the edge of the tree line.

Walking in my father's shoes.

And also trying to put myself into his head.

As I'd said to Fleming yesterday, the vast majority of my work involved looking after my patients—men who had already been caught for their crimes—but I had also contributed to three active cases. Each time, I had provided a carefully considered profile of the potential offender. Doing so involved research and statistical analysis, not magic or mind reading, but there was also an element of empathy. In some ways, it wasn't so different from my more everyday work. It was a matter of looking at the available facts, trying to work out how someone might be thinking and feeling, and then attempting to see the world through their eyes.

I didn't have enough evidence yet to understand why my father had ended up at the Reach, but I had a lifetime of experience to help me understand him in other ways.

I pictured him walking slightly behind me now.

Why didn't you go to the police with the photograph? I asked him.

And then I allowed my subconscious to answer me with his voice.

Talk to Liam Fleming? I imagined him saying. *Have you lost your mind, my son?*

I almost smiled.

But it would have been the right thing to do, I thought.

Maybe. But I always had a complicated relationship with the job.

A hesitation.

Actually, I probably wouldn't have put it like that, would I? But we both know it's true.

Yes, I thought. We do.

I mean, I loved it. But it never felt like I made much of a difference. Maybe just in a few small ways, here and there. But there was never a big case—not like in those books I love so much. And by the end, I was pretty much a joke to everyone. That old dinosaur, right? The new guys made fun of me behind my back.

Go on, I thought.

It was a little life, all in all. And I suppose that when I found her body, a part of me didn't want to be sidelined like I always had been. And it seemed to me that it was my job to take care of her. You know how strongly I felt about things.

Yes, I thought.

That makes sense to me, Dad.

I continued along the trail, my shoes crunching softly on the pine needles strewn across the path. Still picturing my father walking patiently behind.

Why didn't you tell me about the body?

He was silent for a moment. Perhaps my subconscious didn't want to provide an answer. My father and I had rarely talked about the work I did with my patients, because he had indeed *felt things strongly*, and I knew he had struggled to see such people as worthy of empathy or understanding. But even so, he must have known my expertise could have been useful. And yet he had chosen not to talk to me.

Why didn't you tell me, Dad?

Maybe exactly because of what you just thought.

I frowned to myself.

What does that mean?

Because you've done work that matters. You've caught killers.

I looked down at the trail, considering that. I always tried to downplay my occasional role in cases. That wasn't out of modesty, but realism; the way I saw it, the police would have got there eventually without my help. And yet the truth was that my work really had helped to catch three men that I knew of, and most likely before they had gone on to hurt others. I had talked to my father about that. Perhaps, unlike with my work at the prison, I had wanted him to be impressed or proud. But I hadn't stopped to think that they were exactly the kind of cases he had always dreamed of being involved in and never had been.

Maybe I just wanted something on the ledger that was mine.

Anyway—we're here.

I looked up again.

A few meters ahead, I saw the white branch emerging from the tree line, poking down crookedly into the undergrowth at the edge of the path. The surprise was such that I actually turned and checked behind me—but of course the trail was empty. My father wasn't really there. I had just been lost in thought, and my subconscious had noticed where I was a few seconds before my mind actively registered it.

I approached the tree.

It had been over a month since the woman's body had been found, and no evidence remained of it ever having been here. The foliage by my feet was undisturbed. There were no scorch marks. But then, the news reports I had read indicated that police believed she had been killed somewhere else and then brought here afterward.

Why would someone do that?

Without access to an actual case file, it was impossible even to begin to answer that question. When constructing a profile, you always had to be cautious—to stick to the available facts and remember that the same act could have multiple explanations. Burning the victim might have personal meaning to the killer. It might have been an attempt at hiding her identity. Or perhaps it had seemed like the most straightforward method of destroying evidence. Or a combination of all three, along with any number of other possible motivations.

But the *location* was curious.

Some killers kept their victims' bodies, but the majority of patients I had worked with or studied had either destroyed or disposed of them. The intention was almost always that the body would not be discovered for as long as possible. There were plenty of wilder, less accessible spots on the island that would have been more effective dump sites than this, but the killer had gone to the effort of moving the dead woman, with all the risk that entailed, and then left her where she was certain to be found.

Why would he do that?

I imagined a different presence standing behind me now. Not my father. A more shadowy and insubstantial figure this time; a man made mostly of smoke for the moment. And while the woods remained quiet, and the early morning sun continued to hang like mist between the trees, the world seemed to darken slightly.

I steeled myself.

Why did you bring her here? I thought.

Silence.

What were you trying to say?

Silence.

But then, I didn't know nearly enough yet to give the killer a voice in the same way I had with my father.

I shook my head, then reached into my jacket and took out the photograph. Using the distinctive branch as a guide, I moved myself closer to the exact place in which my father had been standing. One foot here; the other there. Then I turned, angling my body so I was facing in the direction he had been when the photograph was taken.

And then held my breath.

The woods around the trails were dense, but there was a slight break in the tree line ahead of me now. In the distance, the land rose steeply, and distant crags—bare outcrops of rock—overlooked the spot where I was standing. Not impossible to reach, but a long way off the path.

I looked down at the photograph.

I could still sense that shadowy, voiceless presence behind me but I didn't ask it anything. For the moment, I didn't need to.

Why had he brought her here?

Perhaps so that he could watch when she was found.

• • •

I marked the crag as best I could on the GPS map on my phone and then set off through the undergrowth.

There was no clear path, and within a few minutes I was fighting through the foliage, snapping off branches and pushing through tangled grass, sticks cracking beneath my feet. My destination was soon out of sight, but the phone kept me more or less on track, heading in the right direction and pushing my way slowly uphill through the forest.

What exactly was I doing?

That was a perfectly reasonable question, but one to which I had no immediate answer. The chances of finding anything out here after all this time were remote. But while I knew the woods around the crime scene would have been searched, the crag was far enough away that it would probably have escaped attention. And it was the most likely vantage point from which to take the photograph.

Eventually there was a break in the trees and the land opened up ahead. Pale stone stretched sharply upward, with a rough path in the rock that was dotted with shivery patches of grass and scrub. I started to climb carefully, using roots in the rock as handholds. The rough shingle was loose beneath my feet, and the breeze grew colder and stronger with every cautious step.

Would my father have been able to climb up here?

I thought so. He was old but active—a long way from being infirm. And as I knew very well, he had been nothing if not determined. Assuming he hadn't gone to the police, I was sure he would have followed the evidence in the photograph at least this far. And on a less rational level, I felt a connection with him as I climbed: the strange sensation of him being right here with me, just at a different time.

I was drenched with sweat as I approached the top, despite the wind, and the woods seemed dizzyingly far below me. I clambered up and round onto a wide ledge of rock that stretched out several meters ahead.

Then I stood still for a few seconds, catching my breath.

My heart was beating hard.

Here you are, I thought.

A short distance ahead, tucked away out of sight of the edge of the outcrop, were the remains of a campsite. There was an old tent, the thin red fabric tattered and ripped and flapping in the wind. It was held in place by tight, spidery ropes attached to nails hammered into the stone.

I dusted my hands against my thighs and made my way across.

Closer to, the sound of the tent's torn material made a frantic cracking sound, like a bird tethered to something trying to escape. I crouched down and peered into the entrance. It was small inside, and I could see the rock pushing up sharply through the taut canvas. If someone had slept overnight in here, they must have been hardy and used to the elements.

Whoever that was had left something behind.

After a moment's hesitation, I reached inside and picked up the single item inside the tent. It was a brown leather wallet, worn from being carried for years. It felt light and baggy in my hand, as though it had been full once but had been emptied out before being placed in the tent. And *placed* was exactly the right word, I thought. Because there was nothing else inside, and I didn't believe that this had been left behind by accident.

None of this felt like an accident.

I flipped the wallet open. It wasn't entirely empty. There was a driver's license inside, and a small photo of a man stared out at me from the left-hand side. On the right, there was a name—Darren Field—and an address.

I stared at it for a moment, committing the details to memory, then put the license back into the wallet and placed it back where I had found it. Assuming my father had come here, he had clearly decided to leave it, and so for the moment—following in his footsteps—I would too.

Then I stood up and walked as close to the edge of the crag as I dared. The fabric of the tent was still cracking desolately behind me, and the woods stretched away below. I took out my phone and turned on the camera, angling it down, trying to keep my aim steady as I zoomed in as far as I could. The foliage on the screen was shaky and blurry. But after a few seconds, I was able to locate the spot in which my father had been standing when the photograph was taken.

The angle was exact.

I lowered my phone.

And then I imagined that silent presence behind me again.

What kind of man are you? I thought.

No answer.

You brought the body of a woman out here to the woods, I thought. You took a photograph of the moment she was found. And then you sent it to the person who did so, knowing full well that it would lead them to the scene you left behind.

Why would you do that?

Once again, the figure behind me said nothing. But then I heard a man's voice, raised finally from my subconscious, but still so quiet for the moment that it was barely louder than a whisper.

Isn't it obvious? he said.

And then a sigh, almost lost to the wind.

I did it because I wanted to be seen.

James

"Look at this!" his mother says. "We made it."

James glances up expectantly. He is eleven years old and has never been to the seaside before. He's seen it on television and in brochures, though, and for the last few weeks the images have been locked in his head, waiting to become real. Warm yellow sunshine; blue skies and seas; everyone smiling and happy. He's been so giddy that he's found it hard to sleep.

But as his mother takes the turnoff for the campsite now, it's nothing like how he imagined. He leans down to peer out, and his heart sinks a little. It's not very different at all. The sky through the windscreen ahead is gray and empty—the same one he sees every day out of his little bedroom window in the tower block—and there's no sign of the sea. There's just grass shivering in the cold wind on the ridges of moorland around them.

It could be anywhere.

Hey! Barnaby tells him. *You're strong!*

You're brave!

James strokes the head of the soft toy lion in his lap.

Barnaby is his best friend. James has had him for as long as he can remember. He had an argument with his mother last year, because the other children at school were beginning to make fun of him for taking Barnaby into lessons, and his mother wanted him to stop. *I'll look after him at home; he'll be fine, I promise.* She'd been pretty full-on about it. But when he finally managed to get it through to her how much Barnaby helped him, she had eventually sighed and looked sad, and then she hadn't mentioned it again.

They pull up on an expanse of gravel at the side of the road.

James looks around. The car park is bedraggled and empty. But that makes sense, right? His mother has told him—over and over—that this is an odd time of year to come on holiday, but that it means the place will be cheap and they'll have it all to themselves. It had sounded like she was trying to convince herself as much as him, and he can tell that she's still trying to do that now, staring out at this windswept, barren place.

She says something now. He doesn't quite catch it.

"Mum?" he asks.

A dot of rain lands on the windscreen.

"I said *I'm sorry*, James. I know it doesn't look that good."

He looks at her for a moment, feeling helpless. It's bad when she's angry at him, but that doesn't happen often and it doesn't matter because he knows it won't last. It's always so much worse when she's like this: angry at herself. Because she doesn't deserve to be.

You know what to do, Barnaby tells him.

"It looks great, Mum." He remembers what she's told him. "We'll make the best of it. There are some nice walks around here. And you borrowed a little gas burner, so we can cook dinner together out in the open tonight. And the sleeping bags are warmer than they look. We'll have fun."

She stares back at him for a moment.

He waits.

Then she ruffles his hair.

"You and me against the world, James," she says quietly. "Right?"

"Yes." He's so pleased. "Always."

They get out of the car and his mother opens the trunk. They begin to collect their gear, and James looks around the car park again. It's empty to all intents and purposes . . . but actually, not quite.

He pauses for a moment, his fingers on the back of the car.

There's an old camper van tucked away out of sight in one corner, dark and dirty. The branches of the trees above are overgrown and hanging down over it. The vehicle looks abandoned, as though it has been sitting there for years, but there's something about it that bothers him.

He stares at the pitch-black windows of the cab.

It's empty, or it looks it, but—

"James!"

He flinches suddenly—then moves his hands away quickly just as the lid of the boot slams down.

The sound echoes around the car park. His mother stares at him.

"Just pay attention," she says. "Please?"

He's not sure if she's talking to him or herself, but he nods anyway.

Then he collects his share of the bags at the back of the car, and follows his mother over the ridge ahead of them. And while he can still feel that old camper van behind him, he doesn't look back.

James helps his mother pitch the tent—or at least, he tries to. The whole thing is baffling and impossible. He struggles to click the sticks into place and then bend them through the loops on the thin fabric. The frustration becomes almost overwhelming, and he bites his lip in concentration. Everything starts shaking. The tent, the sticks, his hands. Then the end flicks away upward, and he falls back on his heels.

"It doesn't want to be built," he says.

His mother is struggling too and seems to be about to lose her temper.

"Don't do this, James."

"I wish Dad was here."

That's the anger talking. There's probably nothing he could have said that would hurt his mother more. The stupid thing is that he isn't even sure if it's true: it's been such a long time since James has seen his father that he can't even really remember what he looks like. It's more like he's an absence that would be comforting to fill.

But he knows that's not how his mother feels. James wrote a letter to his father just before Christmas, talking about life, and how he wished they were all still together. He even drew him a picture. But when he gave it to his mother, she'd tried to argue. So he'd got upset with her, and just as with Barnaby, she'd eventually sighed and looked sad, and promised to send it. But he isn't sure if she did.

She takes a few deep breaths now, and then puts her hand on his arm.

"I'm trying," she says.

"I'm sorry."

"You don't need to be. Just work with me, okay?"

There is a look of resolve on her face: a determination to make the best of it, despite the shabbiness and smallness of it all.

"Okay," he says.

When they finish building the tent, it looks barely sufficient to protect them from the elements, but James feels happy with it.

Are you proud of me? he thinks.

That's all he ever wants, but as usual he doesn't dare to ask the question. What if she doesn't reply? Because he's let go of the anger from earlier, but he's not sure his mother has. Emotions come and go quickly for him, but he knows that grown-ups hold on to them for much longer, and his mother more than most. So he just *thinks* the question instead: concentrating on it so hard that it seems impossible she won't be able to read his mind.

Are you proud of me?

"I'll just get some things from the car," she says.

"I'll come with you."

"I just need a minute to myself, James."

He hesitates. "Okay."

And then he waits by the tent, hoping that she'll be better when she gets back. The seconds tick by. She returns a few minutes later with a bag of their belongings: a blanket and towel; a Frisbee. And he's relieved to see that her mood has settled and she looks a little brighter.

"*All right, then,*" she says. "Let's go and find the sea."

It's a longer walk than he's expecting, down a trail lined with more of that shivering grass. There are signposts warning that it's not safe to swim here because of the currents. Which doesn't matter to him— learning to swim is one of many things he hasn't had a chance to do yet— but it does make him wonder why people come here. And when they get to the beach, it turns out to be more rock than sand, and the sea is a vast gray expanse: nothing like the way he imagined it. The tide is going out, leaving a web of scummy froth between the pebbles, and the shingle crunches beneath his feet.

But.

Just work with me, okay?

They play with the Frisbee for a while. It's okay at first, and James feels good whenever the feathered plastic edge lands solidly in his hand. But his mother is already finding it hard.

"The wind!" she keeps saying.

It's not that windy though, and he's managing to throw it to her without a problem. As time goes on, she begins to fumble her catches more, and then James starts having to dart forward as her attempts to throw it back to him fall shorter and shorter.

"I'm sorry," she says.

Her voice sounds tired. Smeared.

And James realizes why she wanted to go to the car by herself. At home, his mother keeps the pill bottles hidden away on the top shelf of the bathroom cabinet, but she's lost track of how much James has grown recently, and he can reach them now if he stands on tiptoes. The bottles are very old, the original labels all but worn off. He thinks his mother used to get the pills from the chemist, but that at some point she started getting different ones from somewhere else instead.

"It's okay," he tells her.

"I just . . . all this exercise. Maybe I need a little lie down."

She sets out the blanket and curls up, and within a minute she's fast asleep. James spreads the towel over her as best he can. He knows from experience that it'll be an hour or so before she wakes up, which means that he's alone for now. But that's fine. For one thing, Barnaby will keep him safe.

And anyway, there's nobody else here.

You're brave! Barnaby tells him. *You're very brave!*

Yes, James thinks. I am.

The stretch of coastline here is formed of a series of inlets, separated by steep ridges of rock. The tide has retreated enough for him to walk around the edge of this beach and into the next, which turns out to be a little wider than the one behind, but just as stony underfoot. The wind has picked up a little now. It's cold, and comes in sudden gusts that he can see rippling on the surface of the gray water like gooseflesh.

He stands as close to the edge of the sea as he dares.

The sight of it stretching out all the way to the horizon makes him feel small. But it's odd. He spends most of his life feeling that way and hating it, but the sensation is different here. It's not like when he's lying in bed at night, staring at the damp on the thin wall and listening to the baby crying in the neighbor's flat. Not like when he's being bullied by the other kids, or ignored by the teachers. Here, it's strangely comforting, as though the world is telling him that deep down it's the same for everyone, and it's just that most people don't realize it.

He closes his eyes.

Breathes in deeply.

And then he hears something.

He opens his eyes and turns slowly, scanning the beach. The sound is delicate—barely distinguishable from the wind—but it sounds like someone whistling. Where is it coming from though? There's nobody in sight. And he hasn't seen another living soul the whole time they've been here.

He looks up at the ridge behind him.

It's dark against the sky, the grass shivering at the edge.

Empty.

And yet the whistling sound is a little louder than before. It's a tune of some kind. There's something familiar about it, even though he doesn't think he's ever heard it before. How can that be possible? And suddenly, everything feels off-kilter. The empty beach; the ethereal music. It's as though when he rounded those rocks and left his mother behind him, he stepped out of the real world and into a different and more dangerous one.

He clutches Barnaby to his chest.

You're strong, James! the lion says. *You're brave!*

But maybe you should go back now.

And he wants to do that, but it doesn't feel like he can. He won't be able to wake his mother up, and what would he say if he managed to? He wants her to be proud of him, not think he's a silly, scared little boy. Except that a scared little boy is exactly what he is right now. And there's a hypnotic quality to the whistling that is holding him in place.

He looks back up at the ridge again.

The top is no longer empty now. A man is standing there, silhouetted against the sky behind. He's so black that it is impossible to make out anything about him at all.

Run! Barnaby says.

But James remains frozen.

The man begins walking steadily down the embankment toward him.

Run!

But he can't. And then it's like time begins to blur. As the man approaches him, and the whistling grows louder, James sees his mother waking up an hour from now. She is groggy at first, because it always takes her a little time to come around, but her first proper thought will be of him. Because he knows that she loves him. She'll sit up carefully and call his name. When he doesn't shout back, she'll feel a small curl of panic against her heart, but she won't be properly worried, not at first. He'll be at the tent, she'll think. Everything will be fine, because of course it will be, and—

The whistling stops.

"Nobody sees," the man says.

He ruffles James's hair with a rough, dirty hand.

"And nobody cares."

PART TWO
ANGER

Eight

"I'm sorry about your dad."

Two hours later, I was standing in the car park at the Reach with Craig Aspinall, the man who had spoken with my father here, and who had then noticed his car was still here the next day. Aspinall was in his seventies, his complexion weathered by a lifetime spent out in the elements. There was a watery gleam to his eyes as he spoke. He was trying to keep himself together on the surface, but the emotion he was feeling was clearly visible underneath.

"Thank you," I said. "I'm sorry too."

"I just keep thinking . . ."

But then he trailed off and shook his head. He took a sip of coffee from the lid of the thermos flask he was carrying.

There was no need for him to finish. It was easy for me to imagine what must be going through his head. Some variation of *what if?* What if he had done things differently that day? What if he had paid a little more attention and noticed that something was wrong? It was an almost ubiquitous reaction to trauma, and right now he was wearing the guilt as plainly as the wax jacket he was pulling around himself against the cold.

"I understand," I said. "But it's important to remember that my father chose to do what he did. It wasn't your fault."

"It feels like I should have realized."

"Perhaps," I said. "But however you or I might feel about it, it was *his* decision. And there's another way of looking at it too. You knew him, right?"

"Yeah." He nodded. "Pretty well."

"So you know the kind of man he was."

"Stubborn as hell."

"Exactly," I said. "Which means that it wouldn't have mattered what you said or did, because once he'd made his mind up about something, there wouldn't have been any changing it."

"Yeah. Maybe."

He hesitated.

"Do you have any idea why—?"

"No," I said quickly. "I don't."

Which remained true, but the question had taken on additional nuance since Fleming had asked me it yesterday. I glanced at the footpath that led away from the car park toward the Reach itself. I knew a little more about my father now. I knew he had been keeping a secret. But whether that had played into whatever happened here remained a secret in itself.

"How was my father when you saw him?" I said.

"Pretty much the same as always."

"Did it seem to you like he was . . . troubled by anything?"

"I don't know." Aspinall frowned. "When I look back on it, all I keep thinking is that it seemed like he wanted rid of me. Like I was interrupting something, or holding him back. But maybe that's just me overthinking things because of what happened."

"Maybe," I said.

I glanced over at my father's car, which was the only vehicle parked here right now. Aspinall was a walker; like me, he had arrived here on foot. He followed my gaze and took it as a prompt.

"Ah, God, sorry. You'll be wanting these."

He got the keys out of his pocket and passed them to me.

"There's no need to apologize," I said. "But yes, I do. Thank you."

"I locked it for safekeeping. I'm sure it would have been okay, but you get kids up here messing around sometimes."

"I remember."

I unlocked my father's car and eased myself into the driver's seat. Out of habit, I started to place my hands on the steering wheel—*ten-to-two, my son*—but that conjured up a memory of him attempting to teach me to drive, and I released my grip. Our growing frustration and impatience with each other back then had quickly put a stop to those lessons.

Pay attention.

Was that his voice or mine? I glanced around the car. My father had driven to his death in this vehicle, and yet it was as clean and well maintained as the house. There were no signs of disarray. Nothing that suggested a distressed state of mind. Nothing that—

Aspinall tapped on the window.

I wound it down.

"Look." There was an awkward expression on his face. "I'm not sure if this is the right thing to tell you or not, but if I don't then it'll just bother me until I do. And I don't know when I'll get the chance again."

"Then you should do it now," I said.

"When your father and I were speaking . . . well, I asked about you. Just casual conversation, you know? The way you do. And he said you were doing great."

"Did he?"

"Yeah." Aspinall paused. "He said he was very proud of you."

"Well," I said. "It's a shame he didn't tell me that, isn't it?"

Aspinall blinked quickly.

"God. I'm sorry, Dr. Garvie. I just—"

"It's fine."

"It's just . . ." Aspinall trailed off, looking sad and wounded. "It's just what a father would want their son to know."

"Thank you."

And I was about to close the window, but he was still hovering there, unwilling for some reason to end our encounter.

"What are your plans?" he said.

"I'm sticking around for a while."

"That's the thing about this island, right?" A note of bitterness entered his expression. "You think you've got away, but the place keeps dragging you back."

"No," I said. "Just until things are sorted."

He nodded to himself, as though that was what everyone said.

"So what are you going to do now?"

I looked out through the windscreen. What was I going to do? I had been turning that question over in my mind ever since finding the makeshift campsite up on the crag. It would have been possible for me to overlook the photograph, or fail to understand its significance, but it was much harder to ignore what it had led me to. My father had decided not to go to the police, and so far I had respected his wishes, but whatever duty I still felt to him, others were beginning to press on me now.

And yet perhaps there were still a few of his footsteps I could follow in first.

I put my hands back on the steering wheel. Thinking about the name Darren Field, and the address I'd read on the driving license that had been left so conspicuously in the tent. Like a breadcrumb on a trail.

"I think I might go for a drive," I said.

I arrived at the terminal in time to catch the midday ferry.

After parking in the hold, I stood out on the passenger deck above, watching the empty sea ahead as I left the island behind. After my previous visits here, it had always been a relief to do so. But this time, I knew I would be returning later, and any prospect of escape was tempered by the thought of what I might discover in the hours ahead.

I suppressed the anger that had surprised me back at the Reach, and imagined my father standing behind me.

Did you make this journey, Dad? I thought.

He offered no response to that. Any reply he gave could only come from my own subconscious, and that wasn't a question I was capable of answering. Time would tell. One thing I was sure of was that, if he had done, he would have been standing out where I was right now. Whenever we journeyed off the island together, he insisted on doing so, even when the weather was bad and I tried to persuade him to sit inside where it was warm.

What? I imagined him saying now. *And miss this view?*

I smiled.

"Plus it's bracing, right?" I said quietly.

That's right.

He sounded pleased that I remembered.

Keeps the senses sharp, my son.

When the ferry reached the mainland, I returned to the car and joined the steady stream of vehicles rolling slowly down the ramp. Within a few minutes, I was away from the terminal and driving along country roads. I had Darren Field's address programmed into my GPS. The town I was heading to was about an hour's drive away. I turned the radio on. I didn't recognize the name of the station my father had it set to, but it turned out to be the kind of gentle conversation that was exactly what I needed right then. As I drove, I listened to people talking about nothing, allowing their voices to wash over me, until it was almost a surprise when I realized I had arrived at my destination.

The address was in a nice neighborhood. Detached houses curled around horseshoe-shaped streets, with trees spaced out neatly along the grass verges. I parked and looked out the window. Field's house was as well maintained as the ones around it, but it seemed to have a melancholy air, as though someone had stopped taking care of it, but too recently for the cracks to have begun to show.

I tapped the steering wheel.

Doubting myself now.

What was I hoping to achieve by coming here? The idea that it might be dangerous to do so had been lingering at the back of my mind throughout the journey. The worst-case scenario, I supposed, was that I was parked outside the home of a manipulative killer. But that didn't make sense to me. In my experience, murderers did not tend to leave clues that led directly to their front door. If there was a link between this address and the body my father had found in the woods, I was sure the connection would be more oblique than that. But it was hard to imagine what it might be.

There's only one way to find out.

My father's voice, from the seat behind me.

What did you do now? I thought.

What do you imagine I did? Don't overthink things. Just go and knock on the front door and see what happens.

I nodded to myself.

After locking the car, I made my way up the drive. But my arrival must have already been noted, because the front door opened before I reached it. Only a little though. Whoever was inside had kept it on the chain. As I drew closer, I saw a woman there, standing back from the slightly open gap.

She looked suspicious. Nervous, even.

"Can you stay back, please?" she said.

"Of course."

I stopped a short distance from the door and smiled lightly. She was maybe a few years older than I was, but it was hard to be more precise, as both her pale skin and the shadows beneath her eyes suggested she wasn't sleeping well or taking care of herself. There was a restlessness to her too. Her body was moving slightly, as though there was some energy inside her that wouldn't allow her to keep still.

"I'm sorry," I said. "Is this a bad time?"

She considered that.

"It is a bad time," she said. "Yes."

"I'm sorry to bother you then. I was hoping to speak to Darren Field?"

"He's not here."

"Okay."

"Yeah," she said. "That's kind of why it's a bad time."

I was about to reply but then the woman glanced over my shoulder, and the look of suspicion on her face deepened.

"Wait a minute—is that your car?"

"Yes," I said. "Sort of."

She pointed at it. "That's the car *the man* was driving. I'm sure of it."

"The man?"

"The weird old man who came to talk to Darren."

I didn't think my father would have appreciated that description much. But at least it cleared up one question. He *had* followed the trail this far. At the same time, it raised others. Presumably he had come here looking for Darren Field, and now Field *wasn't* here, and from the woman's demeanor there was clearly something very wrong about that.

"It's my father's car," I said. "*Was* his car, I mean. He died a few days ago."

She didn't seem in the mood to offer condolences.

"Why did he want to speak to Darren? Why do *you*, come to that?"

"I found Darren's name and address in my father's files," I said. "I don't actually know who Darren is; I'd never heard of him before. And I don't know why my father came to see him. I suppose the reason I'm here is that I'm looking for answers myself. When was this?"

"A couple of weeks ago. The day before Darren left."

"Darren's your husband, right?"

"Your guess is as good as mine." She held up her hand, showing her wedding ring. "I don't know if he's still wearing his. All I know is that your father—if that's who it was—came to see him, and then everything went to shit. The day after that, Darren was gone. I haven't seen him since."

The information sent a ripple of alarm through me.

My father had a strong sense of justice, but he was also an impulsive man who struggled with his temper. Given the reason for his visit here, I hoped he hadn't done something stupid. The idea seemed ridiculous, and I tried to tell myself that. Except it was clear that he had kept this investigation to himself, and equally obvious that I had no real idea what had been going through his head these past few weeks. Perhaps the answer to *why* he had taken his life was that he'd snapped and done something his conscience wouldn't allow him to live with.

But I didn't want to believe that.

"So you don't know where Darren is now?" I said.

"Probably with *her*, whoever she is."

"What do you mean?"

"You got a sister?"

I shook my head. "No."

"I just wondered. The two of them went off into another room to talk, and I couldn't hear any of that. But your father said something about an island, and that he wanted to talk to Darren about a woman. He was too old to be someone's angry husband, so I thought that maybe Darren might have been messing around with his daughter."

I didn't reply.

The island. The woman.

I knew exactly who my father had been referring to, but of course there was no way I could explain that to Darren Field's wife. A moment later, she mistook my silence for awkwardness.

"It's fine, by the way," she said. "I don't give a shit about that. I've got used to it over the years. Don't ask, don't tell. A part of me always knew what I was getting into when I got involved with him, but I never thought the bastard would actually leave me. Although I should be glad he's gone, shouldn't I? Strike that, actually—I *am* glad he's gone."

She was too hurt for that to be true.

"Did my father seem angry?" I said.

"Not really. The two of them were both very serious, though. When they came out of the room, they both seemed kind of *grim*. Darren wouldn't tell me about it. No surprises there. We hadn't been talking much anyway. He was a bit shaken about something, though, and I was worried about him." She laughed without humor. "What a fucking idiot, right? He was just building up to making his decision. I see that now."

"I'm sorry."

People come up with explanations based on the facts they have and, in terms of Darren Field's disappearance, it was clear to me why his wife had settled on the one she had. But she didn't have access to the same facts that I did. My father had come here to talk to Field about a murdered woman.

And then Field had vanished.

If my father hadn't seemed angry, then that was something to cling to, at least. And Field had not left with him that day, which was probably something else. But the feeling of alarm had not lifted.

"I'm sorry," I said again.

"Don't be." She shook her head. "I already told you. I'm glad he's gone."

"Well, then. I'm sorry to have bothered you."

I turned away.

"But you'll tell me if you hear from him?" she said quickly. "I mean— you might right? Because if your father knew him, he might get in touch? About the funeral, or whatever?"

I looked back.

The suspicion on her face had been replaced by quiet desperation now, and her fingers were clutching the edge of the door. I felt slightly sick inside. She needed reassurance I was in no position to give, and she was asking me to make a promise that I might not be able to keep.

And yet it seemed unfair to leave her with nothing.

"I'll try," I said.

Nine

John's on the motorway when Daniel finally phones him.

It's not the most opportune time—it's raining and the traffic is heavy—and for a second he thinks about not taking the call. He doesn't use the hands-free in the car much and doesn't want to fumble around with it in these conditions. And perhaps more importantly, he doesn't want to have to lie to his son.

But the thought is only fleeting. They've not spoken for what feels like an age, and he wants the connection. He turns the radio off, and a moment later, Daniel's voice sounds in the car.

"Dad?"

"That's me," John says, pleased with himself for getting the phone to work. "But I'm driving, my son. Can you hear me okay?"

"Yes, I can hear you fine. What are you up to?"

"Nothing much," he says. "Just out and about."

The lie comes surprisingly easily.

He navigates the traffic carefully, the windscreen dappled with rain that the wipers smear away. The two of them talk about nothing much. That should please him, because it means his son called for the sake of it rather than for a particular reason, but today puts him on edge. He has to be careful. A conversation without a focus has the potential to find one.

He asks what Daniel's been up to, but it's just work, and there's no real news on that score: steady therapeutic work rather than consulting on some exciting case. There's been no woman in his son's life since that breakup last year—or none that Daniel's mentioned, at least, as John isn't naive enough to imagine he's privy to everything. Their relationship is better now than he would have dreamed possible, but it's still a house with its fair share of locked rooms. He knows how tightly his son keeps some of those doors closed, and that nothing good will come from pushing at them.

Of course, he has a secret of his own now.

He thinks of the photograph. The tent on the crag it led him to.

"What have you been up to?" Daniel asks.

John glances out of the passenger window.

"Nothing much," he says.

"You're okay, though?"

"Yes," he lies. "I'm fine."

Except is it really a lie? That question occurs to him after the call is over—when it's just him and the rain and the radio again. There are butterflies in his stomach and his nerves are singing a little. While he's full of doubt about what he's doing, it's also been years since he's felt quite as *alive* as he does right now. He's a man who had grown used to walking the same trail every morning, and who now has a different one to follow.

A short while later, he parks outside the address.

He sits in the car for a couple of minutes, with the radio off now and the rain tapping gently on the roof. He hasn't exactly thought this through, and he's not sure how to play things now that he's here. The conversation he's about to have with Darren Field might have been easier if he'd brought the man's wallet with him.

Here, he could say.

I found this on an isolated outcrop where someone photographed me standing next to a murdered woman's body.

Do you want to tell me what it was doing there?

Well, perhaps nothing quite as direct as that, but it would provide a way in. It's a moot point though: he decided to leave the wallet in the tent on the cliff.

If that was a mistake then there are probably a bunch of other things he should have done differently too. When he arrived home after finding the tent, he was aware that the correct course of action was to go to Fleming and tell him everything. But he also knew that he wasn't going to. He can rationalize that decision if he tries. Not enough to go on; maybe it didn't mean anything; need a stronger case. And so on.

But deep down, John knows it wasn't about logic or common sense or doing the right thing. It was about the way his life feels so small and pointless these days, like there's nothing worth sticking around for. It's about a path that doesn't lead him to the edge of the Reach, kicking pebbles into the void. It's about the butterflies he could already feel gathering inside him.

They're stronger than ever now.

He gets out of the car and approaches the house. Should he be nervous? Maybe. But even though he's no longer police, he knows he can still project some of the authority he gained in his years on the job. And while there has to be some kind of connection between Darren Field and the remains he found, he's pretty sure he's not walking toward the home of a killer right now. If he talked it over with Daniel, he imagines his son would tell him the same thing his own intuition is. Murderers don't tend to lead you straight to their front door.

So whatever he's going to find here will be something . . . else.

He knocks and waits.

A woman answers the door. She's in her forties, and pretty, but she also looks tired and maybe even a little apprehensive. He glances down and notes the wedding ring. When he looks up again and smiles, she doesn't smile back.

"Good afternoon," he says. "I was hoping to speak to your husband."

"You and me both."

"Is Darren in?"

"What do you want with him?"

The question suggests that Field is somewhere in the house. John has most likely just arrived in the middle of an argument, and the woman is more than happy to take her frustration out on a random stranger on the doorstep.

"It's a private matter," he says. "If you don't mind, I'd prefer to discuss it with Darren in person."

She stares at him for a few seconds, looks over his shoulder at the car parked at the bottom of the drive, then shrugs and calls loudly into the house.

"*Darren.* Someone here for you."

A muffled reply.

"No fucking idea," she shouts back. "How would I know?"

There are a few seconds of silence, and then John hears a door opening somewhere behind her in the house. A moment later, a man arrives at the front door. Darren Field is tall and good-looking. John guesses that, with a suit and some hair gel, he'd be the type given to acting the alpha at work and in the wine bars afterward. But right now he's wearing a dressing gown and his hair is messy. He has the air of a man who's been drinking too much and sleeping too little, and who maybe hasn't been into work for a while.

John smiles.

"Darren?"

"Yeah." Field stares at him. "Do I know you?"

John starts to shake his head—but then, suddenly, he's not sure that's true. The sensation is eerie. He's not convinced the two of them have ever met, but at the same time, there's something familiar about the man, and he feels an itch at the back of his mind that he can't put his finger on to scratch.

Field's wife has retreated a little, but he can see her standing near a doorway inside, still close enough to hear.

"No," John says. "You don't know me. But I think there's something the two of us need to talk about. And I was hoping we could have that conversation in private. It's about the island."

Field shakes his head.

"I don't know anything about an island."

John hesitates. Maybe that's true, but he can tell Field isn't anywhere near as relaxed as he's trying to come across as being. There's something wrong here. Field doesn't know who he is, but he also doesn't seem remotely surprised to have a stranger knock on his door wanting a private chat.

John decides to take a chance and leans in as close as he can.

"It's about the woman."

The change in Field's demeanor is immediate and obvious. There's a sharp intake of breath and a stiffening of his body. He tries to hide it a second later, but he's no actor. And as John leans away again, he thinks that maybe Field doesn't *want* to hide it. He has the air of a man with a weight inside him he's desperate to unload, and the heaviness of whatever he's holding is right there on his face.

God, John thinks.

He looks like he's struggling not to cry.

Field looks out past him, as though he's checking the road at the bottom of the driveway.

Seconds pass.

Then he looks back and nods.

"We can go to my study," he says quietly.

It's a study in the sense that John's a police officer. There's still some of the right furniture, but its role is clearly very different these days. It's just the smallest room in a three-bed house. There's a desk along one wall, but the rest of the room is taken up by a packed clothing rail and cardboard boxes, and the air smells musty and old. There's a computer and a mess of paperwork on the desk. Space enough for two chairs. Old habits die hard; John waits for Field to sit down in one seat before taking the other.

"Talk to me, Darren," John says.

Field stares at the floor, rubbing his hands together.

"Are you police?"

"Why?"

"Because it matters."

"Have you been you expecting—?"

Field looks up suddenly, his expression deadly serious. The meaning there is clear. This conversation is going nowhere until he gets an answer to the question he just asked.

"No," John says. "I'm not police."

"Who are you then?"

"I'm the man who found her body."

Field flinches at that.

John leans forward.

"You know who I'm talking about, don't you?"

Field looks down again and then nods miserably. The tears the man was suppressing at the front door are coming now. His face is out of sight, but his shoulders are beginning to shake, and John glances at the closed door. The stairs had creaked as they made their way up, and he hasn't heard anything since, so Field's wife is probably out of earshot. But if Field starts sobbing loudly enough then she might come up.

"It's okay, Darren. Just talk to me."

"I don't know what to say."

"Start at the beginning."

Field doesn't say anything for a few seconds. Then he seems to gather himself together and he takes a deep breath. For some reason, it reminds John of a man crossing himself.

"It was dark," Field says. "And it was cold."

Ten

It was dark, and it was cold.

That was all he was aware of to begin with, and both those realizations came gradually. He was drifting awake, and for a few seconds he found it hard to distinguish between reality and the unconsciousness he was emerging from. Dark and cold. What else? His body was juddering slightly, and a quiet rattling noise filled the air.

Where am I?

All he could tell was that he was horizontal and in motion. When he tried to move his arms and legs, they were held in place. There was something restraining him. He was strapped down on a gurney of some kind, and even his head wouldn't turn; all he could do was flick his eyes from side to side. The darkness and the shuddering movement of the trolley beneath him made the world hard to make sense of. He caught flashes of what looked like foliage, and there was a dusting of stars above him. The night sky. So he was outside somewhere.

Had there been an accident?

Was he being taken to hospital?

He was moving feetfirst. While he couldn't tilt his head back to look, he was aware of a presence just behind him, pushing the trolley along.

He could hear a ragged breathing sound, as though they were struggling with the effort.

A doctor perhaps.

"Hello?" he tried to say.

And realized there was tape covering his mouth.

Panic flared inside him at that, and he tried to fight against his restraints with more urgency, pushing and pulling with all his strength. But there was no give in them at all. His mumbles from behind the tape became muffled screams, which continued until he felt like he was about to vomit.

If he was sick, he would choke to death.

Whoever was behind him seemed oblivious to his distress. The trolley carried on at the same speed, rattling like a shopping trolley with a broken wheel that wouldn't stop spinning and stalling.

He forced himself to breathe slowly through his nose, and after what felt like an age the nausea subsided slightly. But his heart was punching hard inside his chest, as if it were trying to find a way out.

Think.

How had he got here?

It was hard to gather his thoughts. Dim recollections drifted through his mind, the way threads of smoke in the air might—but that image brought a sharper jolt of memory. *Smoke in the air.* He remembered that. He had been in the outside area of a bar with a cigarette, watching the smoke he exhaled swirling in the air beneath the light of a heater and then disappearing away into the night. He remembered thinking that it was kind of beautiful to see the air made real like that.

Marie wouldn't have approved of him smoking, but he was a couple of drinks down by then, and she wouldn't have approved of that either. He didn't care; that was the point of being in the bar in the first place. It was a stupid habit he'd fallen into. A lot of the time when he was at home, it felt like he couldn't do right for doing wrong, and so a couple of nights a week he'd taken to pretending he was working late, but stopped instead at whatever brightly lit bar happened to call out to him from the side of the road.

Just a little me time.

Marie probably thought he was cheating on her. The thing was, he never had and never would. It was like he used to tell her: even if they weren't always great together, they were always good. But she was the jealous type, and that had got worse recently. And if he was going to end up doing the time for a crime he hadn't committed then he figured he might as well commit one of some kind.

The gurney's spinning wheel caught a snag of undergrowth. Whoever was behind grunted softly and pushed harder to get it moving again, but the moment's stillness gave Darren Field a chance to glance to either side and see that the world was no longer as dark as it had been.

And then they were moving again.

But that brief moment had been enough for him to see that there were loops of small fairy lights strung between the trees. The sight was so incongruous that, for a few half-delirious seconds, he imagined that the man had taken him out of the real world, and that the two of them were now in a different one entirely.

"Do you think you were abducted from the bar?" John says.

Field nods cautiously.

"I left my drink inside when I went out to smoke," he says. "Someone could have spiked it then. I don't remember much after that."

"Why did you leave your drink?"

"You don't worry about it as a guy, do you? The place wasn't all that busy, and I had a table out of the way round a corner that I wanted to keep. I didn't want to talk to anyone there."

There's a helpless expression on his face.

"I just wanted to sit with my phone. That was all I *ever* did. Catch up on the news a bit; read a few updates on social media. Maybe play a few games of chess if I couldn't get reception."

He spreads his hands, the question clear.

Is that too much to ask?

The answer, John thinks, is that it shouldn't be, but that's not the way things work. If you let your guard down once, the chances are that you'll be okay. But if you do it a hundred times, the odds are going to catch up with you eventually. Which to his mind is more than enough reason to keep your guard up the whole time.

"Can you remember the name of the bar?" he says.

"No. I didn't even look at the sign when I parked."

"You could drive the route. Check in a few places. You'd recognize it if you were there again."

Field shakes his head. "No."

"It could help. There might be security footage."

"It wasn't the kind of place with CCTV."

Which is just a stupid excuse, and John feels frustration rising inside him. The familiar anger is probably only a short distance behind. On one level, he gets it: returning to the place he was taken from would be traumatic for Field, and it's the last thing he wants to do. But the woman in the woods deserves justice, and he finds it hard to control the urge to grab Field and shake him until he sees sense.

He can't do that, of course, but how else can he persuade him? Daniel would be so much better at this than he is, John thinks. What would his son suggest?

Keeping calm, probably.

"Even so," he says. "Someone there might have seen what happened?"

"He's not the kind of man other people see."

And John is about to reply—maybe even give into the frustration and reach out the way he knows he shouldn't—but Field's choice of words give him pause.

He's not the kind of man other people see.

A beat of silence in the study.

"Okay," John says. "Let's leave that for now."

Field looks down at the carpet. He knows what's coming next.

"Tell me about the woman," John says.

He couldn't tell how long he was pushed on the trolley for, but eventually it came to a stop. His gaze flicked frantically left and right. The space he was in now was more open than the path through the undergrowth. That had felt like a woodland trail, whereas he could tell this was a clearing of some kind. The fairy lights had been left behind them, and there was a different kind of illumination now.

The man behind him was breathing heavily.

And then he became aware that the man was moving around to the right-hand side of the gurney. Instinctively, he looked in the other direction, blinking quickly, keeping his gaze fixed on a line of trees that were almost lost in the shadows.

Don't look.

Don't look at him.

The man began grunting softly. A few seconds later, still restrained, Field felt his body moving. It took him a moment to understand what was happening, and then he understood. The gurney he was lying on juddered as it was rotated slowly upward. While he remained strapped firmly in place, he was being moved from a horizontal position to a vertical one.

The prickling of stars above receded backward in a series of jerks, each one accompanied by a grunt of effort from the man at his side. Field felt delirious. The constellations above him appeared to be swirling. He thought that if he could just get them to settle then perhaps he could remember them and somehow be able to work out where he was.

And then he was upright.

It was easier to make sense of his surroundings now. It was indeed a clearing, somewhere deep in a forest, and it was lit by bright bulbs screwed into the tops of the wooden posts that were dotted around. A swirl of cables was spread out over the ground, and he could hear a generator humming away out of sight. The scene had a dreamlike quality to it. It reminded him of a movie set at night.

Ahead of him, he could see a series of wooden pens, and he had been positioned so as to be facing directly into one of them. When he saw the woman there, his mind suddenly became cold and clear, as though a glass of iced water had been thrown at his face.

She was lying on the ground, curled up on her side, illuminated well enough by the lights for him to see that she was alive and awake and looking back at him. A wooden post had been driven into the ground in the center of the pen. She was chained to it.

The two of them stared at each other for a few seconds.

Even though Field had never been as terrified as he was right then, he still felt a desperate urge to break free and help her somehow. To rescue her. To stop whatever he had been brought here to watch from happening.

And then he became aware that the presence beside him was gone.

"No," he tried to say.

The man walked over to the pen. Field could see him now. He was dressed entirely in black, apart from his face, which was obscured by a featureless white mask.

He had a knife in one hand. A can of petrol in the other.

Darren Field's heart started beating even harder—*no, no, no*—and he strained frantically, impotently, stretching against his bonds as he watched the man approach the woman. And then—

"Stop," John says.

He holds up a hand. It's enough.

He remembers what Sarah told him when they sat together at the seafront last week. *She'd been hurt before that. There were knife marks on the bones.* Maybe if he were still police, it would be important to hear Field's testimony as to what happened next, but it's not something he wants or needs to listen to now.

Field is looking down. Focused on the floor. Crying quietly at the memory. It looks like he's reliving the trauma of what he was forced to see.

"He made you watch him kill this woman?" John asks.

Field shakes his head quickly. "I don't want to say what he did."

"You don't need to."

"But he was so ... *angry*. In my head, that's all I can see of him: he's reds and blacks. He's fucking *screaming*. It's just rage. And he keeps looking at me the whole time, like he wants me to see every second of it."

A beat of silence.

John tries to think.

"What happened afterward?"

"Everything goes dark," Field says. "Maybe he gave me an injection of some kind. Or I drank something. I don't know; I can't remember. But at some point, I woke up, and I was back in my car. For all the world, it was like I'd just pulled over at the side of the road to take a nap. But my phone was gone. My wallet was missing. I'd lost close to two days."

John leans back in his chair.

Thinking again—or at least trying to.

He has never been involved in a major investigation, and he is nowhere near as good at this as Daniel would be. But he has decent instincts. He knows when someone is lying to him, and there's none of that with Darren Field. At the same time, the story is so outlandish that it's hard to know what to make of it.

He glances at the closed door.

"What did your wife say?"

"She was pissed off with me," Field says. "I mean, what do you expect? I hadn't been answering my phone the whole time. I'd worried her sick, she said. Although, honestly, she didn't seem all that worried. She thought I'd been off with someone, or out on a bender or something. She probably *still* thinks that."

"You didn't try to tell her?"

Field looks at John incredulously.

"You're joking, right?"

John takes the force of that. He found the woman's remains, and so he knows there must be some truth to Field's account, but even he isn't sure what to make of it. He can imagine the reception the story would receive from someone else. It's so outlandish that who would believe it?

At the same time, he can't understand why Field wouldn't have at least tried to tell someone. How could you carry an experience like that without buckling under the weight of it? And if the story is true then there must be evidence out there to corroborate it. *He's not the kind of man other people see*, Field had said, but that was magical thinking. Field's phone data can be tracked. There will be footage of his vehicle and its movements. If the story is true then the man who did this thing is not invisible. He *exists*. There will be traces of him everywhere.

"Darren," John says. "You need to talk to the police."

Field shakes his head again, more quickly this time.

"No."

"Why not?"

"Because maybe it wasn't real. Maybe I imagined it all. I was out of my mind, and it was all just some terrible dream. That's probably true, right? And if it wasn't—"

"Darren—"

"*And if it wasn't*," Field interrupts him, "then it matters even more."

"Why?"

Field stares at him for a few seconds.

Then he takes another deep breath.

"Because of what the man told me would happen next."

Eleven

Night was beginning to fall as I parked in the driveway outside my father's house. When I turned off the engine, the car ticked gently in the silence.

I'd spent the journey back from Darren Field's house going over the conversation I'd had with the man's wife. The more I thought about what she'd told me, the more they formed a chain that held firm. My father had found the body of a murdered woman, and a photograph had been taken of him at the scene, seemingly designed to point him in the direction of Darren Field. He had gone to Field's house and spoken to him.

And then Darren Field had disappeared.

I locked the car and entered the house, then headed upstairs to my father's room. I looked around. The bed, neatly made; the careful filing system in the shelves above his desk.

The computer I couldn't fucking open.

Finally, my gaze settled on the punch bag, hanging on its chain in the center of the room.

The boxing gloves on the floor there.

When I was fourteen, my father bought me my own pair. This was after I came home with a split lip and the beginnings of a black eye. There had been an incident after school on the recreation ground I walked through on my way home. Liam Fleming and a couple of his friends were picking on a boy in the year below me. They had him pinned to the ground, one arm up high behind his back, and he was shouting out in pain. There had been a moment when he looked directly at me, scared and helpless, and the expression on his face had stopped me from walking past.

And so I got the shit beaten out of me.

Who did this? my father asked.

I didn't say, of course. That wasn't how things worked.

Did you start it?

No, I told him. I had been sticking up for someone even *less* capable of looking after themselves than I was. I didn't tell him why; maybe I didn't need to. But maybe I'd at least expected some kind of recognition for it: some kind of approval for having tried to do the right thing. But there had been a blank expression on his face, as though he was disappointed in me.

It was a few days later when he bought me the gloves.

"Here," he said.

Then he tried to teach me to box. And I tried to learn. Over the days that followed, I punched the bag the way he showed me, this way and that, over and over. *Get angry,* he told me when he thought I was being too timid. *Keep going,* he said when I was tired. A part of me wanted to impress him, but all it did was reinforce that feeling of shame—that sense that I was worthless and weak—and his attempts at training me hadn't lasted long.

But I still remembered the sadness and depression that had filled my father back then. The black moods. The thuds of the punch bag echoing through the house. The closed doors and the silences.

The anger.

I visualized him standing behind me now, and then attempted to get back into his head. I willed my subconscious to give him a voice that might provide me with some answers.

Did you hurt him, Dad?

You know I wouldn't do that.

Do I?

I wasn't sure. Perhaps I was only imagining him saying that because it was what I wanted to believe. The truth was that, for years now, I had seen my father a handful of times a year, and spoken to him on the phone only occasionally in between. That wasn't enough contact to know someone. People can hide things away from you in the spaces between seconds, never mind weeks and months.

When I imagined him speaking again now, he sounded angry.

You know I wouldn't do what you're thinking.

So what did happen then, Dad?

A beat of silence.

You're clever, aren't you, my son?

I don't know, I thought. Am I?

Sure you are.

So why don't you fucking figure it out for yourself?

I turned around quickly. There was such rage in the voice that I half expected to find him standing there, fists clenched at his sides. Even though the room was empty, the air seemed to throb with emotion.

Anger. Resentment. Guilt.

And I realized my own fists were clenched.

You are detached, I told myself.

You are calm.

I breathed in and out slowly for a few seconds and then relaxed my hands.

Then I went downstairs, closing the door to my father's room behind me. In the kitchen, the fridge was humming quietly. Yesterday, it had felt wrong to cook a meal in here, as though it would be moving on with unseemly speed. But that wasn't my fault. My father had made his decisions, hadn't he? Left me to deal with the detritus of them and clean up the mess.

Fuck you, then, I thought.

I opened the fridge and began to gather ingredients.

And then—later—the karaoke bar again.

I wasn't sure why I went out. Given the events of the day, and the way I was feeling, I had no desire for random socializing. And yet, when I walked in to find Sarah sitting at a table at the back of the room with a bottle of beer in front of her, I was immediately glad to see her. I raised a hand in greeting and she waved back and beckoned me over. I got myself a beer and joined her at the table.

"Hey, stranger," she said. "How's tricks?"

"Strange. Tricky."

"Well, aren't they always?"

I glanced back toward the bar. "You're not working tonight?"

"No." She nodded at her drink. "But this place is like a second home to me these days. And coming here gives me an excuse to sing if I want to. It doesn't feel right to be belting stuff out alone at home in the kitchen by myself."

"That would be a waste of your talents, I agree."

"Very gracious." She tilted her head. "I thank you."

"Except that you're not singing."

She picked up her bottle. "Right now, I'm drinking, and coming here gives me an excuse to do that too. I refer you back to my reasoning about doing things alone in the kitchen."

"Got you."

I picked up my own beer.

It was not lost on me that, whatever the status of Sarah's relationship with Fleming, her last two answers suggested that at least they weren't living together. It almost surprised me that I was pleased by that.

"So, you and Liam," I said. "What *is* happening there?"

"Why do you want to know? Are you worried he might arrest you for drinking with me?"

"I don't think he can do that."

"I'm not so sure he wouldn't try." She hesitated, then sighed. "He has his good qualities, like I said, or it would never have happened. We were together for six months or so. It was never a long-term thing to me, but I guess he saw it differently, because he started to get a little bit too *possessive* for my liking. Not quite as *nice* as before. So I called it a day a couple of weeks ago."

I thought back to my conversation with him yesterday.

"Does he know that?" I said.

She laughed. There was no humor in it.

"He knows I need space," she said. "I'm engaged in what I choose to describe as a very carefully managed *extraction*. Sometimes you can just end it and everything's cool. But with some guys, this is just the safest way of managing things. If you tiptoe out a step at a time, they can tell themselves they never really wanted you and it was their decision all along. Not that I expect you to understand, by the way."

"I understand a little."

"Oh really? Psycho ex-wife about to burst in through the door?" She frowned and put her drink down. "Actually, I shouldn't say that. I apologize in advance if it's possible that might happen."

"Don't worry. I never got married. And my exes are all surprisingly lovely."

She smiled.

"That doesn't surprise me. How come things never worked out?"

"Apparently I'm too closed off. I don't let people in."

"Yeah, that doesn't surprise me either."

I smiled in return, but only briefly. It was a joke, maybe, but there wasn't anything funny about it. It made me think of Laura leaving last year, and the way she'd seemed more frustrated than angry. All my relationships had followed a similar pattern. Women were often intrigued by me at first, and maybe they imagined I'd eventually allow them inside. But even when I wanted to, I never could. The panic kicked in. The shutters came down. I watched people walk away, while a voice in my head told me that I was *detached* and *calm*, and that everything was fine.

My defense mechanisms had served me well in so many ways, but they had also protected me from so much more than I needed them to. They were like old friends who had kept me safe once, but who kept sabotaging me now. I knew I should let go of them, but I didn't know how. Perhaps a part of me was even scared of doing so.

I shook my head.

"What I meant before," I said, "is that I've worked with men like that in the past. My patients are on a different level, obviously, and I'm not saying Liam is anywhere near as bad as that. But there's a scale there in terms of behavior."

"Any advice you want to offer as a professional?"

"I'm sure that you know what you're doing."

She looked at me for a moment, on the verge of saying something else, but then Fiona at the karaoke machine shouted over.

"Sarah—you're up."

"On my way." She looked back at me. "Hey, you want to duet?"

"Maybe later." The idea of standing up there in front of everyone—exposed like that—filled me with horror. "By which I mean, several drinks later."

I watched her bound over, and then listened as she belted out a note-perfect rendition of "Rolling in the Deep." There were so few people in that she might as well have been singing alone in her kitchen, and yet she was totally in her element, the microphone held loosely in her hand, lights flickering on the disco ball rotating above her.

A star on a small stage, perhaps, but a star nonetheless.

After the song finished, she stopped by the bar and brought us both a drink back. We talked more casually then, and before I knew it, it was my round. Then we chatted some more.

She sang another song. Bought more drinks.

For me, the alcohol and conversation helped to loosen the tension of the day, and the bar began to feel like some kind of warm cocoon into which the nagging questions my father had left me with couldn't reach. But I could still feel them there, waiting for me back home, and I knew I couldn't avoid them forever. And I could also tell that Sarah was getting very drunk.

"How are you getting home?" I said.

"Walking."

"Happy to walk you then."

She looked sad. "No duet?"

"Maybe another time."

The two of us walked arm in arm. There was nothing openly romantic about the gesture. If anything, I thought she might be a little unsteady on her feet and wanting to hide the fact from me. Was this how she spent all her evenings, I wondered? Not that it was my place to judge. She was a grown adult. And the last thing she probably needed right now was another man trying to tell her what to do.

She hadn't mentioned where home was, but I figured she'd be in her mother's old house, and we drifted that way naturally. It wasn't far, just a little way along a quiet lane on the edge of the village. As we reached the driveway, she unlinked her arm from mine.

"Thank you," she said.

"You're welcome."

"I'm sorry, by the way. I realized I hardly asked about your dad at all."

"That's okay. I don't feel like talking about him anyway."

"No? How come?"

"I guess I'm pissed off." I shrugged. "What he did. What he didn't." I put my hands in my pockets, choosing my next words carefully. "Everything he's left me to deal with."

"Oh, Dan." She put her hand on my arm. "It's natural to feel that way. But he was a good man. He loved you. You know that deep down."

"I guess so."

"Has there been any news?"

I shook my head.

"Maybe tomorrow," she said softly.

"Maybe. Good night."

I headed back down the lane.

Now that I was alone, I noticed how quiet it was here. The night breeze seemed much colder than it had a minute ago, and I pulled my jacket around me as I walked, my breath misty in the air beneath the streetlights.

There were bushes toward the end of the street, and I registered the man there a fraction of a second before he stepped out in front of me. I held back a pace out of instinct and raised my hands in a fence: a loose boxing stance, but with my palms open and my demeanor less aggressive. It had come in useful on the wards from time to time, helping to control the space between me and a potential assailant.

For some reason, I wasn't remotely surprised to see Liam Fleming standing in front of me now. He seemed a little shocked, though. I imagined he must have stepped out in time to collide with me, and he looked taken aback by the speed of my reaction.

"Whoa." He raised his own hands slightly. "Calm down there, Dan."

"I am calm."

Even so, I didn't immediately relax my guard. Instead, I tried to evaluate the level of threat he represented. His voice was slurred; he was more than a little drunk. And this encounter was clearly a deliberate one. Neither of us was a teenager anymore, but he was still larger than me. And while he was out of uniform right now, he was police, and there was nobody else around. Anything that happened between us here would be his word against mine.

I lowered my hands a little.

"You startled me, Liam."

"Yeah, I can tell," he said. "Sorry about that."

"What are you doing here?"

"Checking on my girl." He nodded down the lane. "Making sure she got home safe. She doesn't always make the best decisions when she's been drinking."

"Who does?" I said.

A beat of silence.

"Two of you seemed pretty cozy," he said.

"She's an old friend. We haven't seen each other in a long time. It was nice to catch up."

"Is that right?"

"Yes," I said. "That is right. And obviously, I also wanted to make sure she got home safely. And so here we both are."

He didn't reply.

If something was going to happen, it would be now. His body language was difficult to read, but I could almost see the attack he was thinking of in his posture, just not quite fully formed yet. For a couple of seconds, the situation was balanced on a knife edge, and the tension sang in the air in the short distance between us.

Then I felt him relax a little.

"Here we both are," he said. "That's right."

"And now here you are, because I'm going home. Good night, Liam."

He was blocking the pavement, and clearly had no intention of moving aside for me. But I allowed him his moment of dominance, stepping into the road, aware of that tension circling around me as I walked past him.

I was about to turn the corner when he called out behind me.

"Just watch yourself, Dan."

I didn't turn around. "In what sense should I watch myself?"

"Remember why you're here. That's all. You're very *clever*. So do what you need to do, and then go back where you went."

He probably intended his tone to be menacing, but I also detected an undercurrent of resentment to his words. Like so many of the people who grew up on this little island and never left, perhaps in his own way he felt trapped here too.

Do what you need to do, and then go back where you went.

"Yes," I said. "I will."

"And you know what? If it had been me there that day at the rest area, I'd have done something."

I waited.

"I'd have done something to save that poor kid."

And again, I said nothing. The temptation to turn back was strong, and I didn't quite trust myself not to give into that if I replied.

So instead I just nodded to myself. And then I walked away.

Despite my jacket I was shivering slightly as I reached my father's house. The confrontation with Liam had not only dumped adrenaline into my system, it had left me angry. I knew that it was better to walk away, but doing so had brought back that same sense of shame I remembered from childhood.

Which brought my thoughts back to my father.

After locking the front door, I headed straight up to his room.

What Sarah had told me earlier was true. Whatever his faults, my father had been a good man. He had loved me. The words I had imagined him speaking in here earlier had come from my subconscious: a reflection of my own thoughts. It had been the grief and anger and frustration that were simmering inside me releasing a bubble to the surface.

I stood in front of the desk, conjuring him up behind me again. Concentrating hard. Until, after a moment, I could almost feel him standing there.

Maybe we should both stay calm, I thought.

That might be a good idea.

What happened, Dad?

Because I need to know so I can figure out what to do next.

You know I can't tell you that.

His voice sounded sad.

In that case, I asked him, Why did you leave me to deal with this? Even if you didn't want me to help you at the time, you must have known I'd stumble onto it eventually. You left a note, didn't you? You told me to come. And you knew I'd find the photograph when I did.

And?

You set me off on a path without giving me any kind of direction at all.

Do you really *think I'd do that, my son?*

I closed my eyes. He still sounded sad, as though it hurt that I would imagine him doing such a thing. And I knew that part of the anger I was feeling was because he *shouldn't* have left me floundering in the dark—that it wasn't fair of him to have done so. But until now, it hadn't occurred to me that he might not have done. That it was possible he had left me something else, and that I might simply be missing what it was.

But what? I thought.

You tell me. Think carefully now.

You kept your investigation from the police, I thought. And so any clue you left behind wouldn't be obvious to them. It would have to be subtle. Something that only I would understand.

He laughed softly.

You're clever, aren't you, my son?

They were the same words I'd imagined him saying before, but this time there was no sneer to them, no mockery. Not only did it sound like he genuinely meant them, but also as if they had been delivered with a knowing wink.

I opened my eyes.

What had just occurred to me seemed ridiculous. Even so, I reached down and turned my father's computer on. Because he had left a message for me, hadn't he?

Notify my son.

The meaning of those words would appear straightforward and obvious to everyone else. There was only me who might think of his voice speaking them out loud, and hear them a little differently.

The password screen appeared on the computer.

I typed Notify and pressed return.

My father's desktop loaded.

The computer was old, and it took a few seconds for it to settle. Window after window flicked back open, one at a time. The final one was a browser, showing the website my father had left open before closing the machine down.

A wall of text. The title at the top was in a larger font.

THE PIED PIPER

Twelve

It's close to midnight.

Andrew Sanderson is supposed to be off shift by now, but he was called out to a domestic violence incident late on and still has to sign the car back in at the department before heading home. The call was a nothing. He was well acquainted with the couple in question by now, and also with the concerned neighbor that kept phoning. The visits always ended the same way. Everything calm by the time he arrived; a few things thrown and smashed, but nobody physically hurt; neither of them wanting to talk to Sanderson. And everyone, including the neighbor, ending up resenting him being there almost as much as he did himself.

He's driving back now along a curling country road, hungry and tired and eager to get home. Sally will probably be in bed by now, but she'll have left him dinner, and there'll at least be a sleepy cuddle on the horizon when he finally slips into bed beside her. Which makes him think of the couple he just left. He and Sally never argue; he can't imagine either of them even getting angry enough to shout, never mind throw anything at each other. Thirty years on the job and some people still baffle him.

He glances out to the right.

About a mile away, he can see the gridded lights of the airport. To his left, at a similar distance, are the lazy yellow floodlights of the college campus. But right here, in the middle of nowhere, everything is dark. The fields directly to either side are black expanses. There are no streetlights, and no other vehicles out at this time of night. Anything oncoming, you always see a good few minutes before you reach each other.

His own car headlights play on the road ahead, the tarmac flashing along like static.

It's the kind of road on which you could really put your foot down if you knew the turns, and given his desire to get home the temptation is there. But Sanderson keeps his speed steady. It's easy to imagine a deer darting out suddenly in front of the vehicle; he's seen that happen before. Always better to be careful.

Regardless, it's this caution that saves his life. He glances down for a second as he rounds a corner, and then up again just as his headlights illuminate something small and bright in the road ahead, and he *slams* on the brakes more out of instinct than anything else. A pale shape is speeding toward him, resolving a second later into the back of a camper van, stopped in the middle of the road. His tires screech desperately on the tarmac, and he comes to a stop just a nose away from the back of it.

And then sits there for a moment, staring down at his hands. They're gripping the steering wheel, and his heart is pounding.

Shit, he thinks. *Shit.*

But then he lets out a nervous laugh and looks up. His car's headlights form bright white circles on the back of the camper van, revealing dents and scratches in the metal, and dirt that seems to be smeared everywhere. There is a door in the back, with a little black window and an old steel handle. Perhaps it had been the handle that had reflected the light and saved him. It certainly wasn't the number plate, which is so thick with mud that it's impossible to read.

Sanderson flicks on his hazards, then grabs a torch and opens the door.

Outside, the night is silent and still, with just the faintest rush of air from the open field to his side. The airport and college are out of sight be-

hind now, and he imagines himself as a single speck of light at the heart of
a pitch-black void. But for some reason, standing there in the empty road,
he doesn't feel *alone*. There's a crawling sensation inside him, as though
something is out there in the darkness watching him.

He shivers.

Get yourself together.

The camper van is backlit by his own headlights, and enough of that
light creeps around the vehicle for him to see it's half off the road, the
front angled into a thorny hedgerow.

He turns on the torch and walks forward slowly, playing the beam
along the side of the van as he goes.

He stops halfway down. The metal here is as dirty as the back, but
there's what looks like a series of small, smeared handprints close to the
ground, as though a child has knelt down in the mud and pawed at it.

He moves the torch beam up.

Here is a window, the black glass protected by a screen of rusty iron
mesh that has been screwed into the metal. He can't see in properly. Is
there something covering the window on the inside too? It looks like
it's been papered over. Standing on tiptoes, he angles the light down,
illuminating a little of the sill between the glass and whatever has been
plastered on the inside. The sill is coated with what appears at first to be
lumps of dirt but which, as he stares closer, moving the light here and
there, reveals itself to be a ridge of dead flies.

He stands still for a moment, listening.

There's a soft tapping coming from inside.

Sanderson breathes in, and realizes there's an unpleasant smell leak-
ing from the vehicle: a faint trace of something rotten and vile escaping
through the cracked seams of its metal.

He feels a cold fingertip tracing up the length of his spine. Almost
real enough for it to flick the hair at the nape of his neck. *Certainly* real
enough to make him turn quickly and angle the torch into the field
behind him.

The light moves over the tangles of gray grass and shadow close to
him, dissolving into darkness farther away.

Again: *get yourself together.*

He turns back to the camper van. None of its own lights are on. The thing looks dead. It can surely only have been here for a handful of minutes without causing an accident, but a part of him can imagine it has sat long abandoned for years in some mirror version of this road, and has just now passed through a veil and shimmered into existence here.

He continues slowly down the side, toward the driver's door.

The window is smeared with more dirt, and the inside of the cab is thick with darkness. But there is *something* there, he can tell. A shadow close to the glass. Almost pressed up against it, but not quite.

Sanderson's heart begins thumping harder in his chest.

He raises the beam of the torch to the window—

—and immediately recoils, stepping back so quickly that he almost loses his footing in the road. Somehow the torch remains pointed roughly at the window, illuminating the dead man behind the glass.

The festering wound that covered one side of his face.

His open eyes staring sightlessly out at the world.

And the impossibly long, yellow teeth, bared in a final rictus of anger and pain and *hate.*

That was the first body.

Sanderson discovered the second in the ten-minute window between calling for assistance and the other officers arriving at the scene. Afterward, he would justify levering open the back door of the camper van and disturbing the crime scene on the grounds that he had been worried someone inside might be hurt. Which was reasonable. But in all the years that followed, he would have given anything not to have done it.

The door crunched open. He shone his torch inside.

The interior managed to be both sparse and cluttered at the same time: a space that felt at once cramped and confined and yet still somehow infinite. There were none of the fixtures and fittings you might have expected. There was no bed to sleep in; no seating area; no toilet or shower. All the standard amenities for living had been ripped out. Because this was not a place in which anyone was intended to live, exactly.

His torch beam moved over shelves and cabinets scattered with tools. As he stepped up into the van, the headlights behind cast his shadow over the base, but he could tell that a section of the floor had been stripped back to create a kind of pit. When he pointed the torch down at it, the flies that were gathered there erupted and clouded the air.

The remains in that pit would be identified as belonging to Robbie Garforth, a ten-year-old boy who had gone missing from woodland a few weeks previously. A friend had been with Robbie at the time. That second child told police that they had been playing hide-and-seek, and that the two of them had entered the wood through a car park on a nearby trail. The second boy remembered seeing what he thought was an old camper van pulled up there, and that there had been a man he didn't want to look at in the driver's seat.

Why didn't you want to look at him? the police asked him.

Because he felt bad, the boy told them.

He felt *wrong*.

Investigators assumed abduction from the start, and swiftly joined forces with other departments around the country. Because over the previous three years, other children had gone missing in similar circumstances. Sean Loughlin, Paul Deacon, and Charlie French. In each case, witnesses recalled seeing an old camper van, and a man they found hard to describe. A long coat. Dirty work boots. A face with something behind it that made you want to look away again very quickly.

To *not see*.

The postmortem on the man in the driver's seat revealed that he had died of a catastrophic heart attack, most likely brought on by the infection that was ravaging his system. There was extensive burning to the left side of his face, where his cheekbone was partially exposed, and patches of his hair were charred down to an ugly black fuzz. Similar injuries were found on his hands. The injuries had clearly been left untreated for some time, until his body finally succumbed to them. Perhaps it brought some small degree of comfort to the children's families to know their killer had spent his final days in a state of delirium and agony.

If so, that was to be the only real closure they did receive. Forensic analysis detected traces of all four boys in the camper van, but Robbie Garforth's was the only body recovered; the remains of the other three victims were never located. And the man who had murdered them remained a mystery. Beyond the evidence of his crimes, nothing was discovered inside the van that enabled the police to identify him. The old wallet in his trouser pocket contained no credit card, driver's license, or money; his fingerprints—or at least, what remained of them—were not found in any records; and searches for his DNA in genealogy databases returned no matches. The vehicle he had been driving yielded no clues either. It had clearly been extensively repaired over the years, assembled from the parts of other vehicles, with any identifying numbers filed away from the metal. The license plate was unregistered. It appeared to be handmade.

And while the investigation into the killer—dubbed the Pied Piper by the media—continued for a time, it ultimately stalled. In the end, despite extensive inquiries, it seemed very much as Andrew Sanderson had thought when he was standing beside the van that night. That the killer and his vehicle had appeared from nowhere, slipping sideways into this world from some terrible adjacent place.

And eventually the world moved on.

But not mine.

Thirteen

THE PIED PIPER

The house around me was silent. There was nothing but the gentle hum of my father's computer, and the menace of those words, right there in front of me in red capital letters on the screen.

The website itself was clearly a relic from the early days of the internet. The background was a repeating beige tile, so badly designed that the patterns were misaligned at every edge, and most of the black text beneath the title was small and hard to read. A primitive animated icon of a man was digging beside the title. Site under construction. Given how old and out of date the page appeared, I wondered how many years that animation had been mindlessly playing for. The site had the feel of a place that had been abandoned a long time ago.

I scrolled down.

Even if the website had been forgotten now, it was immediately apparent that at some point it had been obsessed over. The whole thing was a single page: a wall of text running down one column on the left of the screen, with occasional photographs and document scans on the right-hand side, each of those encased in white, window-like frames.

As I scrolled down, the slow progress of the bar at the side of the screen suggested the page was very long indeed. And the text itself was densely written.

But it was at least arranged roughly into sections. The page began by describing the discovery of the crashed camper van, and the fruitless attempts to identify the killer found dead behind the wheel. Then there were lengthy sections devoted to each of the four victims. I leaned down carefully on the desk, as though the surface might burn my hands, and scanned the screen to see if whoever had compiled the website had done their homework.

—the age of 9, he was already showing an aptitude—

I leaned back.

They had.

But it wasn't necessary for me to read the on-screen text too carefully. Just as I didn't need to look at any of the photographs of the boys that ran down the right-hand side of the screen.

Because I knew everything that had been written here already.

Even after all this time, I still knew it by heart.

A memory.

I was sixteen years old. I was in my room in the attic, lying on my back on the bed, with a book held open awkwardly over my face.

It wasn't a heavy book, but for some reason my arms still ached from the effort. Which was silly, really. I didn't need to lie down; there was a chair I could sit in. And yet I always chose to read the book that way. Perhaps a part of me believed that it should be an uncomfortable experience.

That I deserved to suffer.

Robbie was something of a child prodigy, I read.

At the age of 9, he was already showing an aptitude for chess and had started a club at his primary school.

The book was *The Man Made of Smoke* by Terrence O'Hare, and I had read it more times than I could count. The front cover showed a man's face composed roughly of misty jigsaw pieces. The blurb on the back gave a lurid account of the contents, teasing atrocities that were provided in several of the more speculative chapters inside. But in some ways, it was the sections focusing on the victims in life that were the hardest for me to read.

> *Following his disappearance, Robbie's friends and family joined the—*

I was distracted by the noise from downstairs. My father was shut away in his room, hitting the punch bag, and the sound of his blows reverberated up through the floorboards.

Thud. Thud. Thud.

Heavy. Repetitive. Mindlessly angry.

I kept reading.

> *Following his disappearance, Robbie's friends and family joined the local community in searching the woods for the boy. They were committed and remained hopeful. For a day or two, it was almost as though the game of hide-and-seek begun by Robbie and his friend was still being played.*

The photographs in the book were all in the middle, printed on slightly thicker pages. I held my place but flicked through to one of the pictures of Robbie. It was a portrait from school: one of those ones taken close to Christmas so that your family can order a print for a frame or a keyring. Robbie had a side-part and a sweet smile. He appeared very young, like a little brother you wanted to protect. But there was nothing distinctive about him. He looked like any child, or every one.

I returned to the previous passage.

> *Like many boys his age, Robbie was fascinated by dinosaurs. He would have his parents test him, asking them to question him on*

the pictures. Which dinosaur is this? He would always answer without hesitation.

Reading about Robbie helped me to visualize him as a person, which was also a way of punishing myself for what I had failed to do. The two of us would always be connected—we *all* would be. Because in a strange way, the victims of the Pied Piper had become more real to me at that point than the boys I walked past in the corridors at school. There were even times when I might have thought of them as brothers. Except that I had been in a position to save one of them and I had failed, and my cowardice in the face of their killer would mean that they would surely have rejected me.

The dinosaur names were often long and obscure. They were creatures—monsters in a sense—that Robbie's parents might also have recognized when they were children, but whose names they had forgotten since. The nature of adulthood, after all, is to leave childish things behind.

But it was an interest that Robbie would not be allowed to grow old enough to grow out of.

There was a creak on the staircase outside my bedroom door.

I flipped over quickly, closing the book and sliding it under my pillow in one smooth moment.

My father had already made me throw the book away once, and he would be angry to discover me with it again now. He hated the fact that I tortured myself by reading it. He knew how much it hurt me to do so, and he wanted to rescue me from it—protect me from what had happened—but he could no more do that than I could bring myself to throw the book away myself.

The stairs creaked softly again.

I stood up and walked quietly across the room to the closed door.

After a moment, I could sense my father there, standing on the other side. We were deep in the trenches at that point, he and I. It wasn't just

the book. It felt like we were sharing a house but living separate exis-
tences that were diverging more and more by the day. We had nothing to
say to each other, and whenever we tried it went wrong.

And yet a part of me yearned for him to knock and ask to come in. I
would ignore him or say no, of course . . . except that, right then, it felt
possible that I might say yes. That I would open the door. And perhaps
the two of us could talk in a way that the words actually met in the middle rather than drifting past or drowning each other out.

I waited.

And then I heard the soft creaks on the stairs as he went back down.

I stood there for a moment longer, until I heard his door close on the
floor below and the sound of thudding return. Then I went back to my
bed and lay down with the book again.

*But it was an interest that Robbie would not be allowed to grow
old enough to grow out of.*

I flipped through to the photographs in the center of the book.

Past the portrait shots of Sean Loughlin, Paul Deacon, and Charlie
French—the other victims of the Pied Piper—to the sheets dedicated to
Robbie Garforth.

To the picture that had been taken at his school.

To the sketch that I had helped the police to draw.

And then, bracing myself, to the photograph reproduced below.

Standing in my father's room now, I scrolled down to the bottom of the
web page he'd left open and read the headline of the section there.

The Sighting at Rampton Rest Area

The infamous photograph of Robbie Garforth was posted to the side.

It was a low-resolution, black-and-white image—perhaps even
scanned from O'Hare's book—but it still had the power to shock, because anyone who saw it knew that it had been taken by Robbie's killer.

It showed a close-up of the boy's face, as he turned his head to one side to look back over his shoulder. The image had been captured in a moment of motion that smeared almost everything apart from the fear in his eyes.

The picture had been cropped, but it was still desperately upsetting to look at. And of course, I was the one who had found the original photograph at the rest area that day. The picture here might have been gray and faded, but I had seen the full image in color—vivid and real—and as I looked at the image again now, my mind filled in the details that were hidden outside the edges of the frame. The floor where a section of boards had been removed to create a pit; the hammers and screwdrivers and lengths of cable arranged around the sides, surrounding the terrified little boy.

And for a moment, I was back there. I could smell the stale air of the toilets. Hear the nasal hum of the flickering green lights. See my hands shaking as I stared down at the photograph I was holding and realized what it showed.

I looked away, at the text on the screen, reading this section of the website more closely than I had the ones above.

> The photograph (R) of this little boy was found by 12-year-old Daniel Garvie and his father, John. The image was left in the bathroom at Rampton rest area and the boy has been identified as Robbie Garforth, the final victim of the Pied Piper.

Seeing my name there made my heart beat a little faster.

The cropped version of the photograph had featured heavily in the media at the time, along with the details of my encounter with the killer and the boy. I had seen my father's name mentioned in print occasionally, but I supposed that was understandable: he was a policeman, after all, even if he had never been involved in the investigation itself. There was a lengthy section in O'Hare's book describing the incident. But this was the first time I had ever seen my own name published in the public domain.

A feeling of unease crept through me. Once again, there was the unsettling sensation that I had left a door unlocked and something had snuck in without me realizing.

I forced myself to read on.

> Daniel Garvie encountered the killer and Robbie Garforth in the rest area toilets that day. He was probably lucky to escape with his life!

My heart rate went up again, this time because reading even a bland description threatened to take me back there again. Back into that toilet, with its flickering lights and alien atmosphere, and the man standing outside the flimsy door of the cubicle as I cowered inside. I felt faint, my mind momentarily unable to differentiate between the past and present.

I focused on the screen.

The words there.

> Daniel Garvie encountered the killer and Robbie Garforth in the rest area toilets that day.

I remembered being interviewed by the police at the time. They had been careful with me at first, and then become a little more belligerent as the days passed. They were always professional, but it was obvious that their impatience with me was growing with every meeting. Because there was no doubt that the boy in the photograph was Robbie Garforth. And almost all the witnesses who had seen the boy at the rest area that day were sure it had been him.

All of them except for me.

On the very first day, the police showed me the same school photograph of Robbie that would eventually be printed in O'Hare's book.

This is Robbie Garforth, they told me. He was abducted from the woodland last week. Is this the boy you saw in the toilets?

I stared at it for a long time. There was a superficial resemblance there, but the boy's face was still seared into my mind at that point.

No, I told them. It wasn't Robbie I saw.

They showed me pictures of Sean Loughlin, Paul Deacon, and Charlie French, the other known victims.

And I told them again: no.

The boy I had seen was someone else.

The next day, they came back with that same photograph of Robbie. They'd interviewed the other people at the rest area, they told me, and they all disagreed with me. It was strange, in hindsight, how they flipped the logic of the situation. All these other people had only glimpsed the boy, they said, and yet *they* could manage to be sure. So why couldn't I?

But I am sure, I said.

It wasn't him.

That was when they brought the sketch artist in. I worked with her to produce an image of the boy I'd seen. And I kept insisting on changes, because it had to be right. The end result was as faithful a likeness as I could manage, and while it bore a passing resemblance to Robbie Garforth, it was a different boy.

A few days later, the police returned and told me that, despite an extensive investigation, and my sketch being circulated in the media, they had found no evidence of a missing child in the country matching the description. They showed me the photograph of Robbie Garforth again, and asked me to think back over what happened as carefully as I could.

Because memory was often so unreliable, wasn't it?

And the thing is, my memory really *was* becoming unreliable by then. I had seen that photo of Robbie a number of times, not only in the police interviews, but in the media as well, and his face had begun to merge in my mind with that of the boy I had seen. When I looked at the sketch again, it was the similarities I saw to Robbie now, rather than the differences.

But.

No, I told the police.

I still don't think it was him.

Close to two weeks later, they came back one final time. This was shortly after Andrew Sanderson had found the Pied Piper dead, with

Robbie's remains in the back of the camper van. My heart had broken when I heard the news. I hadn't realized how much I had been holding on to the hope that he was alive—how much it *mattered* to me that he was. In a single moment, that hope was extinguished, like a tiny light blown out inside me. I was flooded with the contempt I felt for myself: for my cowardice, my weakness, my failure.

Because of my age, my father had sat in on all the interviews. I looked at him, and his expression was difficult to read.

"Just tell them the truth, Daniel," he said.

He kept his tone even and his face blank, but his arms were folded, and it felt like he was annoyed with me. After everything else I'd done, I was embarrassing him in front of these officers.

In that moment, I had an overwhelming urge to do anything I could to make amends. To do *something* right. Even if that was just going along with a narrative that would win everyone's approval and bring the pressure—the horror of all this—to an end.

It might have been Robbie, I told them.

Might have been?

It was, I said.

It was him.

Daniel was probably lucky to escape with his life!

I read those words again now. Perhaps it was true. And yet in the years after the encounter, I had lived with the guilt of doing nothing. I had wallowed in it to the point that it almost drowned me. Because if I had been braver then that boy—*Robbie Garforth*, I had to keep telling myself at the time, *it was Robbie Garforth*—might still be alive.

I could have saved him. I should have done.

In the years since leaving home, I had worked hard to push such thoughts away. Detachment and calm had become my watchwords, my defense mechanisms. But the old guilt returned now, along with the self-disgust that had filled me back then.

I shook my head.

Assuming my father had left the note as a clue for me to follow after his death, why had he led me to a web page about this trauma from my past? He must have known how much it would hurt me to revisit this. And he had always been so adamant in the past that I didn't, to the point I'd had to hide O'Hare's book from him until I finally made the decision to leave it behind myself.

Why, Dad?

I forced myself to read on.

At the very least, I was relieved to find no further mentions of my name. The rest of that section was taken up by accounts given by some of the other people who had been at the rest area that day. They had all identified Robbie as the boy they saw. But beyond that, they had been unable to provide much information to the police.

And then I reached a paragraph that made my body go still.

> We know exactly how long the Pied Piper and Robbie spent inside the rest area that day. They arrived at four p.m. in a camper van and departed exactly an hour later. This was confirmed by another witness: a teenager working in the hotel adjacent to the parking area.

The silence in the room began to ring.

> "I go for a cigarette break every hour," Darren Field (19) told police. "I watched them arrive, and I watched them leave."

Fourteen

John is hitting the heavy bag. The mindless repetition is sending a percussion of thuds through the house and shaking his muscles and joints. A bit of brute force. Sometimes that's what you need. And that turns out to be the case right now, because it's when the answer finally comes to him.

Not the answer to the question of what to do. It has been two days since he visited Darren Field's house and listened to the man's story, and John is no clearer now on how to deal with what he was told than he was at the time.

Why wouldn't Field tell the police what he'd been through?

Because of what the man told me would happen next.

And as Field explained, John had understood. He still does now, however much it frustrates him. Field is never going to report what happened to the police: not a chance in hell. And while John could take matters into his own hands and talk to Liam Fleming, he is sure that Field would deny every word of it, assuming it even got as far as him being interviewed. John can easily imagine the pleasure Fleming would take in mocking him. The derision would be obvious on his face. *Look at the old man. Taken in by a wild story. Still trying to play policeman.*

Thud, thud, thud.

Thud, thud, thud.

But there's another important consideration, and that's the danger he might be placing Field in by bringing the man to the attention of the police. John has weighed the risk of that against the memory of finding the dead woman in the woods—balanced it against the suffering she endured, the justice she's owed, and the duty he feels to her—and he's still not sure which way the scales tip. He doesn't know what the right thing to do is. And that's left him adrift and angry, punching the bag a little bit harder every night, but with none of the release that usually brings.

Thud, thud, thud.

Thud, thud, thud.

Thud, thud—

But then he stops.

When he met Darren Field, he had been convinced that there was some kind of connection between the two of them. The sensation has not left him. It has been nagging at him ever since. He knows Field from *somewhere*, but the link between them is too obscure for him to put his finger on.

But suddenly a possible answer has come to him.

For a moment, it seems too ridiculous to be true. But there's also a feeling of rightness to it, like a puzzle piece clicking into place. It was even there in Field's choice of words, when the man had said his abductor was a man that other people didn't notice.

The punch bag creaks back and forth on its chain.

Nobody sees, John thinks.

And nobody cares.

Even though John knew the world did not work that way, it often seemed to him over the years that the encounter with that man at the rest area changed everything. The Pied Piper had driven away that day and disappeared. And then he had been found dead. The rational part of his mind knew those things. But it still felt as though the killer had come home with them that day instead, and been haunting the shadows in the corners of the rooms ever since. Whenever John thought back to the months and years that followed that afternoon, he pictured the man's grubby, broken fingernails reaching into the cracks in his family's life and prying everything apart.

It was later that year that Maggie left the island.

John doesn't blame her for leaving him. He's not sure that he even did back then. If she'd stuck around, her life would have been as small as his has been. But a part of him hated her for leaving him to raise Daniel alone, especially in the aftermath of what their son had gone through.

Because Daniel changed that year. What happened at the rest area affected him so badly. There were times when John could almost smell it in the air, as though his son had been wounded that day, and the injury left untreated, and now an infection was spreading that John had no idea how to treat.

That fucking *book*, for one thing.

When he first found Daniel reading it, John followed his instincts and threw it out. Then he sat his son down and tried to talk to him. Obsessing like that wasn't healthy, he told him. It wouldn't help anyone or change anything. It wasn't his *fault*. A part of John knew that he was talking to himself too, because out of everyone present that day, surely *he* should have noticed something? But he took those thoughts out on the punch bag, along with the rest of his failures. He didn't dwell on it the way that Daniel did.

Days passed.

Then the book reappeared—the same copy; his son had retrieved it from the bin outside—and John was furious. Daniel wouldn't talk to him about what had happened; he wouldn't talk to a therapist; he wouldn't work his feelings out on the bag the way John encouraged him to. He just tortured himself by going over the crimes, again and again. It made John furious. Why wasn't his son listening to him? But all his anger and frustration did was close doors between them: metaphorically at first, and then literally as time passed. John's failure to help his son became yet another weight for him to bear. One more source of pain to take out on the punch bag.

The day that Daniel left for university, John went up to the attic.

As he looked around his son's empty bedroom, he began to cry. He didn't realize he was doing so at first, and it shocked and then shamed him when he did. He prided himself on bearing up to things: taking the disappointments of life on the chin without flinching or folding. The harder the world tried to beat you down, the more resolute you needed to be; whatever happened, you had to *keep going*. But Daniel's bedroom was so strange and unfamiliar to him right then that it might have belonged in a different house. John had the terrible feeling that he had lost something that could never be recovered, and he was crying like a child.

He walked across to Daniel's desk and opened the drawer.

The book was there.

He had long since stopped telling Daniel not to read it, just as he had given up attempting to understand the young man his son had grown into. John picked it up now, noting the tattered cover and well-thumbed pages as he flicked through it.

Were there answers in here to the question of who Daniel had become? There must be, he thought; it felt like the book had raised his son more than he had. Perhaps there were clues as to what had gone wrong between them. Maybe even—the faintest of hopes, this—some hint as to how that damage might be repaired and begin to heal.

John stared down at the book for a long time. There was a lot within its pages that he had no desire to face up to: a lot of history that was best left undisturbed. But that was what he did, wasn't it? And so after he had pulled himself together, he closed the drawer, left the room, and took the book downstairs with him.

He read it from beginning to end that same day. The first reading was a guilty one, as though he was observing his son surreptitiously from a distance. It also brought an ache of sadness. How could Daniel have immersed himself in this, and how much must it have hurt him to do so? John wanted to step backward in time and do more. Wrap him up. Save him in some way.

Days passed.

Daniel didn't call.

John read the book over and over. In one sense, the story inside it was complete. It had ended when the Pied Piper had been found dead by the roadside. Even if the man remained unidentified, his crimes were over, and he couldn't hurt anyone now. And yet John found himself returning to the section in the book that discussed his son's sighting of Robbie Garforth at the rest area and the photograph that had been left behind.

He remembered how adamant Daniel had been when the police interviewed him back then: absolutely certain that the boy he saw had not been Robbie Garforth. He had been determined to make the police believe that, and John had sat there watching him, proud of the way his son stuck to his convictions in the face of that pressure. *Keep going*, he had thought. *Don't give in.* And when Daniel had looked at him for support, John had done his best to reassure him.

Just tell them the truth, Daniel.

But the expression on his son's face had changed at that, and John had realized he'd managed to say the wrong thing yet again—even if, as was so often the case, he couldn't understand how. And Daniel had changed his story and agreed with the officers.

But then . . . surely it *had* to have been Robbie Garforth?

Robbie had been abducted a week before the encounter at the rest area. No other child matching his description had been reported missing, and nobody had come forward when Daniel's sketch was circulated. If it really had been a different boy there that day, then it was as though they had never really been alive at all, or only ever existed in that short window of time. Which was impossible.

But John still found himself thinking: *What if . . . ?*

Days passed.

His son didn't call.

John started making notes. If he was going to work the case (and he barely allowed himself to think of it that way, at least to begin with), it felt important to have his own casework to refer to. He was tentative at first, but his efforts accelerated slightly every evening. By the end of the first week, the paperwork he'd accumulated was scattered chaotically across the desk.

Daniel phoned that evening.

His son said sorry for not being in touch before, but apparently there was only one pay phone in the hall of residence, and there was often a queue. He was settling in well though. Getting on well with his flatmates so far, and already enjoying the introductory lectures in his psychology degree. John had to put his hand over his other ear to make out what Daniel was saying. People were talking in the background, and there was music playing, and it was difficult to hear his son properly.

"What did you say?"

Daniel raised his voice a little. "I asked how *you* were, Dad."

John looked over at the mess of papers.

"I'm good," he said.

After the call, he stood with his hands on his hips for a minute, surveying his desk. The next day, he walked into town and bought his very first box file.

John pulls off the boxing gloves now, wipes his palms on his tracksuit bottoms, and walks over to that old desk.

His collection of box files has grown substantially since then. They are filled with information about the various unsolved crimes that have caught his attention over the years. Inside them are newspaper reports, and printouts, and the scribbled notes he's made while poring over everything, sketching out his own theories.

He picks out that very first box file now—the one that started it all—and blows the dust off its cover. It creaks as he opens it. This first box file contains the core of his research into the Pied Paper case, including all the reports about the encounter at the rest area.

He takes the paperwork out and reads through it carefully.

There is no mention of *Darren Field*. But he did make records of the witness statements given at the time, and one of them calls to him.

> *"I go for a cigarette break on the hour, every hour,"* a worker at the neighboring hotel told the police. *"I watched them both arrive, and I watched them leave."*

John frowns at that, working back through his memories.

He's gone over what happened that day many times, and while much of it is little more than smoke in his mind after all these years, there are still patches of clarity. He recalls that teenager, standing outside the hotel. For some reason, he had caught John's attention: leaning against the wall in his kitchen whites, smoking a cigarette. John can still remember an impression of his face, and when he superimposes it over Darren Field's now, he feels something in his subconscious stir. When he had half recognized Field, he had wondered where it could be from.

Now he wonders if a better question might be *when*.

Those butterflies are back in his chest again: little flutters that tell him he's onto something. Even if he hasn't been able to establish a connection conclusively yet, it *feels* right. He just needs to relax and let the insight come, the way it does for the detectives in the books he reads.

Finally, he turns on the computer.

Follow those damn butterflies.

Fifteen

I went downstairs and got a bottle of good red wine from my father's cellar, then sat at the oak table in the kitchen. I poured myself a glass. Then after a moment's hesitation, I got a second glass from the cupboard, poured a measure of wine into that, and placed it carefully on the table across from me.

Then I sat down and stared at the chair opposite until I could almost see my father sitting there.

It was the same technique I'd employed throughout the day, but I made it more deliberate now, more concentrated. As before, there was no magic to it; it wasn't like conjuring a ghost. Any answers I received would only ever come from inside me. But that in itself could be revealing, because the subconscious often catches its fingertips on textures that the conscious mind skims over.

What's happening here? I asked my father.

A moment of silence. And then:

That's a very good question, my son.

Why don't you talk us both through it? First principles, right?

First principles, I thought. Yes.

What is happening is that you found the remains of a dead woman in the woods. Someone took a photograph of you standing there at that moment and then delivered it to you.

Sure. And we have to assume that was the killer, don't we?

Yes, I think it has to be.

Tell me about the photograph?

It was taken from a particular vantage point, I thought. You realized that just like I did, and when you went up there you found a wallet belonging to a man named Darren Field.

I did. I imagined my father nodding. *It looked like it had been placed there to me. It wasn't an accident—more like a breadcrumb on a trail. The intention was to lead the person who found it somewhere.*

And so you followed that trail?

I did. I went to Darren Field's address to talk to him, and the two of us had a chat. I mentioned the island, the woman. And then the very next day, he vanished.

And nobody's seen him since.

That's right.

I knew better than to ask whether my father had been involved in Darren Field's disappearance. While it remained possible, I didn't want to accept that. Equally, there was no point in asking what he and Darren Field had spoken about that day. The island and the woman's body: I knew that much. I assumed my father would have wanted to know how Field's wallet had found its way to the campsite, but whatever Field might have told him was beyond the scope of the method I was using right now. My subconscious hadn't been there. Anything it told me now would only be guesswork.

I looked down at my glass.

And Darren Field was at the rest area that day?

I imagined my father nodding again.

I recognized his name pretty much straightaway. I'm guessing that you probably did too, right?

No, I thought. Actually, I didn't.

Really?

My father sounded surprised.

I supposed that, given my obsession with the case as a teenager, he might have expected me to be an expert on every little detail. Once upon a time, I had been. But the truth was that I hadn't thought about the Pied Piper very much at all since I left the island. While I hadn't been able to bring myself to burn Terrence O'Hare's book on that last night at the beach, I hadn't taken it with me to university either, and I hadn't read it since.

I wasn't sure if that had been a conscious decision. All I knew was that at some point in my first year at University, detachment and calm had found me, and it had felt safe to be with them. Afterward, my work had helped me as well. However horrendous my patients' crimes might be, they were only men. There was no such thing as monsters, and no sense in revisiting a time when I had believed differently.

That's probably a good thing, my father said softly. *But I'm sure you would have made the connection eventually. You've always been very clever.*

I started turning the glass of wine between my hands.

What am I supposed to do now, Dad? Go to the police?

I don't think that's a good idea.

But—

Hear me out, my son. Not yet, *is what I mean.*

A part of me wanted to argue, but I recognized that there was a degree of sense to the answer I had provided him with. What exactly could I tell Fleming right now? And after our little altercation tonight, I was even more reluctant to talk to him than I had been before. Given our personal animosity, I could easily imagine what his reaction would be if I tried to explain any of this. He'd called me *clever* too, but to Fleming that was probably an insult. I was some kind of mind doctor, not a cop, and I suspected he would take great pleasure in telling me to stop playing at being one.

I kept turning the glass.

What then? I thought. What's the next step?

Another good question. Maybe it's not a step you need, so much as a leap.

Meaning?

You've found one connection to the Pied Piper. Maybe there's another.

No. I shook my head. What happened that day is ancient history.

I wish that was true.

He sounded sad.

You can't just erase history like that, my son. You can look away. You can pretend it's over and done with. But it's always there.

I stopped turning the glass.

Then I looked up. The chair across from me was empty, of course, but I still imagined a presence lifting, as though my father were easing himself out of his seat. A moment later, the air in the kitchen seemed to lose weight. But it didn't feel like he was gone. It was more like he had stood up and left the room, wanting to lead me somewhere.

I picked up the glass of wine and made my way upstairs to his room. The computer had gone into standby in my absence, so I reentered the password and was met by the browser window still open on the website about the Pied Piper.

You can't just erase history like that, my son.

I opened a new tab and clicked on one of the menus at the top.

It's always there.

My father's internet history appeared before me now. There should have been a list of every site he'd visited recently, but aside from the website there was only one. I frowned to myself. Was that really all there was? Or had he manually deleted everything else for some reason? There was no way of knowing.

I clicked on the link to see what was left.

An address search opened on the screen.

Rosemary Saunders
The Blue Flower, Pitch 19, Newland Lock, Rampton

I stared at that for a moment. Rampton was the location of the rest area where I'd encountered the Pied Piper and Robbie Garforth. The address surely couldn't be a coincidence. And a part of me recognized the woman's name too, even though it took a few seconds for me to remember where from.

I clicked back to the tab about the Pied Piper and scrolled a little way down.

"I don't know if he was talking to himself," Rose Saunders (23) told the police afterward. "But he definitely wasn't speaking to me. There was something scary about him. So I acted like I was busy, and I was just glad when I looked up and he was gone."

I read through the rest of the page, searching out the details of the other people who had been present at the rest area that day. Rose Saunders was the only female name I could see listed.

I felt my father's presence solidifying in the air again.

Like I told you, he said. *A leap.*

I stared at the address on the screen.

You thought this might be her? I thought. The woman in the woods?

Well, there were already two links to the Pied Piper, he said. *And both of them were connected to the remains of a woman who nobody had been able to identify. It made sense to follow up on that, if only to rule out the possibility.*

I nodded to myself. It did.

But then I realized what he'd just said.

There were already *two* links? I thought.

Silence for a moment. The air was ringing.

Dad? I prompted.

Are you sure you want me to answer that, my son? You left all this behind you for a reason. I was glad that you did—and perhaps that's why I made this trail hard for you to follow. So that you'd have to choose to do it. So you'd know what you were getting yourself into.

Because it might be dangerous.

Tell me, I thought.

He sighed quietly.

Do you remember what I said to Sarah?

The ringing in the air went up in pitch.

And then disappeared. Yes, I remembered. He had told her it was a good thing it had been him who found the woman's remains in the woods. Better him than a tourist—that had been the rationale.

But thinking about that now . . . who else could have found her?

Earlier today, I had wondered why the killer would make the effort to carry the body out into the woods, only to leave it where it would be discovered so easily. But my father's routine in retirement had been predictable. He had walked that same trail through the woods every morning. And anyone familiar enough with him would have known that.

Two connections. Darren Field. My father.

I reached down to the computer and scrolled a little way up the page, back to the photograph of Robbie Garforth that I had found at the rest area that day. And I thought about the boy I had seen there that day. Despite my initial doubts, I had convinced myself that it must have been Robbie too. Because how could it be anyone else? How was it possible that another boy had disappeared without anyone ever noticing or caring?

And then I felt a different presence behind me.

The figure at my back remained opaque for the moment. Still little more than a shade hanging in the air. But when I shifted angles in my subconscious to allow it a voice, it spoke more strongly now than it had this morning on the crag.

You thought I wanted to be seen, it told me. *And you were right.*

But not just by anyone.

I waited.

I wanted to be seen by you.

James

Click.

James is lying on the dirty mattress when the key turns in the lock. The sound makes him draw his knees up to his chest. It's instinctive; it won't do anything to protect him. But when faced with danger, we all have a desire to curl up. To make ourselves small and unseen.

The door opens slowly.

In the first few months after he was brought here, James was kept in one of the wooden pens outside, tethered by his ankle to a post in the ground. He would lie there shivering at night under a black sky full of implacable stars, and there were moments when he thought he would die, and then ones in which he thought he might already have.

But at some point in the last few weeks, the man had brought him inside. Now he sleeps up here, in a small, windowless room on the first floor of the house. It had been a relief at first. And yet there was also the crawling sensation that all of this was happening by design. That the man had waited until a part of James really *had* died outside—lost somewhere between winter and spring—and that the man was now intending to fill the gap that dead part had left.

The door creaks to a halt.

It's pitch black in the room, so whenever he's locked in here, it's impossible to tell if it's day or night. But there's a window at the far end of the hallway outside the door, and the dim light in the corridor right now suggests to James that it's either dawn or dusk. He doesn't know which; time is difficult to keep track of. It feels like the man usually only keeps him locked in here overnight, but James has the impression that he has been left alone for longer this time.

That's not good.

Because despite the fear and horror, he is alive. The man hasn't killed him. But any shift in routine could mean that is about to change.

The man steps into the doorway.

As always, James avoids looking at his face. The man doesn't like that. But the truth is that there is nothing to see there anyway. Even lying in the darkness, with nothing to distract him, James finds it impossible to picture his features. Ever since that first day at the beach, he has been a black space in James's mind, not so much a presence as an absence. The man is as vast and unfathomable as that night sky outside.

But even out of the corner of his eye, James can see it.

The man is usually empty-handed when he arrives on a morning. There have been times when he brings a camera with him: a bulky old Polaroid contraption. He will hear a click and a whir and then become aware of the man wafting the photograph in the air.

But today, he's holding a knife.

James closes his eyes quickly. Instinct again; if we can't see the monster then it isn't really there. That was something his mother used to say sometimes when he woke up scared in the night. A lot of growing up, she'd tell him, gently stroking his forehead, is about pretending there's no such thing as monsters until you eventually realize that it's true.

Except she was wrong. There is such a thing.

His heart patters in his chest.

"Get up," the man says. "Follow me."

Despite his fear, James knows better than to disobey.

"Yes, sir."

And when he opens his eyes, the man is already gone. James listens to the heavy sound of his footfalls moving away down the corridor, then scrabbles quickly off the mattress and through the doorway. The man's enormous frame fills the hallway ahead. He leads James past the closed doors up here, then downstairs, then through the stale, smoky air of the front room.

And then outside.

Something about the quality of the light in the trees tells James that it's nearly dawn, and he blinks a little as he follows the man down the wooden steps from the house's rickety porch. The camper van is parked at an angle in front of him. Beyond the vehicle, the rest of the farm stretches away, still draped for now in the night's receding shadows.

The farm.

James always thinks of it as that, even though it's really a compound, somewhere deep in the woods, with tight webs of barbed wire strung between the trees. There are wire cages in which the man keeps chickens, and a row of wooden pens where emaciated animals are tied to posts. The air stinks of petrol from the generator that's constantly *putt-putting* away close to the tree line. A farm though. It's easier to think of it as that than some of the other things he might call it.

Prison.

The place he's going to die.

The man walks around the side of the camper van, striding confidently over the dry ground, his boots raising misty puffs of dust. He's holding the knife loosely down by his side. And he doesn't look back— because even though he's leading James to his death right now, he also knows he'll follow. And James does, of course. Because what choice does he have? There's nowhere to hide here. No chance of escape. No use in shouting for help.

Because nobody is coming to save him.

He remembers his first few days here at the farm. Back then, he had tried to convince himself it was a nightmare that he would wake up from soon. When he accepted it was real, he still thought it was going to end.

Because the police would be looking for him, wouldn't they? He remembered the shows he and his mother used to watch on their little television: the ones in which the detective never gave up hope, and the victim was always rescued in time. Away from the farm, the whole world knew that James was gone, and so everyone would be searching for him. His father might never have replied to the letter James wrote, but his mother wouldn't forget about him. She wasn't going to rest until she found him and brought him back home where he belonged.

You and me against the world, James.

But then the days passed.

And then the weeks.

And *nobody* came for him.

During that period, there were times when the man left the farm. On each occasion, James had watched the old camper van disappearing down the trail between the trees, waited until the sound of its engine had faded, and then *screamed* with all the strength he could muster. Calling out for his parents. Shouting for someone—anyone—to come and save him. But his calls disappeared into the trees, and his voice failed him, and there was only ever the insistent *putt-putting* of the generator in reply.

And each time, it was only the man who returned.

Nobody sees.

And nobody cares.

He follows the man across the farm now. Past the lines of wooden pens, where the animals stand motionless inside. Toward the empty pen all the way down at the end. The one closest to the woods, which used to be where he slept. Its gate is open. Perhaps the man has decided to move him back out here? Perhaps that's all that's happening? Except he knows it isn't. Because the man is turning the knife around in his hand, and there's a sense of purpose to him: a kind of dark energy buzzing around him like flies.

There's a dirty old shovel leaning against the post in the center.

James falters. Even with his back to him, the man seems to register it.

"Get in there," he says. "Pick up the shovel."

James walks past him slowly, and then into the pen. He takes hold of the shovel. He can barely lift it. The wooden handle is old and soft, but the metal blade at the bottom is heavy. It's caked with mud and rust.

"Start digging," the man says.

James stares down at the surface of the ground.

And he wants to cry. He doesn't need to be told what he's digging here. It's his own grave. But the thing that sickens him the most is how ashamed he is. Because he feels so weak, and the earth here is hard and solid. His shoulders begin to hitch a little as he tries to keep the tears in. How worthless he is. Everyone has forgotten him. All that's left is the man, and all the man wants is this one final thing from him, and he can't even manage to do that right.

"Start digging," the man repeats.

James gathers himself together. He plants the tip of the shovel against the earth as best he can. Looks at the metal edge at the top of the blade. And then he stamps down on it with the arch of his bare foot as hard as he can.

As James digs his own grave over the next few hours, he forgets about the pain in his body. The trembling muscles. The heat of the sun as it begins to burn his shoulders. The fact that his right foot is so badly hurt now that it won't support his weight. He's determined to do this. He will keep going.

The whole time, the man is whistling softly behind him.

The tune is the same one as always, as maddening and strange as ever. James hates the way that it has begun to worm its way into his mind. Every night in the darkness of his room, it plays in his head, and sometimes he's even found himself humming it without realizing. It's as though the tune is an infection that's gradually spreading to him from the man.

He doesn't want it to be the last thing he ever hears.

But he knows it will be.

Eventually the whistling stops. James assumes that's the man's way of signaling that he's done enough and that the grave is ready. With his hair bedraggled and sweat running down his face, he leans on the spade and looks down at the hole before him. A shiver of pride runs through him. His body is weak and the ground is hard, but he's done a good job. The hole is long and deep. And he's so exhausted now that he just wants to lie down in it, and for this all finally to be over.

Except . . . that's not quite true.

He looks up at the sun streaming through the mist between the trees, and for a moment he thinks he sees his mother standing there, half illuminated by a ray of light. It's only his imagination—a vision driven by the delirium. He knows that. But he still feels a small fire burning inside him. He wants to go home. He doesn't want this monster to beat him.

He wants to live so very badly.

He leans there, breathing heavily, his body trembling.

Waiting.

From back up the farm, he hears the sound of the camper van door slamming shut, and he realizes the man is no longer standing behind him. He hadn't even been aware of him moving. But that's no surprise— it's one of the powers the man has. He seems able to appear and disappear at will.

James risks glancing in that direction.

And what he sees there catches his breath.

The man is walking back toward him again. As always, his face is a black absence, but James's gaze is drawn instead to the figure beside him.

The little boy that the man is dragging by the arm.

With his heart pounding, James looks down at the hole he has dug. Not his own grave at all. The relief that understanding brings washes through him like ice-cold water. But it also brings a burst of shame. He only saw the boy for a second, and he looked nothing like James, but it still feels as though he was seeing a reflection of himself.

But he's done a good job, hasn't he? He needs to cling to that.

He is still alive.

A part of him knows that's what the man wants him to think. That there is a purpose to everything he's doing. That out of all the words James might use to describe this place, the worst one of all might be this:

Home.

But all that, along with the shame, is overwhelmed by the relief. He is still alive! He hears the man and the boy approaching. And as he looks up again at the trees ahead of him, he sees that his mother is gone now.

PART THREE
BARGAINING

Sixteen

Dawn was breaking as I arrived at the ferry terminal the next morning.

I stood out on the deck, watching the gulls wheeling above, like calligraphy etched onto the rose-gold sky. The sea air was freezing, and within minutes I was shivering from the cold. *Bracing*, I reminded myself. And God knew, I needed that this morning. I had slept badly, and the takeaway coffee I was holding was barely warming my hands, never mind taking the edge off my tiredness.

When we reached the mainland, I followed the instructions on the GPS as I drove. The journey took me down a stretch of motorway that I had always been able to avoid until now, but half an hour later, I found myself driving along it for the first time in decades.

My heart began beating harder as I approached the exit to the Rampton rest area. The site was occluded by trees but my skin started to crawl as I reached it, and then a sick feeling settled inside me as I looked up and watched it disappear behind in the rearview mirror.

Because it felt like I'd picked up a passenger.

Please help me.

The voice from the back seat was not the same one I'd imagined last night. That had been the voice of a killer, whereas this was that of a child, scared and desperate. I made sure to keep a careful grip on the steering wheel. The presence behind me wasn't real.

Please help me.

I kept up with the traffic in front.

If you'd helped me then none of this would be happening.

Concentrate, I told myself. It was just the old guilt surfacing: the idea that if I'd only acted differently then everything would be better. And that wouldn't help me right now.

A woman had been murdered. Leaving aside the identity of the killer for the moment, the circumstances around her death allowed me to make a handful of tentative deductions.

Killers could be categorized in a number of different ways, one of which referenced the level of planning that went into the crime. A murderer might be organized or disorganized, for example, or some mixture of the two. Disorganized killers acted on impulse, made mistakes, and were generally easier to catch. But if the body had been left in the woods for my father to find, and the killer had arranged to take a photograph and deliver it to him, that suggested the opposite: an intelligent and highly organized offender. A man who had done precisely what he set out to do, made no mistakes, and left behind only the evidence that he wanted to be found.

The hardest to catch.

Rampton.

I took the exit and then followed the directions through a series of ever-winnowing residential roads. The presence behind me disappeared. And a short while later, I parked on a dusty spread of land at the edge of the canal. Newland Lock. It was a few ramshackle buildings clustered in a circle, all of them shuttered up and closed.

I got out of the car.

Nobody in sight. Everything silent. A crooked wooden lock spanned the water, the sides adorned by blackened cogs that reminded me of rusted clockwork. I crossed it carefully, the wood soft and fragile beneath my feet, a trickle of water spattering out quietly far below.

All the barges here were moored a little way ahead, tethered to iron rings in the ground by thick ropes, and lined up bow to stern along the bank like rides in an out-of-season fairground attraction. Most of them were weathered and ancient, their small gray windows cracked and webbed. But when I reached plot nineteen, I saw that the vessel moored there was in better repair than its neighbors. The sides had been decorated with painted flowers, but also with ornaments glued to the wood: dried flowers pressed behind glass in frames; plastic boxes of seashells; a battered acoustic guitar. The barge looked rickety but cozy, resting in the water like some decades-old arts-and-crafts project.

A man was sitting on a chair outside on the deck.

He was in his fifties, long white hair swept back in a ponytail, and he was wearing a black waistcoat dappled with paint, and a white shirt with the sleeves rolled up. Apparently, he was oblivious to the cold morning air. Or perhaps to everything, I thought. Because even though he was holding a cup, the expression on his face as he stared down at the water suggested he might have forgotten it was there.

I stopped on the bank.

"Excuse me," I called up.

The man turned his head to look at me, but his blank expression didn't alter. As his gaze settled on me, it was like he wasn't really seeing me, and when he spoke he sounded weary.

"What do you want?"

"I was looking for Rose Saunders," I said. "Does she live here?"

The name focused him slightly, bringing him back into his own head a little. While he didn't answer me immediately, it was obvious it meant something to him.

"Rose," he said finally.

"Or Rosemary?"

"No. Always just Rose. That's *important*." He frowned to himself. "And what exactly do you want with my Rose?"

I hadn't prepared an elaborate story in advance, because I hadn't known what I would find here. But given that the address had been in my father's search history, it felt safe to make at least one assumption.

"Because I think my father might have come to see her," I said.

The man said nothing for a few seconds. His gaze moved steadily over my face. Trying to focus. Trying to remember.

"The policeman?" he said.

I hesitated. But my father would have needed a way in. And if that was what he had decided to tell this man then I supposed it had been close enough to the truth.

"Yes," I said. "He was a policeman."

"You look like him, you know."

"I'm not sure that I do."

But the man nodded slowly anyway, then looked away. The focus he had briefly gained was already drifting a little, and as the silence panned out I wondered if there was something stronger in his cup than tea or coffee.

I was about to prompt him when he finally spoke.

"My Rose is gone," he said.

Then he sighed and eased himself carefully to his feet.

"So I suppose you'd better come inside."

The man's name was Brian Gill, and he was Rose Saunders's partner.

Or at least, he had been.

There was a clock mounted to the wall of the barge, and I found myself staring at it as he spoke. The clock had stopped at 8:34, although I had no idea on what day. But the second hand was stuttering in place, and there was something mesmerizing about each little flicker.

"It was a couple of months ago," Gill said. "That was the first time Rose disappeared."

"What happened?" I said.

"She went out one morning, the way she always did. The library in town. The park. But she didn't come back. Rose had always been a free spirit. She liked her space. But it had been a few years since she'd gone off on her own, and it wasn't like her not to let me know where she was."

"Did you talk to the police?"

"Yes, the next morning. But they didn't take it seriously. And then she came back that evening. Except that she was . . . different from before."

Droplets of white paint had congealed and dried on the edge of the table between us. I glanced down the galley. The remains of old flowers were scattered on a makeshift counter there. They had probably been fresh when Rose first gathered them, but they were dark and brittle now, like leaves blown into the corner of an abandoned garage.

I looked back at Gill.

"Where had she been?" I said.

Gill explained it falteringly. When Rose returned to him after that first disappearance, she was shaken and disturbed. She had been kidnapped the day before, she told him. She couldn't remember the details; just that there had been a bench and a man whose face she couldn't recall, and then everything had gone misty. The next thing she knew, she was in the woodland somewhere.

Tied down and unable to move.

Facing a makeshift animal pen.

"There was a man in there," Gill told me. "He was chained to a post."

"Did she describe him?"

"No." Gill shook his head. "She couldn't because of what happened next. And she couldn't tell me much about that either. But the man who had taken her killed the other man. That was all she was sure of. He made her watch it, and whatever happened was so horrible that she couldn't remember it afterward."

I waited.

"And then," Gill said. "He let her go."

The next thing she recalled, he told me, she was back on a bench in the park. Disorientated and a little disheveled, but otherwise unharmed. It was as though she had blinked out of the world for thirty-six hours and then reappeared. Everything was the same as it had been apart from the visceral images—the trauma—that her abductor had left her with.

And the decision that she remembered he had given her.

"The man told her that if she kept what had happened to herself then she would never see him again," Gill said. "Her life would continue as it always had. She'd be safe. But if she went to the police and reported what she'd seen, he would come for her. He would take her back to that place again. And she would be the one to die next."

I thought about my next question carefully. There was something obvious I wanted to ask, given the nature of what I'd just been told, but it seemed better to approach it from a respectful angle.

"Did you believe her story?" I said.

He nodded to himself. Not to say that he did, but acknowledging what I was actually asking.

"I told you that Rose was eccentric," he said. "The truth is that she was ill a number of times over the years. She was sectioned by the authorities on four different occasions that I know of, each time because she suffered a break with reality. When Rose was ill, she said a lot of things that weren't true. So when she told me this . . . I thought it might be the same thing. That she was getting sick again and needed help."

"That's understandable."

"No, it isn't. Because the thing is, she was never lying to me. All those times over the years, it was always real *to her*. And if you imagine that you're scared or in pain, then . . . you really are, aren't you?"

"Yes," I said. "That's true."

"So even if I didn't believe her," he said, "I had to believe *in* her. I had to try to support her and do what was best."

"And she wanted to go to the police?"

"Yes. Because that was the right thing to do."

Despite the threat, she had been adamant that she had to report what happened to her. Rose—Gill told me—had been a woman who felt things deeply. That the murdered man deserved justice. That the killer had to be caught and punished. That the system would protect her.

And that if the police didn't believe her, she would *make* them.

"I drove her to the police station," Gill said. "I waited in the car. Not long after, an officer came out and tapped on the window. He wanted me to go inside to help them calm her down. Which I tried to. She was raging. Desperate. Panicked. It was touch and go whether they were going to call a doctor there and then."

Having dealt with patients with similar histories in the past, I had a degree of sympathy for the authorities for their response. You could only work with the facts available to you. The story Rose had given them was extraordinary, she had a documented history of mental illness, and her behavior in that moment would have led them to a conclusion that was perfectly reasonable. Especially given that the alternative explanation— that her story was true—seemed so wild and unlikely.

"They didn't believe her," I said. "And then she disappeared again?"

"A couple of weeks afterward. She went out for a walk and didn't come back. I went to the police again, of course, but they didn't take her story any more seriously than they had before. They assumed she would come back, like she had other times. And then, when she didn't, they made certain assumptions."

"Yes."

"There was an appeal. Did you see it?"

I shook my head.

"No," Gill said. "Of course you didn't. There hasn't been much coverage, and most of it was down south. She lived there for a while, you see. The police think she's left me and is staying somewhere with friends."

"Maybe that's true."

"No, they're just sweeping her under the carpet. They're not interested. Because of the type of woman she was. No steady employment; no real social network; just living here on this boat with me for years, as off the grid as we could manage. Someone like my Rose was never going to be front-page news. Never anyone's priority."

He grimaced and took a sip of whatever was in his mug.

Then he closed his eyes.

"Nobody cares," he said.

The light in the barge seemed to darken at that. It was only my imagination, but it was as though someone had stepped into the galley behind me, and I felt a tickle at the back of my neck. I glanced over my shoulder. There was nobody there, of course.

Concentrate, I told myself.

Think.

However right Gill might have been about certain people slipping through the cracks, he was wrong about at least one thing.

"But my father came here," I said quietly.

Gill's breathing was growing shallow now. He was falling asleep in front of me.

"Yes," he said. "He did."

For some reason, it felt important to emphasize that point. Even though Gill couldn't see me, I leaned forward, determined to press it.

"So *he* cared."

"Suppose."

"And you told him Rose's story? Just as you've told it to me?"

Gill didn't open his eyes, but frowned slightly.

"He already . . . knew."

"He knew?"

"Working her case, wasn't he?"

And then he started snoring.

"Yes," I said quietly. "He was."

Gill still had the mug clasped loosely against his solar plexus. I stood up and took it away from him, putting it on the small table between us. He grumbled, the way I imagined an infant might, but his eyes remained shut.

I went back outside into the sunlight.

The brightness and fresh air were a shock at first; I hadn't realized how dismal and stale it had been back there in the barge. I looked down at one of the small gray windows on the side, and a swirl of grime on the glass threatened to resolve itself into a face.

I turned my head away quickly and made my way back toward the lock, imagining my father following a few steps behind me.

You told him you were police? I thought.

Well, I might *have done. Or perhaps I hinted that I was to get him to talk to me. Or maybe he just assumed. Who knows?*

I kicked at the dust on the path in frustration. But I did know one thing for certain. To the extent that there had been an investigation into

Rose Saunders's disappearance, my father had been nowhere near it. I also doubted he had any friendly local contacts to call on who would have provided him with the details.

And yet.

Gill told me you already knew Rose's story, Dad.

He did, didn't he.

But how could you have?

That's a good question, isn't it?

Maybe work through it from those first principles of yours.

Assuming what Rose Saunders had told Gill was true, she had been abducted and forced to watch a man being murdered. If she reported what had happened to the police then the same thing would happen to her. And when she did so anyway—because it was the right thing to do—she was not believed. Nobody had listened to her. Nobody had cared.

And the killer, true to his word, had returned and taken her.

My father prompted me, sounding impatient.

But what happened next?

A woman's body was left by a trail in the woods, I thought. Apparently placed there for you to find. A photograph of that moment was delivered to you, which led you to Darren Field, and the two of you had a conversation of some kind. Then Field vanished too. It was after that—after you'd found the connection between Field and the Pied Piper—that you came here looking for Rose and talked to Brian Gill . . .

I stopped as I reached the lock.

Finish the thought, my son.

You knew because you'd already heard the same story from Darren Field, I thought. Hadn't you, Dad? Field told you that he watched someone being killed—let's assume it was Rose—and that he'd been given the same instruction afterward.

A moment of silence.

Maybe so, my father said quietly.

That sounds plausible, doesn't it?

My subconscious had given my father different tones of voice over the past two days, but I was struck now by how sad he sounded. For a moment, that didn't make sense; the revelation felt like a breakthrough. But then I realized what the implications of it might be. If Rose Saunders had been taken, it was because she had gone to the police of her own accord. But if Darren Field had chosen not to—if the police, in the form of my father, had come to his door instead—then it might have been my father's visit that had caused his abductor to return a second time.

Which made his death my father's fault.

It would have been inadvertent. Worse than that, my father would effectively have been tricked into doing so. But I still found it easy to imagine the effect that would have had on him. The guilt it would have caused. He had always been a man who carried the weight of the world on his shoulders. Like Rose, he had been someone who felt things very deeply indeed.

Dad, I thought—

But then quiet music broke the silence, and the spell along with it. I felt a vibration against my side. My phone ringing. I took it out of my jacket pocket and looked at the screen.

[island—police]

The same number that Fleming had originally called me from.

I took a deep breath now and accepted the call.

"Yes?"

"Is this Daniel Garvie?"

A man's voice. Not one I recognized, and certainly not Fleming. But I imagined that after our encounter last night, he would be more than happy to palm off the task of updating me to one of his subordinates. But that didn't change the fact that if someone was calling me then there must have been a development of some kind.

I braced myself.

"Yes, it is," I said. "What's happened?"

There was a faint crackle of static in the background. I imagined the officer reading whatever he was about to tell me from a computer screen, or possibly even just a hastily written note. To his credit, he at least managed to sound sympathetic when he spoke next.

"It's your father, Dr. Garvie."

"Yes."

"I'm very sorry to have to tell you this," he said. "But his body has been found."

Seventeen

The island is still stuck far enough in the past to have a handful of working public telephone boxes, and this one is close to the end of the pier. John has chosen to use it over the past few days partly for convenience, but mostly because he knows that, despite its handy location, it exists in a CCTV black spot. In the event that anyone traces the calls and searches for evidence, there will be no proof that it was him who made them.

Not that you're doing anything wrong, he thinks.

But he doesn't believe that.

It feels more likely that he's done *everything* wrong.

He glances around the street, and then steps into the booth and closes the door. It's cramped and grubby inside, and when he picks up the handset it feels slightly greasy in his hand. Claustrophobic. Dirty. Difficult to get a grip on. That all seems fitting. It's how his whole world has felt since he talked to Brian Gill on the barge and confirmed what had happened to Rose Saunders.

He feeds coins into the slot and dials a number from memory. Then he leans against the side of the box, staring out through the plastic at a gray smear of sea and hoping to God that it will be a man's voice that answers his call this time.

It rings for a while.

When someone eventually picks up, they say nothing.

John waits. There's an obvious presence in the silence on the other end of the line, and he can tell that they sense him here too. The two of them are stuck at an impasse right now, and, for their own very different reasons, neither of them is prepared to break it. This is the third day in a row that he has dialed this number, the first being immediately after returning from that visit to the barge.

Darren Field's wife had spoken to him that time.

No, I'm sorry, she said.

Darren's not here right now.

That's fine, he told her. *I'll try again tomorrow. Not a problem.*

After hanging up, he'd done his best to convince himself that what he'd just said to her was true. That there was not necessarily any kind of *problem* at all. When he'd spoken to Gill, he'd taken the initiative a little: second-guessing what Rose's account of events might have been. The fact that he had been right, and that it echoed what Darren Field had told him so closely, could hardly be a coincidence. However outlandish the stories might have been individually, they corroborated each other.

But that didn't mean anything had happened to Field since. Even accepting the stories at face value—*even if every word of them was true*—Field had done what the killer told him, hadn't he? There was no way in which Rose deserved what had happened to her, but she had broken the rules and gone to the police. Whereas the only person Field had spoken to about what had happened was John.

And he isn't police anymore.

But he had begun to wonder about that. Whoever was responsible for this had not only taken a photograph of John in the woods with the woman's body, but had hand-delivered it to the house afterward. The killer knew that much about John. And even if he was aware that John was no longer police, perhaps to him that was a distinction without a difference.

John had tried the number again yesterday, and Field's wife had answered the call again. This time, she had sounded more frightened, and he had heard the desperation in the *hello* she'd offered, followed immediately by the frustration when John had asked her if Darren was home. It

was obvious she had been hoping the call would have been from someone else.

No, he isn't, she'd said. *I don't know where Darren is.*

Who is—?

John had hung up.

He waits now, the silence heavy in his ear. There's no point in asking
the question. Darren Field isn't there. He can sense the same feeling of
desperation as yesterday, and realizes he doesn't want to take the hope
away from her by speaking and revealing himself once again. Because
deep down, whatever he tries to tell himself, he is certain that he has
already done enough damage to this family.

The silence stretches out for a few more seconds.

"Darren?" Field's wife whispers.

John says nothing.

"Is that you, baby?"

She starts crying.

"Please come home. I'm sorry. I'll do anything, I—"

John hangs up.

What have you done?

His vision stars over suddenly, and he places a hand against the dirty
plastic of the phone box to steady himself. Then lowers his head and
takes a series of deep breaths.

Minutes pass.

And then, finally, he looks up and nods to himself.

What have you done?

That question stays with him all the way home. It feels like some
variation of it has been with him his whole life. The self-hatred and
worthlessness have been inside him since childhood, like a well of lava
that erupts occasionally, shattering the crust. The last few years might
have been peaceful on the surface, but the feelings have always been
there, only ever hidden slightly underneath. And they emerge with ferocity now.

You're worthless.

You're stupid and small.

A failure. A fool.

As always, it doesn't matter whether these things are true, only that it feels like they are. Before now, he's always been able to deal with them, the shame and disgust like pieces of food stuck in his throat that just need to be fought down and swallowed. But this time the consequences of his failure are too much. By the time he gets home, they're choking him.

He locks the front door and heads up to his room.

For a moment, he stands looking up at the shelves of box files above the desk. The cold cases he's investigated over the years. All that research; all those scribbled notes. *Playing policeman.* If so, it had always seemed like a game without stakes: a harmless hobby for an old man to fill his time with. What damage could it do to investigate them? And people might laugh, but nobody really knew what he might end up achieving.

Because people underestimated him.

His very first box file is still open on the desk, all the old paperwork from the beginning of his investigation into the Pied Piper strewn around it. His original cold case, begun all those years ago. His and Daniel's.

He leans on the desk, staring down at it.

Remembering.

In the first year that Daniel was away at university, it took John a while to get used to being in the house by himself. Even though he and his son had lived almost separate lives for the past few years, he felt Daniel's absence keenly. The door to the attic might have always been closed, but it was different knowing there was no longer anyone behind it. That if he worked up the courage to go up those stairs and knock, there was nobody there to answer.

So he threw himself into his new project.

After coming home from work every day, he dedicated his evenings to his research. Over the course of that first year, he read every article he could find on the Pied Piper. He accessed all the available information on the police investigation, ordered copies of old newspapers, joined on-line forums, and made pages and pages of notes. He became gripped by the idea that in solving the mysteries at the heart of the case, he might come to understand his son and heal the damage that had been done to them both.

If I do this, everything will be okay.

And the year had passed.

By the end, his research was an all-consuming mission, but one increasingly driven by a sense of panic: the feeling that time was running out. At the start, he had dared to hope he might find something that everyone else had missed, but all that year proved to him was how thorough the official investigation had been, and how ill-equipped he was to add anything to it.

There was no obvious way forward in identifying the Pied Piper. And if the boy at the rest area had not been Robbie Garforth then he was an enigma: a boy who appeared to have left no discernible trace on the world at all, either before that day or after it.

When Daniel returned for the summer holiday, there was no reconciliation between them. They spent that handful of weeks together much as they had in previous years: retreating to their separate spaces; closing their doors. Only now, it wasn't a lack of courage that kept John from going up the stairs and knocking, but shame.

He had hoped that by identifying the boy Daniel had seen at the rest area that day he might be able to bridge the distance between himself and his son. And he had failed.

Worthless. Stupid. Old man.

At the end of the holiday, Daniel headed off back to university.

John, hungover, had given him an awkward hug at the dock, and noticed that Daniel seemed broader and stronger than he remembered. Away from home (and it was impossible for John to shake the thought: away from *him*), his son had begun to flourish. A part of him had understood that Daniel was leaving the island behind him in more ways than one.

At that point, John had turned his attention to other cases. Just as a hobby. He began to expand his collection of box files, focusing on one cold case after another, flitting between them whenever some new development offered a fresh angle. They were distractions; he never held out real hope of solving any of them. Perhaps that was even part of the appeal. They were like stories in which he could just study chapters over and over, losing himself in the detail, never worrying about reaching the end. They didn't matter to him. They weren't personal.

But he always left that original box file apart from the others, with space beside it on the shelf. It was as though a part of him knew he wasn't done with it just yet. That his worst crime after that first year hadn't been failing during it, but giving up at the end.

Because that was not who he was. He was not a man who gave up.

He was a man who kept going.

What have you done?

John looks through the paperwork from that first file again now.

He remembers how it felt the other night as he was searching for the connection that was eluding him. But the butterflies in his stomach are long gone now. There is only guilt and self-disgust. What on earth had he been thinking? Had he really expected that he might be able to deal with this himself?

He puts the paperwork away and slides the box file back into place on the shelf. There is no gap beside it now. Over the years, that space has been taken up by the seven others he's filled since, and as he stares at those, a different question occurs to him.

Not what he's done.

But what he didn't.

That brings another sharp stab of guilt, and he blinks quickly and turns away to face the punch bag. Worthless. Stupid. Whenever his emotions have erupted, he has taken them out on that, but the ones inside him right now are too huge, too damning. He might have caused Darren Field's death, and that's a weight and pain he can't bear.

The sight of the bag reminds him that he was hitting it when he realized what his connection to Field might be. At the time, he'd been wondering what the best thing to do was.

The emotions inside him now provide an answer to that question.

He sits down at the desk, picturing the Reach, the place that has called to him so often over the years. In the past, he's always resisted. But a voice in his head now demands: *how much better would the world be if you hadn't?*

He takes out a fresh sheet of paper.

Notify my son, he writes.

Eighteen

The traffic and the ferry times meant that it was close to three hours after the phone call when I finally parked by the side of a road on the northeast of the island.

The whole journey, there had been a white-hot sense of urgency inside me, and one that burned more brightly with every passing mile. For some reason, it felt vitally important that I was there when they brought my father's body up from the rocks where it had washed ashore. On one level, I knew that made no sense at all. But even though I understood he was already gone, it still felt possible that I might miss him, and relief flooded through me when I arrived and found that I had not.

The road here curled along the cliff edge, the land open to the right before the world dropped away. A section of the terrain there had been cordoned off by the police and rescue services, but there was less of an official presence than I had anticipated. A single police car and ambulance were parked, along with a couple of unmarked vehicles. A handful of officers were standing around. A helicopter murmured in the sky overhead.

I stared out through the windscreen. A man was standing at the back of one of the cars with coils of yellow rope laid out on the grass nearby. Closer to the cliff edge, metal rings had been hammered into the ground, and more cords of rope were looped through them, pulled taut against the lip of stone by the weight below. My father's body had been spotted by boat, but the rocks meant the vessel itself couldn't get close enough to retrieve it. On this stretch of the coastline, it was almost always easier and safer to send a rescue team down from above.

I got out of the car.

Fleming was standing close to the edge, staring off into the distance with his arms folded impatiently; his body language suggested this was just another instance of my father making life difficult for him. A small crowd had assembled outside of the cordon, the people waiting quietly and respectfully. News traveled fast on the island. It didn't surprise me that a handful of its older residents had gathered here to witness my father's return.

I spotted Craig Aspinall among them. He caught my eye, and for a moment seemed about to nod or raise a hand in acknowledgment. But then he stopped himself. Faltered. Looked away again.

I understood. What was there to say?

There was woodland behind me, but the cliff edge itself was exposed, and the cold wind numbed my face as I leaned against the car. There was the hum of the helicopter high above, the soft sound of lowered voices, the background rush of the sea below. The conversations mingled to form their own quiet, strange language, and the effect was soporific. Within a minute, I felt vaguely hypnotized.

I stared at the loops of metal.

The tightness of the ropes.

I tried not to imagine what state my father's body would be in by now, but it was impossible. The sea was cold here, and that would have preserved him a little, but not entirely. And of course there was the damage he had taken from the initial fall. The Reach was a much higher point on the island than this, and the rocks at its base were slicker and sharper than the ones here. The water might have kept hold of my father all this time, but it hadn't been the sea itself that killed him.

Despite myself, I pictured him falling through the air, the churning world below arriving like a punch you only have a fraction of a second to see coming. The distance must have seemed vast from the top of the cliff, looking down. And yet the speed of the fall must have shocked him.

Detached.

Calm.

My gaze moved to Fleming.

It didn't seem right to me that—however briefly—he would be in charge of my father's body. But there was no escaping it. I forced myself instead to think about the volunteers who were bringing him up. They were good men and women by definition. Whatever the state of his body, they would be carrying him up the cliff face with the care and respect he deserved, wrapped and bundled on a stretcher.

The image brought back a memory.

It was from my first year at university, one of the last few occasions when I'd returned to the island for the holidays. Back then, my father and I were still retreating to our separate rooms and keeping the doors between us closed. One evening, late on, I was lying in bed, listening to the thud of my father's punches echoing up from the floor below.

But then there had been a much louder thud that made the whole house shake.

And then nothing.

I remained lying on the bed for a moment, my heart beating hard, and then made my way downstairs. The door to my father's room was closed. I tapped on it hesitantly.

"Dad?"

No response.

After waiting a few seconds longer, I turned the handle and pushed the door gently open. The main light was off, the room illuminated only by the glow of the computer screen on the desk. There were empty bottles next to it, and a half-finished pint glass of wine beside them.

My father was lying on his side beneath the punch bag, which was still swinging ever so softly in the otherwise still air of the room.

There should have been panic at the sight of him—and perhaps for a second there even was. But it went away quickly. *You are detached,* I told myself. *You are calm.* It was a mantra I'd spent the last year training myself to repeat at times of stress. Things couldn't hurt me if I didn't let them. That aside, my subconscious had already recognized that my father was snoring, and any fear was replaced quickly by sadness and embarrassment for him.

He wouldn't want me to see him like this.

I walked over slowly and crouched down. He still had the gloves on his fists, and the first thing I did was unlace them: one hand and then the other, pulling the leather away. There was blood beneath the skin between his knuckles. His fingers were bare, I noticed. After my mother left, he'd continued to wear his wedding ring. I didn't know when he'd decided to take it off, or why, or where it might have been now.

"Let's get you into bed, Dad," I said quietly.

It wasn't so bad. The same thing had actually happened a couple of times when I was younger, and on those occasions I'd struggled to lift him. But I was stronger now, and perhaps he was lighter. I managed to maneuver him in a half shuffle across to the bed, and then lay him down on his side.

Once I had, I looked back at the desk behind me. The computer was open on a website of some kind. The shelves above were empty aside from two box files at one end. They looked new, and I stared at them for a moment. But then I felt my father stirring beside me, and I looked down at him instead.

"Robbie?" he said. "Was that you?"

The name brought a shiver.

"No," I said. "Robbie's dead."

"I'm so sorry."

"You don't need to be."

"But I am," he said. "Wish I was better."

I waited with him until he fell asleep. He kept repeating that phrase—*wish I was better*—over and over, the words gradually becoming quieter and more incoherent. A mantra of his own. I knew my own feelings about that day only too well, even if I had begun to keep them hidden. But perhaps that was the first time I understood how much it haunted my father too. And as I sat with him, it felt like every awful thing that had happened to us stemmed from our encounter with the Pied Piper that day. As though the man was a rack that had pulled the bones of my family's life apart until they snapped.

"Hey," Sarah said.

I shook my head. I hadn't noticed her in the small crowd that had already gathered, or been aware of her arriving afterward, but she was standing beside me now.

"Hey," I said.

I pulled my jacket around me against the cold, and she rubbed my arm in support. I appreciated that, and also her being here, but I also found myself glancing across at Fleming. He had his back to us right now, standing close to the edge and leaning down on his knees to peer over. But then a whistle came from below, and Fleming called something down, and I put any concerns I had about what he might think to one side. Because the implication was clear enough.

My father's body was coming up.

I turned to Sarah.

"Thank you," I said quietly. "For being here."

"Fuck's sake, you idiot, you don't need to thank me." She gave my arm a squeeze, then let go and hugged herself against the wind. "I'm glad I can be here to support you. But I'd be here anyway. Like I said, your father was always good to me."

A couple of the other officers had joined Fleming now. They were shackling themselves onto the metal loops, readying themselves to reach down and help lift the weight of the stretchered remains up onto the cliff edge.

Sarah glanced at me.

"You okay?"

"I'm detached," I said. "I'm calm."

"What?"

"I'm okay."

"Really? You look like shit."

"Thanks. I'm not sleeping all that well."

"Or eating all that well, I'm guessing." She hesitated. "I'm actually meaning all this in a sympathetic way."

"Noted."

But now that she'd mentioned it, I realized how hungry I was. I'd left the house that morning without breakfast, impatient to get to the mainland and find Rose Saunders, and had been running pretty much on coffee vapors ever since. There was a feeling of faintness right now that wasn't entirely down to the events of the day, or the situation unfolding in front of me. Whatever else I did, I needed to start taking better care of myself.

But first things first.

For another minute, nothing happened, but then the activity at the cliff edge ratcheted up a notch. My view of what was happening was partially blocked by the backs of Fleming and his officers, but it was obvious from their body language that the moment was close. The two men shackled to the loops were leaning over, ropes clenched in their gloved fists. I saw them beginning to strain with effort as they pulled the weight below them upward.

I closed my eyes.

"Steady."

Fleming's voice drifting over.

Then:

"Okay. Good."

I left it a few more seconds before opening my eyes. My father's remains were on the cliff edge now: a vaguely human shape sealed inside a black bag on a stretcher, surrounded by coils of rope on the ground. As the officers stepped away, I couldn't decide whether his body looked larger or smaller than I had expected it to be. There was something diminished about it, but at the same time it seemed to fill the world.

Fleming crouched down beside the stretcher. I heard the quiet sound of a zip being undone.

I felt Sarah's hand on my arm again.

"It's okay *not* to be here," she said. "You do know that, right?"

"No."

Fleming tilted his head, still crouched down on his haunches and staring into the open bag. Then he knelt down properly and moved the lining, examining the remains more closely. He stayed like that for what seemed like an age. Then he rubbed the back of his hand over his jawline, lost in thought.

"Jesus," one of the other officers said quietly.

Finally, Fleming stood up and turned around. His gaze moved steadily over the crowd until it reached and settled on me, and then he saw Sarah standing beside me and his face went blank. *Fuck you*, I thought. I stared back and, after a few seconds, he looked away again. But he raised his hand slightly in my direction. Summoning me.

I walked across to the cordon, leaving Sarah behind me. Fleming met me at the tape. He didn't look at me though. Instead, he stared over my shoulder, his jaw clenched.

"Liam?" I prompted.

"It's not him," he said.

"What?"

He turned to me suddenly, eyes full of anger.

"What do you mean *what*?" he said. "Are you deaf? *It's not your father.* The body's been in the water awhile, but nowhere near long enough. And it's a much younger guy."

I stared at him. But he was looking over my shoulder again now.

"And apart from anything else," he said, "he's wearing a wedding ring."

Nineteen

So there was no reason to stay.

I drove Sarah back to her house. The whole time, there was a *thrum* of anxiety inside me. On one level, I recognized that it was a kind of homeless emotion: the unresolved tension between the horror I'd been building myself up to encounter at the cliff edge and what had happened there instead. But it was more than that.

Because I couldn't shake the memory of Darren Field's wife.

He's your husband, right? I'd asked her yesterday.

She'd held up her hand in answer, showing me her wedding ring.

I don't know if he's still wearing his.

I parked outside Sarah's house. We hadn't discussed what was going to happen next, but she turned to me now.

"You're coming in, by the way," she said. "That's an order."

"Is it?"

"It is." She unbuckled her seat belt. "I intend to feed you."

It was strange to be inside her house again after all these years. I wasn't sure the last time I'd been here; I supposed at some point as a teenager. But as we walked inside, I felt an immediate rush of familiarity, threads of childhood memory catching fire and coming alight in my mind.

The two of us had spent so much of our lives together as kids. There had been a time when we had practically lived in each other's pockets, and when we weren't out in the woods, one of us was usually at the other's house. Being in the kitchen again now was like stepping back into the past, and I had the same sensation I'd had two days ago outside the police station. The feeling that, if I turned around, I might see the ghosts of Sarah and me as children, running through a doorway.

That was exacerbated by the fact that nothing seemed to have changed. The oak table and chairs; the floor tiles and cabinets. Everything was exactly as I remembered. There was even the old cuckoo clock, still nailed at a lopsided angle on the wall by the fridge. It had never worked, even back then. You had to open the door and pull the little wooden bird out by hand on its broken spring.

"I like what you've done with the place," I said.

Sarah hung her coat over the back of a chair.

"What, you mean *fuck all*?"

"Yes."

"Yeah, well." She opened the fridge and peered inside. "The plan was always to get out of here as quickly as possible. So at first, I figured: why do anything? Obviously that didn't quite work out. So these days, it's more a *reminder* of that idea. Every morning, I come downstairs, and I remember that I'm actually just visiting this place, not staying forever. Ah—here we go."

She took a Tupperware tub out of the fridge and turned to me.

"Bolognese okay?"

"Great."

"Then make yourself useful for once in your life."

I boiled the kettle and got pasta out of the cupboard, while Sarah set the leftover sauce warming on the stove. As we prepared the meal, I realized how strange it was for us both to be here like this. Our lives had diverged and gone in different directions, and we hadn't seen each other for so long. Perhaps we would lose touch again soon. It was possible that this moment was its own kind of liminal space, and the thought made me feel sad. The idea that our lives are all separate journeys, and that we just intersect occasionally in places a step aside from them, before carrying on again in our different directions.

Which brought the memory of the rest area to the surface.

That *thrum* inside me intensified, and my chest tightened. It was the same sensation you get when you're about to cry, which immediately made things worse. I didn't cry in front of other people. Not ever. And yet, as I put the pasta into the boiling water, I realized my hand was shaking. The tears were there.

"You okay?" Sarah said.

"I'm fine. I'm—"

"Detached?" she said. "Calm?"

"Yes."

She pulled a face but let it go. She probably imagined it was residual anxiety from the cliff top, and it was partly that. But it was everything behind that as well. Just a couple of days ago, my life had been controlled and contained, the ground beneath me stable, but now I felt unbalanced and lost. There were too many questions I had no answers for right now, and every way forward frightened me on a level I found hard to articulate.

What had happened? What *was* happening?

I didn't know what to think. I didn't know what to do.

When the food was ready, we sat at the kitchen table together, but the emotions had tightened a knot in my throat, and I found it harder and harder to swallow with every mouthful. Something was building. I was bracing myself—determined to keep myself under control—but when everything did finally burst out, it arrived not as tears but as a question.

"Do you ever think about that day?" I said quickly.

There was a moment of silence.

Sarah continued to chew her food slowly, but I noticed the subtle change to her body language. A stiffening of the shoulders; a tension in the way she held her knife and fork. There was no need to specify what day I was asking about. Of all the times as kids that she and I had spent together, the afternoon at the rest area cast the longest shadow.

She swallowed carefully.

"Sometimes," she said.

"When?"

"When I'm feeling bad, I suppose." She shrugged. "When you're down about yourself, you think about things to make yourself feel even worse, don't you? It's weirdly comfortable to dwell. Maybe it means you're right about *something* at least. Even if it's just the fact that you're a shit person."

"You're not a shit person."

"Thank you." She pointed her fork at me. "But also. Do you find *telling someone that* generally makes the slightest bit of difference?"

"No."

She gestured with the fork again—point proved—then looked down and absently poked at her food instead.

"Honestly," she said, "I don't think I even *saw* Robbie Garforth that day. I can picture his face, but maybe that's because I saw the photograph afterward and then my mind *edited* him into my memories."

"That's how I feel too," I said.

She shook her head. "But you did see him."

I hesitated.

"I saw *someone*," I said. "But I didn't think it was Robbie Garforth at first. It took me a long time to accept that it was. My father wanted me to. The police did too—they wanted it to be him. And I think that, in the end, one of the only reasons I agreed was because I just couldn't bear it anymore. It was too much. I needed it all to end."

"Nobody *wanted* it to be him," Sarah said. "Robbie was abducted, what, a week or so beforehand? There were no other missing children."

"There are always missing children."

"Not like that."

"But what if it wasn't him?" I said. "What if it was another child?"

She stared at me for a few seconds. Then she sighed and put down her knife and fork.

"Why are we talking about this, Dan?"

I didn't reply.

"Because it's not healthy," she said. "I do know that much. Whatever happened that day, none of it was *our* fault. Not mine, not yours. We were just kids too, for fuck's sake."

"I know that."

"So what could we have done?"

"Nothing."

The obvious answer.

It was what I'd been told as a teenager, but I'd never been able to accept it then. I had always felt deep down that there must have been something—that there *should* have been. Now there was the sickening possibility that my failure was worse than I had ever realized, and that perhaps everything happening *now* was my fault too.

"Seriously," Sarah said. "Why *are* you asking?"

I took a long, slow breath.

Everything inside me told me to keep this to myself. To keep it all locked down. To remain detached and calm. But it also felt like I needed to unburden myself. That—just for once—it might help to let someone in and share the story, even if it was just so I could hear that it was ridiculous. And Sarah was my friend. Even if she hadn't seen the boy at the rest area that day, she had at least been there.

"Dan?" she prompted.

So I made my decision. I pushed my plate to one side.

"Do you have a laptop?" I said.

Half an hour later, I had told her everything.

Sarah's computer was on the kitchen table between us now, the screen open on the website about the Pied Piper. She kept scrolling up and down the page, as though there was something there that would help her make sense of what I had said but she couldn't see it yet.

"Let's start with this woman," she said. "Rose Saunders. She has a history of mental illness, and she has gone off on her own before. So it's possible she's done that again for some reason?"

"Yes."

"And from what you've told me, her partner doesn't sound like the most reliable of witnesses. So his whole story could just be a load of bullshit?"

"Yes," I said. "But then there's the wallet I found."

"Darren Field, right. Do you know where I'd guess he is right now? Balls deep in some other woman. I mean, I'm sorry to be blunt, but I know the type."

"Yes," I said. "That's possible."

Sarah waited.

Then she sighed.

"*But if not*," she said. "Then what exactly are you thinking? Darren Field can't be the man Rose Saunders watched being murdered."

"No." I shook my head. "The timings of the disappearances are wrong for that. Rose saw someone else die. And then, because she went to the police, the killer took her again, and that time she was the victim. Darren Field was forced to watch her being killed. And now he's vanished too."

"Because he went to the police?"

"I don't think he did," I said. "All I know is that he spoke to my father, and maybe that counted. Perhaps in the killer's mind, that was enough."

"And so this might be why your father did what he did?"

"I don't know."

"And you think the killer might be . . . the boy you saw that day?"

"I don't know."

Sarah stared at me for a moment. I could tell that she was thinking things over, and there was something about the expression on her face that made me feel uneasy. It reminded me a little too closely of the one I'd learned to hide whenever I was guiding a vulnerable client toward an obvious conclusion they were trying to avoid.

"Or *maybe*," she said, "if Field really *has* been murdered, that would mean someone else was abducted and made to watch him die. And if that person was your father, he might still be alive. You might be able to save him."

"I don't know."

"And if the kid you saw *wasn't* Robbie then maybe you can—"

"*I don't know.*"

There was a moment in which it felt like I could hear dust in the air.

"I'm sorry," I said quickly.

"It's fine."

"No," I said. "It's not. I'm sorry. I just don't know what to think."

"Yeah, I get that." Sarah leaned back in her chair. "And I don't know exactly what I was going to say anyway. That you can make amends? Or maybe that you can blame yourself *even harder* for what you didn't do? Look at me, Dan. Please."

I had to force myself to.

"Even though we haven't seen each other in years," she said, "I *do* know you. You haven't changed all that much, you know? You're still carrying a shitload of baggage from what happened back then. And just because you don't think about it, that doesn't mean it isn't there."

I didn't reply.

"I know you're feeling guilty right now," she said quietly. "About your father's death. About everything. When something horrible happens, it's natural to look for answers, and to try to make connections and figure out a way to make things right. Because we want everything to make sense. But sometimes . . . things are just fucking shit."

She gestured around.

"They *don't* make sense. You search for answers, and when you don't find them outside of you, you look for them inside instead. And there are *always* going to be answers there, trust me. Those answers will line up one after a fucking other to make their presence felt."

She looked at the laptop screen.

"But that doesn't mean they're right," she said.

And again, I didn't reply.

But as I drove home, I felt more stupid than ever.

Worthless. Ridiculous. Weak.

And the worst thing was that I should have known better. I had taken a chance and opened myself up, and the outcome of doing that was always predictable. I had not remained detached; I had not been calm.

And Sarah had seen a part of me that I should have kept hidden. I was disgusted with myself for that.

But what she had implied made sense on one level. My father had taken his life, which *of course* had knocked my own off-balance. The grief aside, I felt responsible for that: guilty that I had not done enough to help him; ashamed and hurt that he hadn't reached out to me. Negative emotions are like magnets. It shouldn't have surprised me to find that my mind was trying to make connections to an event in my past that had made me feel exactly the same.

There could be some other explanation for my father having the photograph, and for Field's wallet being in the tent. I didn't know if Brian Gill's story was what had really happened. I didn't know what my father had talked to Darren Field about. There were gaps there. And I was a long way from having enough information to justify the conclusions my subconscious had been starting to leap to.

So your father might still be alive.

You might be able to save him.

Night had fallen as I parked.

The house in front of me had a sad, abandoned air to it. It reminded me of how Sarah hadn't changed anything in her mother's home as a reminder to herself that she wasn't going to stay. I opened the front door and turned on the light. The post had been delivered after I left that morning, and there was a spread of junk mail on the mat. I stepped over, but something about it made me pause and look back. There was a thin white envelope lying face up on top of the flyers. No stamp or address. Just my own name, written there in block capitals.

I closed the front door, then knelt down and picked up the envelope carefully. It wasn't even sealed. The end with the sticker was unfolded and rigid, as if it had arrived here straight from a stationery shop.

I reached inside.

There was a single sheet of paper on which a photograph had been printed. It took me a moment to realize what I was looking at, but then a shiver of horror ran through me. I turned my head slowly, looking down the corridor toward the kitchen, and the door to the garden.

And then back down at the photograph.

The image was mostly black, but there was just enough detail visible for me to understand what I was seeing. The photograph had been taken two nights ago, on the evening I had returned to the island. When in a moment of weakness, I had imagined I was alone, and that it was safe to let my guard down and my emotions loose where nobody would see.

It showed me crouched down on the deck in my father's back garden.

My body arched with grief.

And my face a smeared mask of tears.

Twenty

I slept downstairs that night.

Even with all the doors and windows locked and bolted, the room in the attic felt too isolated for safety. The house below offered too much empty space, and I knew my mind would transform every slight creak into the steady approach of a ghost or worse. And if someone did attempt to break in, I wouldn't hear it from all the way up there.

It made little difference; I found it almost impossible to sleep after receiving that photograph. I drifted a little, but mostly just lay on the settee in the darkness, my skin crawling from the knowledge that someone had been watching me. That I had been in such close proximity to danger without even realizing.

But most of all, because of the moment that had been captured.

The circumstances amplified the sense of violation. It was almost unbearable to me. I had allowed myself to be vulnerable in a way I would never have wanted anyone to witness, and the fact that someone had made my throat tighten up with anxiety. It made me feel helpless and exposed. And the timing of the image seemed deliberate to me.

Mocking me.

The night seemed to go on forever.

But at some point, I became aware that the darkness outside was starting to lighten. Ever so gradually, the shadows in the front room began to shake off their cloaks and reveal themselves as objects of furniture. And the blackness of the night eventually resolved into the dismal, dark gray of morning.

I yawned and stretched. Rubbed my face.

Then went through to make coffee.

While the kettle boiled, I clicked open the blinds on the kitchen window. The back garden stretched out behind the house, the grass there ashen in the dull morning light. The hedge down at the far end was solid. Impenetrable. There was no way anyone could take a photograph through the foliage there, which meant that whoever had done it must have been standing *right there*. Just meters away from me. Invisible in the darkness.

Nobody sees, a voice said in my head.

And nobody—

Someone knocked hard on the front door.

I turned around quickly. For a moment, the door at the end of the corridor seemed to be receding from me, but then I shook my head and it steadied. I walked slowly down, unhooked the chain, and slid the bolt back.

Braced myself and opened it.

Sarah was standing on the doorstep.

"You're up!" she said. "That's good. I was worried I was going to have to keep knocking."

"Yeah," I said. "I didn't sleep too well."

That was probably obvious enough from the state of me, but she didn't make the usual wisecrack. In fact, she looked tired too, as though her night hadn't been any more restful than mine.

I frowned. "Are you okay?"

"I'm . . . okay-ish," she said. "Can I come in?"

"Of course."

She stepped in past me.

"So this is going to sound weird," she said. "But after you left last night, I kept thinking about what you told me, and I decided to do a little bit of digging. And I found something really strange."

"Something strange happened here too."

"Oh?"

I closed the front door.

And then, after hesitating for a moment, I slid the bolt across.

"Yes," I said.

The kettle clicked off in the kitchen.

"But I think that maybe we both need some coffee."

Whatever Sarah had discovered had clearly changed her mind about what might be happening, but I still felt the need to offer some fresh evidence of my own in advance. So I went first, showing her the photograph I'd received. Because even if I had been letting my imagination run away with me and making connections where they might not exist, the photograph proved that *something* was happening.

She stared down at it for a while, her body still. We had spent a great deal of time in each other's houses as kids, and she knew this one well enough not to have to look out of the kitchen window in order to understand what the picture implied.

"Someone was in your garden," she said.

"My *father's* garden," I said. "But yes. He must have just been standing there the whole time. Watching me."

She looked up. "He?"

I pictured the little boy in the rest area.

"I think so," I said.

"But you didn't see him?"

"No."

"Fucking hell." She shook her head and looked down again. "Maybe you need to go to the police."

"Maybe."

Except that, even with the photograph, I still wasn't sure exactly what I could say to them. The picture was evidence of trespass, but it was also meaningless out of context. I could start at the beginning and attempt to convince them, but it felt like I had accumulated disparate parts of a story that was difficult and complicated to tell.

But there was more to it than that. The presence of an intruder in the garden was disturbing and frightening, and the photograph made things personal. But it had *already* been personal. Over two decades ago, I had failed to help that little boy, and I might have compounded my weakness afterward by agreeing it had been Robbie Garforth. If that was true, then what was happening in the present was my fault. And my responsibility to deal with.

"This arrived yesterday, right?" Sarah said.

"It was waiting for me when I got back from yours." I sipped my coffee. "Sitting there on top of the ordinary post, so it must have been delivered sometime during the day. There's no stamp or address on the envelope, so whoever left it had to have been here in person."

"Have you got a doorbell cam?"

I almost laughed. There was as much chance of that as my father having secretly constructed a space shuttle in his bedroom.

"No," I said. "Nothing like that."

A beat of silence in the kitchen.

"What about you?" I said.

"Okay. Let me show you what I found."

She pulled a couple of sheets of paper from her bag and passed one of them to me. It was a printout of a news article, dated a few months ago.

I read it carefully.

SEARCH CONTINUES FOR MISSING ACCOUNTANT

As the search for Oliver Hunter enters its second week, police divers today resumed their search of Bridgewater Canal in the hope of finding evidence pointing to the whereabouts of the missing Whitrow man.

Hunter, 45, was last seen drinking with colleagues in the Red Lion pub, Gildersome Lane, on the 9th June, before leaving alone at approximately 10 p.m. Examination of CCTV footage has suggested he may have taken a shortcut home along the Bridgewater towpath, a route he is known to have used frequently, but searches of the water and surrounding fields have yet to shed light on his disappearance.

DCI Callum Griffiths told a press conference, "Our inquiries are ongoing, and we continue to keep an open mind as to what might have happened to Oliver, and where he might be. We ask anyone with information that might help the investigation to come forward. We also encourage Oliver to make contact with us to let us know he's okay. In the meantime, we continue to offer support to his wife, and his three children, who all very much want their husband and their daddy home safe."

Griffiths sought to downplay any connection with Adam Carlton, 22, who drowned in the canal last year and whose inquest returned an open verdict.

"I stress that, as of right now, this remains a missing persons inquiry," he said. "There is presently no evidence to indicate either criminal involvement or any wider risk to the public."

I looked up at Sarah.

"Oliver Hunter?" I said.

"He was working behind the food counter at the rest area that day."

I looked back down.

"And . . . Adam Carlton?"

She shook her head. "No connection that I can see. I'm guessing that was just an accident the locals had started making a link to. But *Adam Carlton*'s body ended up exactly where you'd expect it to be. That guy definitely drowned. But the police never found Oliver Hunter. The search was called off two weeks later. He's still missing."

I read the news report again.

"Fuck," I said.

"Yep. And then there's this."

Sarah handed me a second sheet of paper. Another printout.

POLICE NAME MURDERED MAN

A man found dead in the woodland two weeks ago has been named by police today as Graham Lloyd. The body was discovered in an isolated corner of Carnegie Park by a couple walking on 3 July, but the condition of the remains had frustrated attempts to establish the victim's identity.

Lloyd was last seen drinking in the town center eight days before the discovery, and was known to police.

DI Benjamin Joyce said, "This was a violent and sustained attack on an especially vulnerable member of the community. Our officers are committed to finding the people responsible for this crime and bringing them to justice."

An autopsy established that Lloyd, 74 years old and of no fixed abode, died as the result of multiple blunt force trauma injuries. DI Joyce reported that several lines of inquiry were being followed, but made a special appeal for members of the town's homeless population to come forward with information.

"We would like to speak to anyone who can shed light on the events leading up to this tragic attack," he said. "Any information we receive will be treated in the strictest confidence."

CAN YOU HELP? [Quote CRGS452 in contact]

"Graham Lloyd was there that day too," Sarah said

I thought back.

"The man in charge of the amusement arcade?"

"That's right." She gestured at the piece of paper I was holding. "I found a few other articles about his murder, but all of them were from before this. All just small, local stuff, then nothing afterward. Either the investigation stalled or—and I'm just *throwing out a vague idea here*— maybe he wasn't the kind of victim the police were going to put a huge amount of resources or effort into."

I nodded.

Even with an article as short as this, it was easy to read between the lines. Known to the police; no fixed abode and drinking in the town center; the appeal to the homeless community. All the quotes from Joyce suggested that Graham Lloyd was not the kind of victim likely to end up on the front pages of the national newspapers, and who probably wouldn't grace the pages of the local ones for long either.

"But there's no way of knowing if anything happened to either of them," I said. "If they were forced to watch someone else being killed, or if they reported it to the police."

"Would the police have believed them if they did?"

"Maybe not Graham Lloyd," I conceded. "Oliver Hunter, though."

"Yeah, but as far as I can tell from the dates, Hunter was first," Sarah said. "If you have a chain then *someone* has to start it off, right? So perhaps Oliver Hunter was abducted and murdered, and Graham Lloyd was forced to watch that. Then it was one after another. Rose Saunders watches Graham Lloyd die. Darren Field watches Rose."

I looked down at the news report, unsure what to think.

"What about the other people on the website?" I said.

"What—you mean, you and your father?"

I didn't reply.

"There *was* one other named person," Sarah said. "Michael Johnson. He was the kid working in the shop there. He clocked the little boy—suspected him of being a shoplifter—but he never saw the Pied Piper. I couldn't find any news stories about him. So I was thinking . . ."

She trailed off, waiting for me to finish the thought.

"That maybe we need to find him?" I said. "And see if he's okay?"

"Maybe."

"But how would we track him down?" The name was so common. "There must be hundreds of people."

"There are," Sarah said. "Yes."

But she had a glint in her eye. And a moment later, she passed me a third piece of paper—another printout, but this time not from an online newspaper article. I looked down at lines of text that appeared to be computer code, most of it jargon that I couldn't remotely understand. But close to the top was the name M. JOHNSON, and there was an address underneath.

"What is this?" I said.

"When you register a website," Sarah said, "there are databases that record it. You can opt out and keep the details private, but it seems like this particular *M. Johnson* didn't bother."

I looked up.

"This is—?"

"The WHOIS information for the website about the Pied Piper that your father was browsing."

She smiled.

"Tell me what an amazing person I am."

"Jesus," I said.

"Well, I wouldn't go *that* far. But pretty good, I think. Because this has to be him, right?"

I nodded. It would be too much of a coincidence for it to be anyone else. It might have been macabre that he'd put so much effort into writing about the case, but I supposed that each of us who had been there that afternoon had been affected by it, and dealt with it in our own ways ever since.

"Yes," I said. "It must be him."

"So. What do you think?"

Sarah looked at me, her eyes still bright. It took me a moment to work out what she was suggesting, but then the expression on her face reminded me of how she used to look when she arrived at my doorstep as a kid.

Do you want to go on an adventure?

Twenty-One

The website was so old that I doubted Michael Johnson would still be at the same address, but Sarah had done her research. The domain name had been renewed last month. She'd also checked another online directory and found a current listing for him there too.

An hour later, we were on the ferry to the mainland.

I bought a coffee and a sandwich from the onboard shop, and then sat down inside on one of the sculpted plastic chairs, facing the glass doors to the outside deck. For some reason, I didn't want *bracing* this morning. Sarah went outside to smoke in the drizzle. Her hair was in a ponytail, and I watched as loose strands of it whipped around in the wind. She seemed oblivious to the elements, just leaning on the railing and staring off toward the horizon as we left the island behind us.

Both of us lost in our own thoughts.

I ate the sandwich slowly, trying to put things together in my head.

Oliver Hunter killed; Graham Lloyd forced to watch.

Graham Lloyd killed; Rose Saunders forced to watch.

Rose Saunders killed; Darren Field forced to watch.

And now Field was missing. If he had been murdered—presumably as a result of talking to my father—then that implied someone *else* had been abducted and forced to watch him die.

So your father might still be alive.

You might be able to save him.

Perhaps that was what a part of me really had been thinking, but I had to remain calm and detached. Because that line of thought was dangerous. I sipped my coffee now and considered the situation logically. If it *had* been my father who was abducted and made to watch Field die, why hadn't he been released and given the choice as to whether to tell his story or not, the way the other victims had?

That didn't make sense.

And I also knew that my father had felt things strongly. He had been an impulsive, frustrated man, prone to outbursts and to lashing out: a man who struggled to control his emotions. He would have felt an enormous weight of guilt over what happened to Darren Field; I had no doubt about that. All the evidence still suggested that he had jumped from the Reach. Apart from anything else, it was difficult to imagine him being taken by someone without putting up a hell of a fight.

And Michael Johnson was likely to be part of the killer's chain.

I wondered what we were going to find when we arrived on Johnson's doorstep. Would he even talk to us? If he did, perhaps it would be a comfort to discover he had no idea what we were talking about. But if he told us a similar story to Rose Saunders's partner then I wasn't sure what would happen next. Because if we couldn't persuade him to talk to the police—which seemed a genuine possibility under the circumstances—then we would be no closer to proving any of it.

The killer had been careful and clever.

I watched the rain dappling the glass.

Okay then, I thought.

And then I braced myself and attempted to conjure up a presence in the air behind me. It was more solid now, and arrived more quickly than it had over the past two days. The man was taking shape in my subconscious. And while I reminded myself that it wasn't real and couldn't hurt me, I still felt the hairs on the back of my neck rising.

Who are you? I thought.

You know who I am.

My mind supplied a note of contempt to the voice, because if the man had once been that boy, he would surely hate me for failing to help him as a child. And yet the words themselves weren't quite true. I didn't know *who* he was. Nobody did. All I knew was *what* he was now.

And what is that?

You're a serial murderer, I thought. You're organized and you're highly intelligent. In terms of what motivates you, your crimes don't seem to fall into the hedonistic category. It's possible that you enjoy the control you have over your victims, but I don't think it's the power itself that matters. And you don't seem like a visionary. Which suggests to me that you're mission-oriented. That would certainly fit with your behavior and victim selection.

You seem very sure of yourself.

No, I thought. It's impossible to be sure without meeting you.

You're getting ahead of yourself, doctor. You talk about my behavior. What exactly is it that I'm doing?

You're playing some kind of sick game.

I'm sure you can do better than that.

All right then, I thought. You force a person to watch someone being murdered. If they tell the police then you kill them next, and you force someone else to watch that. You've created a chain of victims, one after the other.

And who do I kill? Not just anyone, right?

No, I thought. That's part of your mission. You've targeted the people who were at the rest area that day. The people who looked the other way. The ones who failed to help you.

The figure laughed.

You're assuming they're the only people I've killed.

My subconscious sounded like it was mocking me. I felt frustration building up inside me and forced it down.

I am, I thought. Yes. But Occam's razor tells us not to multiply entities unnecessarily. So right now, I'm working with the facts I have. Perhaps there have been others—it's possible you've hurt a lot of people over the years—but those are the only victims I know you've targeted.

The voice was silent for a moment.

When it spoke next, the mockery was gone. It sounded serious now. Angry. Because however clever and careful he was, this was a man built on fragile foundations, and he wouldn't enjoy being challenged.

How do I kill them?

I sipped my coffee.

I didn't know the answer to that question for certain, but in two cases I knew enough. Graham Lloyd had been the victim of a brutal, sustained assault; Rose Saunders's body had been discovered with blade marks on the bones. Whatever the actual cause of death, I had no doubt they had both suffered tremendously.

Violently, I thought.

Horrifically.

And what does that tell you about me?

That you hate your victims, I thought. That you see them as blame-worthy. In your mind, they deserve to be punished. They didn't help you that day, and now you want them to suffer for it.

The answer seemed intuitive.

And yet when the figure spoke again, the voice sounded surprised.

Really? it said. *You think it's as straightforward and obvious as that? I'm disappointed in you, doctor. Did you get your degree from one of those books your father used to love?*

I waited.

If I hated them and wanted to hurt them, why wouldn't I just do it?

Doesn't what I'm doing suggest something . . . more?

Again, I didn't reply.

Because that was true; it did suggest something more. If the man simply wanted to punish the people who had been at the rest area that day, he had the ability and opportunity to do so. But instead, he put them through a terrible ordeal and then gave them a choice. If they did nothing, they would be spared. If they did the right thing, they would be killed next.

And that didn't fit with hating them for doing nothing in the past. If the motivation was to punish them for failing to do the right thing back then, why reward them for behaving in that same selfish way now?

Behind me, the figure laughed to itself softly.

I looked ahead of me, through the glass doors. Sarah blew smoke off to one side on the deck, and I watched as it was snatched quickly away by the wind. The rain was picking up too. It felt like the ferry was taking us into a storm.

The truth is you have no idea what I'm doing, the figure said.

You've spent your whole life avoiding thinking about me. Pretending you could just leave what you did to me behind. Protecting yourself. But you were never safe. I was always there.

I watched as Sarah stubbed out her cigarette. Then she turned around, and just for a second, the rain on the glass changed her face into a smear. In my mind's eye, I pictured the photograph I'd found at the rest area that day.

I blinked quickly. The figure behind me laughed softly again.

You said it was impossible to be sure without meeting me, it said.

But don't worry.

You're going to.

Twenty-Two

Notify my son.

John puts the note in the glove box and then gets out of the car.

He looks down at the photograph he's brought with him: at the image taken of him in the woods with the body of a woman he now believes to be Rose Saunders. His arrogance in investigating the photograph took him to Darren Field's door, which in turn has led to Field's death. He's sure of that now, and the guilt he feels is stronger than ever. But perhaps he can at least try to make amends of some kind before acting on it.

Across the road, the police station is lit by an angle of early evening sunlight.

John hasn't been inside since his last day at work the year before. It had been an uneventful final shift that seemed like an afterthought at the time; to all intents and purposes, he might as well have already left. At six o'clock, there was a haphazard informal gathering at which the super had said a few words, but there had been no drinks afterward, no gifts or decorations, nothing you could call a proper send-off. John had been happy enough with that. He had spent most of that last day feeling like an outdated piece of office equipment that nobody would miss when it was taken away, assuming they even noticed it was gone at all.

The building looks strange to him now. It's still familiar, of course; he spent far too many years working there for it not to be. But it's also alien, like an old home for which he no longer has the keys or any right to enter.

The door opens.

Liam Fleming emerges from the police station, a blustery energy about him. John puts the photograph in his pocket and steels himself. It's Fleming he needs to talk to: the guilt demands a confession. He needs to tell the man everything and confess just how badly he's failed. Whatever the resulting humiliation might be, he deserves that and more. And the Reach is always there.

He leans away from the wall and heads quickly across the street, aiming to meet the man a short distance from the door.

"Liam," he calls over.

But he's misjudged the distance. And while Fleming clearly hears him, and sees him approaching, the man keeps walking, and is already past him when John gets to the other side of the road.

"Liam—"

Fleming comes to a stop on the pavement a short distance away. He doesn't turn around. There is a tension to him, though, like a man trying his best to walk away from a bar fight, but who keeps being called back inside against his will.

"What is it, John? I'm really busy."

"It's about her," John says. "The woman in the woods."

Fleming sighs.

"I can't discuss an ongoing investigation with a civilian. You know that."

"I know. But hear me out."

Fleming turns around deliberately slowly. When they used to work together, John often noted a look of contempt on the man's face, and perhaps Fleming sometimes caught a mirror of it reflected on his. But there's nothing at all there now. Fleming's expression is blank, as though he won the battle between them a long time ago, and hasn't wasted much time thinking about John since.

He stuffs his hands in his pockets and gestures out with his elbows.

"What then?"

"I—"

John stops. The emotion has brought him here. He hasn't rehearsed what he needs to say, and now that the moment has arrived, he doesn't know where to start. In the face of Fleming's indifference, he feels even more stupid than before, not just for his mistakes but for his inability to express them. He glances at the wall back across the street, where Daniel used to wait for him sometimes after work, and it occurs to him that his son would be able to explain the situation. Daniel would weave an account together that Fleming would take seriously. Whereas John has only ever been as good with words as he has been with everything else.

Fleming frowns.

"You all right, John? You seem upset."

"I'm fine."

"You look like you've been crying."

And again, John says nothing. Fleming's line is straight out of the bully's playbook: pretend concern designed to belittle. He *hasn't* been crying. Has he? He remembers that time when he walked into Daniel's bedroom after he left for university, and has to resist the urge to touch his face now to check. Perhaps Fleming is right and it happened without him realizing.

"I haven't been crying," he says.

"Well, you look like you have." Fleming's frown deepens, the fake concern going up a notch. "And you look very *tired*. Is it bothering you, or something? I know it's not a pleasant thing to stumble upon, an old man out walking like that."

"No," he says. "I'm glad it was me who found her."

"Okay. I mean, that's a little *odd*. But okay."

As opposed to a tourist finding her, John thinks.

Because I've seen terrible things before.

But he doesn't say those things out loud. It would only buy into

Fleming's narrative and feed him further lines—*not really, John; you never handled anything as serious as that*—but it's also because his words just now have tripped his thoughts and caused them to stumble.

I'm glad it was me who found her.

That was what he'd said to Sarah, but that had been *before* he'd discovered the connections to the Pied Piper. It has become obvious that he didn't really *find* the woman's remains at all. They were left for him personally. He's being manipulated, which means there is some kind of game being played here: one strung with trip wires and scattered with traps. In both of the accounts he's heard, the victims were warned not to talk to the police about what happened or else they would be taken next. Assuming Darren Field is dead now, that might well be John's fault. But if someone else watched Field die, then what if—by John giving his own account to Fleming now—he seals their fate too?

What if he makes everything worse?

It feels like, all his life, he's had form on that score.

"Is it something you forgot in your statement?" Fleming says. "Because I know you're putting a brave face on things now, but I remember how upset you were at the time."

Tell him, John orders himself.

Just get the photograph out and tell him.

But his hand doesn't move, and the words won't come. He looks back over at the wall again. Daniel would know what to do. Not only would he have figured out exactly what to say to Fleming, he would probably have already prepared a profile of the man responsible. Right now, John can hardly think straight.

What is the right thing to do?

Fleming shifts his stance, losing his patience.

"Look, John," he says. "It's highly unlikely you missed anything that's going to help us at this point. We know what we're doing. We've got everything in hand."

"Right," John says quietly.

"What I think you should do is forget about it. Get some therapy or something. Your boy can probably put you in touch with someone, right?

And then maybe just try to enjoy your retirement as best you can. Work on all those little cases you imagine you're going to solve."

The words smart. He had no idea Fleming knew about that. He remembers talking about them with a few of the other officers sometimes, never imagining it going any further. Now he pictures them all laughing at him behind his back. Because why wouldn't they?

"Right," he says again.

"And for God's sake . . . get a long fucking *sleep* or something."

Finally, John looks back at him.

"Yes," he says. "Maybe I'll do that."

And maybe he won't.

He does try though. Instead of driving to the Reach, he goes to the shop and buys food, then unloads it carefully into the fridge. He cooks an elaborate dinner and then eats it alone at the kitchen table with a glass of good red wine from his cellar. He attempts to keep going.

But while he chews slowly and methodically, he barely tastes the meal. When he attempts to read for a time, the sentences are too slippery and he can't get a purchase on them. In the shower before bed, beneath the deafening hiss of the water, he imagines furtive movement in the house beneath him, but each time he cuts off the spray he hears nothing beyond the thud of his own heartbeat.

Last thing of all, he checks the doors and windows and turns off the lights inside the house one by one.

And then he lies awake in bed, the silence ticking softly.

After a time, his eyes begin to adjust to the darkness of the room, and the pale shape of the punch bag becomes a still figure that seems to be hanging in the air watching him.

He imagines it's Daniel.

Why didn't you tell me, Dad?

I almost did, he thinks.

There had been a moment earlier, walking home after his conversation with Fleming, when John had thought about calling his son: telling him everything; asking him for advice; seeking his counsel. He had got close enough to take out his mobile and navigate to Daniel's number, his finger hovering over the green call icon for an age before he put the phone back in his pocket.

Whatever is happening here, it's *his* responsibility. He needs to deal with it himself. But maybe it's not just the guilt that's stopped him. He is proud of Daniel; his son has overcome the trauma of his childhood and grown into an impressive man. And maybe John wants something he can add to the ledger of his own life. All too often, he's felt little more than a footnote or crossing-out in someone else's.

He thinks:

Because I want you to be proud of me too, my son.

So what would I do?

John considers that. If this really is a game, like in one of those books downstairs, then he has to work out the rules. That's what Daniel would do. John needs to know what winning and losing look like and understand the best way to play, and to do that, he has to learn the layout of the board and get an idea of where the pieces are right now.

He has to find the games master.

John reaches out and flicks the light back on. Then he gets out of bed and walks slowly over to his desk.

To the box files waiting for him there on the bottom shelf.

How did you find a child who never existed?

That was the question that had confounded John when he resumed his research into the Pied Piper case. No child had been reported missing. And the police investigation had been rigorous and comprehensive.

But while most of the world accepted that the boy at the rest area had been Robbie Garforth—because who else could it have been?—there were still pockets of speculation online. John read all the theories. The boy's parents hadn't cared enough to report him missing. He'd been sold to the killer like contraband. He was the man's child, and his birth had gone unrecorded.

None of those ideas sat right with John.

He sat there, illuminated by the computer screen, rubbing his jaw in thought. The police investigation had been thorough, but there were always budgets and constraints to consider—always limits in terms of what efforts were deemed reasonable. But there was nobody looking over his shoulder right then demanding results. The only budget that mattered could be paid for with his time. And it occurred to him that a man who did not give up—a man who kept going—might be able to go beyond what was *reasonable*.

Look at it from a different angle, he told himself.

Work from first principles.

He knew the boy had never been reported missing, and so the first assumption he made was that a child must have disappeared without it being recognized as an abduction at the time. Somehow, a boy had vanished from the face of the earth without there being any suspicion of foul play.

The second assumption he made was based more in hope than logic, and it was this:

Someone must have loved this child.

John didn't want to believe in a world in which that wasn't true. But whoever had loved him had not come forward, and there had to be a reason for that. And so, in opposition to the theories that the boy had come from a broken home in which nobody cared about him, John found himself wondering if the real explanation might perhaps be the exact opposite.

If it was possible that someone had cared *too much*.

The data he required was fragmented across different systems, to which he had varying levels of access, and it took several weeks to amass. The number of files he gathered was eye-watering. It turned out that five years' worth of deaths by suicide amounted to many thousands of records.

He opened the first file and read the details of the inquest. It was immediately apparent that there was no possible connection to the Pied Piper. He was looking for someone who had taken their own life after losing a child. But he kept reading the file anyway. It seemed wrong, having opened it, not to read the person's story. It felt important for someone to see, to care, to remember.

One person a night, he told himself. *That's all.*

No pressure. No expectations.

And years passed.

John looks at the bottom shelf now.

The first box file is back where he replaced it earlier. But his attention is drawn to the seven others beside it. The final one fits in perfectly. It's as though a part of him knew how much work would be required when he started—how much space he needed to leave—if not quite how long it would take to do so. That last box was slid into place four years ago. He hasn't touched it since.

He takes it down now.

Opens it slowly and takes out a piece of paper.

I'm sorry, James, he thinks.

I always assumed you were dead.

James

The man whistles quietly as he drives.

James stares out of the windows of the camper van, eager for sensation but also overwhelmed by it. His gaze darts here and there—one side then the other; up through the windscreen—watching the woods outside the vehicle flashing past. There is almost too much for him to take in right now. The trees at ground level form an intricate brown-green blur of texture. He has become so used to his world being static—living in the center of a universe that turns around him, if it moves at all—that it is a shock to find himself in motion.

This is the first time he has left the farm in over three years.

James doesn't remember much of those years. There is too much pain, too much horror, for him to recall any of what he's experienced in detail. But the man has absorbed him into his world by increments. He made him dig the graves before he made him bury the bodies afterward. He made him listen before he made him watch.

He made him take photographs of his own.

James thinks of the image he has in his pocket right now: of the boy in the back of the camper van when the man brought him back to the farm yesterday. James has never taken part in the killing itself. The man has been waiting for him to be broken before trusting him to do that. But that boy is waiting in the end pen back at the farm now. And tomorrow morning, he will be James's first.

The man continues to whistle as he drives.

James has no idea where they are going today or why. What does it matter? The man is God, and he will reveal himself when he is ready. They drive through woodland and then join the motorway. It is difficult to keep track of time, but it's perhaps an hour after they left the farm when the man finally indicates and takes a turning off the motorway. They drive into a rest area car park and come to a stop. The man unclips his seat belt. He indicates for James to do the same.

James's heart starts beating a little harder.

This can't be real, can it?

Outside the camper van, the air is as fresh as it has ever tasted, and the slight rush of the breeze suggests a landscape he might run in forever. He pictures a kite trailing in the blue sky behind him—and then gets distracted. Because there are people here! The sight of them *all around* causes him to blink in surprise. Aside from the man and the boys, he hasn't seen anyone since he was taken from the beach. He's been in a different world. But now he's back in the real one. As he turns to look, this way and that, it feels as though everything is turning around him instead, and the sensation makes him dizzy.

This can't be happening!

"Nobody sees," the man tells him. "And nobody cares."

He slams the camper van door.

"You'll see."

And then the man sets off for the building at the end of the car park. James follows dutifully behind. But the man must be wrong, he thinks. He's going to wake up from the nightmare after all. He looks down at himself. He is thin and disheveled, unwashed. He knows there are bruises on his face. And he still remembers enough of the real world to believe that someone must notice those things.

Because despite the man's best efforts, he has never quite lost hope.

Even after everything he has gone through, there is still something of *him* left inside. A part of him that believes he might mean more to the world than the man has tried to convince him. A part that wants to go home. That hope is small and fragile, like a faltering pilot light in his heart, but it is there. He isn't brave enough to challenge the man alone, but if someone were to ask him if he was okay, or approach him and offer to help, James would tell them everything in a heartbeat. He still has just enough courage left to do that.

And surely someone will.

A young man is smoking a cigarette outside the hotel at the side of the car park. James stares across at him as they walk, willing him to look up. And then he does! James's heart flutters as the two of them lock eyes.

Notice me, he thinks.

Please.

But then the young man looks away.

"Keep up," the man tells him.

The flower van first. The woman working inside is young and pretty, and she has a kind face. *Help me*, James thinks. But not only does she avoid looking at him, she even turns away. And the same thing happens when they go inside. The student behind the food counter is too distracted; the man at the amusement arcade is too angry; the boy in the shop watches him with open hostility. Person after person, the horrible realization settles inside James that nobody is going to help him.

Everything the man has told him is true.

Nobody sees.

And nobody cares.

And then, finally, the bathroom at the end of the concourse.

The man locks himself away inside a toilet stall, whistling to himself. James is suddenly alone and untethered. He feels the air beginning to sing with tension.

Run, he tells himself.

But his body won't respond. It's the same sensation he remembers having on the beach—a lifetime ago now—but it's so much worse. He is long past the point of helping himself; he is only a little boy, one who somehow feels even younger than he was back then. What he needs is for someone to take his hand and lead him to safety. Away from the man. Away from the boy waiting back at the farm.

All it would take is someone—

And then James hears the door open behind him.

He turns slowly. The boy who walks into the bathroom a moment later is about his own age, and the sight of him takes James's breath away. It is like staring at his own reflection—or into a mirror that shows what he could have been if things had been different. They stare into each other's eyes for a second. And the boy *sees* him—he's not like the others here. The boy knows instantly that something is wrong. Perhaps it's because he's a child too. Maybe it takes someone who hasn't quite grown out of their own nightmares yet to recognize when they've just walked into someone else's.

Help me, James thinks. *Help us.*

Because if you won't then nobody will.

The boy stares back at him, and the hope in James's heart flickers a little more brightly. Even just the eye contact, just being *seen*, gives him courage, and he starts to take a step forward. But then the man stops whistling, and James stops and glances sideways at the closed door. Doing so breaks whatever spell exists between him and the other boy. When James looks back again, he sees the boy is already ducking into the far stall.

Pulling the door closed.

Locking it.

Hiding.

And that last little flicker of hope inside James gutters out.

The man emerges from his own toilet stall a moment later. Even after all this time, James still knows better than to look at the man's face, but he can sense the expression of triumph there right now.

The man ruffles his hair as he walks past.

He stops briefly outside the stall where the other boy is cowering. James walks past it afterward, dutifully following the man out, and he reaches out to the door as he does. His fingertips touch the wood so softly that the boy inside cannot possibly have heard, and yet James senses him flinching.

You could have saved us, he thinks. *But you didn't.*

And after a moment's hesitation, he takes the photograph out of his pocket and places it on the floor.

So that's yours now.

When they arrive back at the farm later, the man takes James to the house. A few of the chickens flutter about frantically in their cages, but the man seems indifferent. He doesn't look down the patchy yard either. Past the pens of animals, to the enclosure at the far end, where the slumped shape of the boy waits in the early evening gloom.

But James does.

Inside the house, the man leads him through to the dirty kitchen at the back, then unlocks the heavy padlock on the door there. It opens onto a set of flimsy wooden stairs descending into absolute blackness below. James has never been down here. The man's heavy boots tap solidly on each step as he descends. James's own land more softly behind as he follows him down into this cold, dark space underneath the world.

At the bottom, the air smells of mold and earth.

There's a click as the man pulls on a cord. The single bulb flickers on and buzzes gently, illuminating a small, makeshift storeroom.

James looks around. Every visible surface is thick with dust, and cobwebs trail down from the wooden ceiling. There are bags stuffed full of old clothes against one wall. Open cardboard boxes against another, filled with an assortment of random objects. Crumpled handbags. Broken toys. Indistinct photographs curling at the edges.

Souvenirs, James realizes.

The wall directly ahead is lined with rusted filing cabinets. Above them are a series of handmade wooden shelves the man has nailed into the brickwork. James's gaze moves over the items there. An old kerosene lamp and a crumpled box of matches; the rusted handles of wrenches and hammers; an ornate silver picture frame with no photograph inside. Metal hooks have been screwed into the fronts of the shelves, keys hanging from them at intervals all the way along.

The man opens one of the drawers. It makes a rasping, scraping sound.

"Come and look," he tells James.

James steps across and peers down. The first thing he notices is the money. It has been a long time since he has seen money, and there is almost too much of it here for his mind to make sense of. Hundreds of rolled-up banknotes, held in tight coils with dirty rubber bands. James has no idea where the man got it from, but the implication of what he's being shown is clear.

Look at how powerful I am.

How powerful I can make you be.

His gaze moves to everything else in the drawer.

"Take some of it out," the man tells him. "Look through it."

James hesitates for a second, then reaches in and begins to pick items out at random, one by one. Passports; bank cards; birth certificates; driving licenses. The blank faces of strangers stare back at him, and the details begin to merge as he looks through them. But again, the implication is clear. The man has dark magic. He can change his name, his age, his face. There are so many identities in this room, each one a door that the man can step through, moving from one to the next at will. He is anybody and nobody. He is whoever he wishes to be. He is hurt and trauma passed on from body to body.

And that is what James can be too.

Nobody sees. And nobody cares.

The man has spent so long convincing him of that, and he's proved it to James today. But down here, finally, he is teaching him something else as well.

Nobody except me.

James hears the familiar tune whistled softly in the air.

It takes a moment for him to realize that it's coming from him now.

PART FOUR
DESPAIR

Twenty-Three

Michael Johnson lived in a tower block not far from the canal where Rose Saunders had moored her boat. Aside from a handful of miles at the end, in fact, the route I drove us on was almost exactly the same as I'd taken yesterday, and passing the exit for the rest area brought the same frisson of panic it had then.

But it also occurred to me how close most of us had stayed to the scene of our encounter with the Pied Piper. Darren Field and Rose Saunders had both lived nearby; Michael Johnson still appeared to. Oliver Hunter had moved a little farther afield, but the stretch of canal on which he had vanished was part of the same system where Rose had made her home. And while Sarah and I had moved away, circumstances had brought the two of us back again. It was as though we were all tethered to the place by a cord that could never be broken, only stretched for a while until eventually it pulled us back.

After leaving the motorway, I didn't drive directly to Johnson's address. When I estimated that we were ten minutes away, I pulled in and parked on a residential road.

"What are you doing?" Sarah said.

"Nothing."

I eyed the rearview mirror. When she realized what I was doing, she craned her neck and looked back over her shoulder.

"You think we're being followed?"

"No," I said. "I'm just being careful."

Ever since the ferry, I'd had the sensation that we were being shadowed. A tingle of attention was itching between my shoulder blades. Which made sense, of course; the photograph I'd received proved that someone really *had* been watching me. But I hadn't noticed anything suspicious on the ferry, and I'd kept a constant eye on the traffic around us after we disembarked and drove away. There had been nothing. Even so, I was still watching carefully now, making a mental note of the color and model of the cars around us. I tried to catch glimpses of the people driving them and remember parts of the license plates.

Five minutes later, I was satisfied.

"Okay," I said quietly. "Let's go."

Michael Johnson had a flat in a tower block. It turned out to be one of three, angled so that the blank windows and empty balconies twenty stories above faced each other across a forlorn spread of dirty tarmac. We parked outside Johnson's block. There were large gray bins in a wire-mesh cage by the entrance, but one of them had been tipped over onto its side, and litter was skittering aimlessly across the ground in the breeze. An old set of double doors led inside, the glass there dark.

Sarah leaned forward and peered up dubiously.

"I'm guessing eight twelve means he's on the eighth floor?"

"Probably," I said. "The lift might be working."

"If not, at least we'll get our steps in."

I turned the engine off, and we sat there for a few seconds in silence. Outside the car, there didn't seem to be anybody else around at all. The world was so quiet that the tower block in front of us now felt eerie and deserted.

"You realize we might be doing something very stupid?" Sarah said.

"I've been thinking that ever since we left the house."

She nodded to herself. "As long as we're on the same page."

Then she leaned back and clicked her seat belt off.

We walked across to the block. The entrance doors opened onto a drab corridor that led down to a claustrophobic hall, with narrow stairwells disappearing up on three sides. There were two lifts, one of them working. I pressed the call button and we waited, the half reflection on the swirled metal of the doors turning us into a pair of distorted ghosts. The interior was small and cramped, with torn linoleum on the floor and undecipherable graffiti daubed across the misty mirror. The elevator lurched as it set off and then juddered more alarmingly with every floor we passed.

"We're going to die," Sarah said.

"It'll be okay."

"I don't want to die in a lift."

We reached the eighth floor and then followed the corridor around. There was no natural light, and a number of the strips above us weren't working, so we passed through pockets of shadow. All the doors were shut, but I could hear television programs and music through the thin wood. A couple arguing. A baby crying.

We reached flat 812.

I knocked on the flimsy door. There was no immediate response from inside the flat, and Sarah and I shared an uneasy glance. There could have been a hundred reasons why Michael Johnson wasn't home right now, and most of them were innocent. But I could tell that we were both focusing on the one that was not.

Then I heard careful movement on the other side of the door.

A few seconds later it opened a crack, a chain holding it in place, and a man peered out at us. Assuming this was Michael Johnson, he was only six or seven years older than us, but time had not been kind to him. Even from the little I could see through the gap, his eyes were bleary and his face was pale and drawn. He was wearing a dirty, baggy T-shirt, and a sagging gray beanie in which his head appeared almost lost.

"Michael Johnson?" I said.

"Who are you?"

He sounded suspicious. But I thought there was also an undertone of fear. Once again, there were many possible reasons for that, but I couldn't help imagining the worst.

"My name's Daniel," I said. "This is my friend, Sarah."

"Are you police?"

"No. I'm a doctor. Sarah's a . . . singer."

He looked at Sarah then back at me.

"What do you want?"

How would my father approach this? As far as he had taken his own investigation, I didn't imagine he would have found his way here. *Michael Johnson* was too common a name to pin down, and I was sure that the method Sarah had used to find this address would never have occurred to him. But if he had done, what would he say? What words would he have used to persuade a frightened man to unchain the door and talk to him?

I decided to settle the matter quickly.

"We're here because we want to talk about what happened to you," I said. "About what you were forced to watch."

That got an immediate reaction, if not quite the one I had hoped for. The man's eyes widened in panic and he made to shut the door. But he was slower than I was, and I got there first, sliding my foot quickly into the gap. The wood was so thin that it barely hurt when the door slammed into it.

And then did so again and again.

"Get out," he spat at me. "Get out. *Leave me alone.*"

"Michael—"

"Go fucking away! Get the fuck out!"

"Michael."

I placed my hand on the door. Even with me adding just that small extra pressure, he wasn't strong enough to slam the door against my foot anymore. He struggled for a moment anyway, and then stopped trying.

Which left us at an impasse.

"Michael," I said. "It's okay."

He looked at me. More obviously frightened now.

"You have *no idea* what you're talking about," he said.

"I do. I—"

"You don't know how fucking *dangerous* it is for you to be here."

A surge of anger threatened to rise up inside me. I wasn't sure where it came from, just that it was suddenly there: the desire to shove a little harder, force the door off its hinges, send him sprawling backward . . .

Detached, I reminded myself.

Calm.

"Listen to me, Michael," I said quietly. "This is really important. I understand because I *was there* that day too. All those years ago at the rest area. You know what day I'm talking about, right? Because you wrote about it. You made a website about the Pied Piper."

That made him hesitate. While the terror remained in his eyes, it was obvious that what I'd said had thrown him.

"You were there too?" he said.

"Yes."

He blinked rapidly. Then he made the connection in his head.

"Daniel?" he said. "You're *Daniel Garvie?*"

"That's right. Sarah and I were both there that afternoon."

He looked at Sarah for a second. Then back to me.

Then he shook his head. His voice dropped to a whisper.

"Have you seen him too?"

The question made a shiver run through me. Even without telling us anything else, I knew he'd just confirmed the worst of what I'd been imagining.

"Seen him?" I said. "No, I don't think so. But I think I do know what you mean by that, and how awful it must have been if I'm right. And if so, I think we really, *really* need to talk."

For a long moment, he didn't reply, and I began to wonder whether I'd said too little or too much. It had been enough to knock him off-balance, but for those few seconds it wasn't clear in which direction he was going to fall.

But then he looked away from me, down at the floor.

"All right," he said. "All right."

And he undid the chain.

Twenty-Four

"I don't know why, but it's the lights in the trees I remember most," Johnson said. "Maybe because everything else is too horrible. But it's also because they seemed so out of place—like a fairy tale. Like I was being taken away into a wood by a monster."

"There's no such thing as monsters," I said.

"Fucking hell," he said. "Didn't you listen to a word I said?"

The three of us sat in silence for a moment.

His question was reasonable. The account he had just given us matched what had happened to Rose Saunders. He had been abducted last week, late one night, after drinking in a pub: a quiet, out of the way place, because the ones nearby were always busy and threatening. He had left his drink at one point to go to the toilet. He remembered leaving the pub, and that the cold air had made him feel woozy and sick, and then nothing until the forest and the fairy lights.

Until he had been forced to watch a man die.

I looked around now.

His living room was small and sparsely furnished. There was just a settee and chairs, and a plywood table with a portable television. Johnson was sitting at the end of the settee, Sarah and I on a chair each. A window took up most of one wall, and we were high enough up that it had felt like being in the sky when we first walked in: bright and airy despite the claustrophobia of the room. But everything seemed darker now.

I glanced over at Sarah. She was staring down at the floor.

"And you're sure it was Darren Field?" I said.

"I'm sure." He nodded miserably. "I knew Darren back then. We were the same age, so we hung about a bit. I hadn't seen him in a few years, but he hadn't changed that much. As soon as I set eyes on him, there was this jolt of recognition. And somehow I knew."

"Knew what?"

"That it was about that day. That the man behind me was *him*."

"But the man never said anything?"

"Just what I told you already. What he said afterward: that if I went to the police, then I'd be next. But he didn't need to say anything for me to know who he was. Because think about it: who else could it be?"

"You saw the boy that day."

"Yeah. The same as you did. I thought he was just some little shit looking to shoplift. I didn't realize he needed help."

Not the same as me, I thought. Johnson might have felt culpable for doing nothing that day, but he was only a bystander. I had known for certain the boy needed help, and I had been too scared to give it.

"You told the police it was Robbie Garforth you saw," I said.

"Because they showed me a photograph. It looked like him, so I figured it had to be. And you know what? I think I even *wanted* it to be. That's a horrible thing to admit, but it's true."

"Why did you want it to be Robbie?"

"Because that meant the man was the Pied Piper—that he'd been *right there*. I know that sounds sick, but I was obsessed with serial killers back then. And if it hadn't been Robbie I saw, then it wasn't such a big deal, was it? Not as much of a *story* to tell people."

He shook his head.

On the face of it, he seemed disgusted with himself for having thought that way, but I wondered if that was really true, or if he was attempting to put psychological distance between the past and the present. If he wasn't that person anymore then it was unfair to be held responsible for his actions. *I didn't do it; it wasn't me.* But not only had he created the website, he had maintained it. If his obsession back then really was a source of shame to him, he had done little to hide it since.

I leaned forward and spoke as gently as I could.

"Michael, I want you to listen to me very carefully. *Whatever* you did back then, what is happening right now is not your fault."

"I'm not sure about that."

"You have experienced something terrible," I continued, as though I hadn't heard him. "Something that is beyond most people's capacity to imagine. And I want you to understand that whatever you're feeling right now is a rational response to the trauma you've suffered."

"I haven't suffered."

"You have."

"Not like Darren suffered. You weren't there. You don't know what suffering is."

"That's true," I said. "But I have counseled people who have undergone similar experiences. And I do know that kind of trauma is not something that easily leaves you. Perhaps you weren't hurt like Darren was, but you *were* hurt. You are a victim here too. That's the first thing I want you to accept."

"What's the second thing?"

I took a deep breath.

"That you need to talk to the police."

"No."

"Michael—"

"No!" He shook his head again, more firmly than before. "For fuck's sake, did you *really* not listen to anything I told you? No. *No!*"

"Michael—"

But he put his head down and cupped his hands over his ears, and just kept shouting that word—*No!*—over and over again. Sarah looked at me helplessly, shocked by the sudden change in his demeanor.

Detached, I thought.

Calm.

"I know it won't be easy," I said.

Johnson's voice grew louder; it seemed inevitable that someone in a neighboring flat would hear him. But I forced myself to continue speaking quietly and deliberately. If he saw my words as an attack, I knew that a part of him would be intently focused on them.

"It will be frightening. But it's the right thing to do. Other people who were there that day have been killed. This man has to be stopped. He—"

Johnson looked up at me.

"*That's exactly what I'm doing.* If I don't go to the police, he *does* stop! I mean, are you fucking stupid or something? Do you not understand?" He gestured frantically around the room. "*This* is how I stop him. This is how I save however many of us are left. *By doing nothing.*"

Someone pounded on the wall next door.

Ignore it, I told myself.

You can do this.

"We don't know that will make him stop," I said. "I don't think we know enough about him yet to be sure why he's doing this or what he wants."

"He told me! If I talk to the police—"

"The police can keep you safe."

"Oh God," Johnson said. "They aren't going to believe me. You're out of your fucking mind."

More banging from next door.

"There's corroborating evidence," I said. "I think that—"

"No, I'm going to forget it ever happened. Because I think that's what he wants. He wants to punish the people who were there. He wants someone to take on the suffering and live with it. Because we could have helped him, and we didn't. And now he wants at least one of us to *wallow* in the guilt from that."

"We need to talk to the police," I said.

"No! No, no, no!"

"Michael—"

The pounding on the wall intensified. I could hear shouting from behind the plaster, and then felt Sarah put her hand on my arm.

"Dan," she said. "Stop."

I looked down. Without realizing it, my fists were clenched.

"We should go," Sarah said.

Johnson was incoherent now, his body racked by sobs. Despite myself, I wanted to grab hold of him. Drag him out of here.

Force him to go to the police if that was what it took.

Careful, my son.

At the sound of my father's voice, the anger retreated a little. I took a deep breath and then relaxed my hands. Then I got a business card out of my wallet and put it down on the settee beside him.

"If you change your mind," I said. "Call me. It might help just to talk."

"*Dan,*" Sarah said.

"I'm coming."

But even out in the corridor, I felt the urge to turn back. I stood by the closed door for a moment, trying to think what I could say to convince Johnson. There must have been words, surely? I should have been able to find them. I was supposed to be able to do that.

Sarah was already heading away, back in the direction of the elevator. Finally, I started after her. It was clear that the encounter in the flat had scared her badly, and I imagined she was also worried that one of Johnson's neighbors was about to come out and confront us.

She needn't have worried about that. As I followed her past the flat next door, I could hear that the banging sound had stopped now. Most likely, whoever lived there had just been angry at being disturbed.

Nobody sees, I thought.

And nobody cares.

Twenty-Five

Back in the car, we sat together in silence for a while. I drove slowly and carefully, and Sarah stared out of the passenger window. As we approached the motorway, I said:

"What are you thinking?"

"I'm thinking that I was scared back there."

"Yes," I said. "I know."

The way Michael Johnson had broken down would have frightened anyone, not to mention what he'd told us. I remembered her face this morning. *Do you want to go on an adventure?* But at that point it had still been academic, whereas it was another thing entirely to hear the truth in person, and to witness the effect such an experience had on someone. To have it confirmed that something terrible really was happening, and that you had found yourself caught up in it.

Sarah looked at me.

"Are you okay?" she said. "You seemed angry back there. I haven't seen you like that before."

"I'm okay."

Careful, my son.

The emotion seemed to have caught me unawares in Johnson's flat, but I understood where it had come from now. What Johnson had told us confirmed what was happening here: that someone out there was targeting those of us who had been at the rest area that day, setting up a chain of victims and killing one after the other. But it also removed the possibility that I had allowed myself to consider, even though I'd known it was dangerous to do so. It was Johnson who had watched Darren Field die. Johnson who was the most recent victim in the killer's chain. So while my father technically remained *missing* for the moment, there was no reason to believe that he was the next link in the killer's plan. The most likely explanation for his disappearance remained true.

But understanding my emotions didn't make them go away. I felt stupid for allowing myself to hope, and I was also still angry with myself for failing to convince Johnson to go to the police. There must have been *something* I could have said that would have made him change his mind. The fact that I hadn't been able to find the right words made me feel small and useless.

We joined the motorway and I accelerated.

Sarah sighed.

"What are we going to do now?"

"Go home," I said. "Back to the island, I mean. Try to think."

"We could still talk to the police."

I shook my head quickly. "No."

"We can go to Liam. He'll listen to me."

"I really don't think bringing you into this will help on that score."

She considered that.

"Maybe not," she said. "But you have the photographs. You have the connection between all the people who were at the rest area that day. And you have the same account of what happened from different people."

"I don't have that at all," I said. "I have what Brian Gill told us, and that's pretty much all I have."

"But—"

"*Maybe* Darren Field's story would have been the same. But it doesn't matter now, because he's dead and gone, and he can't tell it. And you and I just heard it from Michael Johnson too, but we can't report what he said to the police. Not without his consent."

"Is that some kind of medical privilege thing? I know you're a doctor, but you're not *his* doctor."

"No," I said. "Think about the repercussions if we did."

It was possible that my father's conversation with Darren Field had led to Field's death—that in the killer's mind it had counted as Field talking to the police. I could imagine the guilt that would have caused my father, but the fact was that he couldn't have known what the consequences might be when he went knocking on Field's door. I wouldn't have the same excuse if something happened to Johnson.

"If I talk to the police," I said, "I'm making the decision for him. I'd be the one putting him in danger. And that's not my choice to make."

"But it's like you said. The police can protect him."

"That's what I told Johnson. But honestly? I'm nowhere near as confident about that as I might have sounded. I don't know much about the man behind this, but I do know that he's smart. He's determined. He's patient. He's a *planner*. He isn't the type to act impulsively. This is someone who's more than happy to bide his time, and the police can't protect Johnson forever."

Sarah thought about it.

"Okay, so what if Johnson was right? If he keeps the story to himself then the killer will stop."

"Does that make sense though?"

"Fucking hell, none of it does to me." She gave a half laugh. "This is supposed to be your area of expertise, Dan. Have you ever encountered anyone like this before?"

"No."

The truth was that I could attempt to categorize him as much as I wanted, but in my experience, killers rarely operated the way this one did. Serial murders were uncommon in this day and age anyway, because most offenders were caught before they could progress beyond one or two victims, but when they did occur, they rarely displayed this level of complexity and planning. They were simple and brutal: the ugly endpoint of a disturbed and fractured mind. Not one that wanted to make a statement or play games.

"Do you have any idea *why* he's doing what he's doing?" she said.

"No."

I remembered what I'd imagined the killer saying to me on the ferry.

The truth is you have no idea what I'm doing.

You've spent your whole life avoiding thinking about me. Pretending you could just leave what you did to me behind. Protecting yourself.

I looked ahead at the motorway and realized where we were.

"No," I said again quietly. "Not yet."

And then, without thinking about it, I signaled.

Sarah looked to the side, confused.

"Where are we going?"

I didn't answer. But as I drove down the exit off the motorway, I saw her settle back nervously in her seat beside me, and I knew that she didn't need me to.

"Have you been back here since?" Sarah said.

There were so many parking spaces that it was difficult to be exact, but I tried to park in roughly the same spot my father had on that afternoon all those years ago.

"No," I said. "You?"

"Of course not. Why would I? I can get an out-of-date cheese sandwich and a packet of crisps anywhere."

She peered out through the window.

"And this is just . . . a place."

"Maybe," I said.

It was a place that hadn't changed much. The motel remained to one side: a different chain now, but no different apart from the signage on the front. The tiled slope ahead that led into the main building was exactly as I remembered it. *Just a place.* That was true on one level. But looking around, I found it easy to picture a figure smoking against the wall of the motel, and a van selling flowers to one side of the entrance. For a brief moment, I even sensed the shadow of a vehicle parked beside us, its dirty metal sides patterned with small handprints beneath a rusty grille over the window.

"Why are we here, Dan?" Sarah said.

"Because I need to talk to him. The man who's doing this."

"What—you think he's here?"

"No. I mean in my mind."

She hesitated.

"You know that sounds really weird, right?"

"Probably," I said. "I've been trying to put myself in his head for a couple of days now, and it's not working, but maybe I spent so long not thinking about him that it's hard to do it properly now. Perhaps if I want to understand him, I need to start from first principles."

I took a deep breath.

"And that means being here."

I opened the car door. I wasn't sure if Sarah was going to follow me, but after a moment, she did.

We walked across the car park together.

And then inside.

It *had* changed in here. The amusement arcade was gone now, replaced by a sprawl of beige tables and chairs. What had once been the burger counter was now a currency exchange window in the wall. And while the shop remained in the same place I remembered, the layout was entirely different. Everything seemed brighter and more open than I recalled it being.

The toilets were still at the far end of the concourse.

"I guess I'll wait here," Sarah said when we reached them.

"That's probably for the best."

"Are you going to be okay?"

I looked at her and did my best to smile.

"I really don't know."

But there was no point in hesitating.

I turned around and pushed open the door.

The corridor had been renovated. The tiles on the floor and the walls were clean and new, and the air smelled of fresh lemon disinfectant. The lights above didn't flicker or hum. There was none of the sense of threat I remembered. No feeling that this was an adult space in which I didn't yet belong. The corridor ahead seemed much shorter than it had when I was a child.

I walked down and turned the corner at the end.

The layout was the same. The toilets were long and narrow, with the cubicles on the right-hand side and a urinal along the opposite wall. The sink and mirror were at the far end, just as they had been back then. My reflection stared back from the mirror. It seemed to approach me as I walked forward.

I stopped halfway across the room and closed my eyes.

I'm here, I thought.

Then I waited.

After a few seconds, the temperature dropped, and I sensed the lights begin to dim and flicker. From somewhere in the back of my mind, the faint sound of whistling drifted free. A shiver ran down my spine at the noise. It was the same deliberate and careful melody I'd heard back then, somehow both familiar and impossible to place. My heart started beating faster. On a rational level I knew that all of this was just my imagination. That I was alone in here. But it no longer felt like I was.

Okay then, I thought.

Let's take a look at you.

I opened my eyes.

The little boy in front of me was exactly as I remembered him. Skinny frame all but lost in the baggy old clothes; a streak of dirt across his cheek; eyes wide and desperate. He did look a little like Robbie Garforth, but it was clear to me now that it was not him, and I wondered how I had ever allowed myself to be convinced otherwise.

The whistling was coming from the closed cubicle beside him. The boy looked at it for a second, and that reminded me of the moment when I had ducked into a cubicle of my own to hide. But this time, I remained where I was. As awful as it felt to be back here, I knew deep down that nothing was going to hurt me right now.

A moment later, the boy's terrified gaze returned to my own.

Help me.

And I wanted to. So desperately. If I had been an adult back then, I would have walked across, picked him up in my arms, and carried him out of here to safety. But it was too late for that now.

I can't, I thought.

Please.

I can't. That's not why I'm here.

I hate you. His face contorted in rage. *I hate you all so much!*

I know.

Then I glanced at the closed door to the cubicle.

Why didn't you run? I thought. When he was locked away in there?

Because I could never be fast enough.

Nobody could.

I kept looking at the closed door. It occurred to me what *arrogance* the Pied Piper must have had to leave the boy out here like that. There had been moments when the boy had been wandering the rest area all but unattended as well. It was hard to imagine possessing that degree of confidence and control. I had no idea what the boy had gone through before that afternoon, but it must have been terrible enough for him to see his captor as all-powerful. For it to be impossible for him to fight back by then.

I looked at the boy.

What did he do to you?

He broke me down. That's enough for you to know.

I'm sorry, I thought. I'm so sorry.

You will be. All of you will.

But there was an itch in my subconscious, and I forced myself to run back through my thoughts, trying to work out what had caused it. The sense of control—that was it. The Pied Piper's behavior that day appeared arrogant and brazen, and there had been no obvious need for him to take the risks that he had. But nothing he did would have been unnecessary; in his own warped mind, there would have been a reason for everything. And that included the way he had put the boy on display. It had been done for a purpose.

Nobody sees, I thought. And nobody cares.

That's right. None of you saw me. None of you cared.

And that's why I'm hurting you now. To punish you all.

I stared back at the boy. His eyes were full of hatred, and I could feel that same emotion mirrored inside me. The guilt and self-disgust rising to the surface, threatening to overwhelm me. I did my best to fight it back down. Because however keenly I felt it, what the boy had said— *that's why I'm hurting you now*—wasn't the whole story.

No, I thought. That's not quite right. Because all of us did the wrong thing that day, and I can understand you hating us for that. I hated myself for it and I still do. But that's not why you're doing this, is it?

The boy didn't reply.

I looked at the closed cubicle door again, chasing the idea.

You give the people you attack a choice, I thought slowly. They can do the right thing or the wrong thing. You reward them for doing the wrong thing—it's only if they do what's right that you punish them. And at that point you hurt them very badly, don't you? The violence is ferocious and out of all proportion. You are *raging* when you kill.

I looked back at the boy.

But it's not *them* you hate, I thought. It's you.

The whistling stopped.

And immediately, the boy's demeanor shifted. All the fury seemed to leave him, and in my mind's eye he was just a child again, one who looked even smaller than before. Emaciated. Frightened. *Broken down.*

And then he began crying.

Nobody sees me, he sobbed. *Nobody cares about* me.

You in particular?

Yes! I didn't matter to anyone. Nobody loved me enough to look for me. Nobody missed me. I meant nothing *to the world. He was teaching me that I was worthless. That I didn't deserve to be saved.*

And he was right, wasn't he?

No, I thought. He wasn't. You were never worthless.

I want to believe that.

The boy wiped his nose with a trembling hand.

I've tried so hard to. I've told myself that it was your fault—all of you— and I've done my best to hate you instead. But it's me that's disgusting. It's me!

He began pounding his small fist against his chest.

The hollow sound echoed around the toilet. It was sickening to hear, and even though I knew there was nothing really there in front of me, I still felt the urge again to walk across and comfort him.

But it was too late for that.

That's why you punish them if they do the right thing?

Yes! If they do the wrong thing, that means they were bad people all along. They're the worthless ones—not me. They don't see or care about anyone. Every second they keep silent, I can pretend to myself that it wasn't about me.

But if they see? I thought.

If they care?

Then it means the man was right.

The boy stopped hitting himself. And then suddenly he was directly in front of me, screaming into my face.

AND I CAN'T BEAR THAT!

Despite myself, I took a step back, bringing my hands up. The wave of white-hot rage burning in front of me offered a glimpse of what his victims must have faced in their final moments. The self-hatred simmering inside him bursting suddenly and horrifyingly into flame, and—

I heard the door to the corridor behind me opening.

Immediately, the vision before me disappeared.

The light was normal again. The boy was gone.

I stepped quickly over to the sink, my heart pounding.

Help me, the boy whispered.

I pressed down hard on the tap. Once. Twice. *Work*. In the mirror, I saw a father and son walking into the toilets behind me. The man was encouraging the child with a gentle hand on his back.

"Just go in there, champ. I'll be out here the whole time, I promise."

I looked back down again. The water was running now. I made a show of washing my hands, watching in the mirror as the little boy stepped nervously into one of the cubicles and closed the door. The lock clicked. His father folded his arms and waited.

I moved over to the hand dryer. The roar of it filled the air.

Help me, the boy whispered again.

I can't, I thought. It's too late.

So what are you going to do?

I tried to get myself under control.

What someone should have done all those years ago, I thought.

I'm going to find you.

Twenty-Six

John parks on the road by the cemetery.

When he turns the car engine off, the world is silent apart from the gentle rush of the breeze outside the car. There is a grand arch of stone beside him, through which he can see leafy trees and neatly tended grass illuminated by the midmorning sun. He has come to this place twice a year for the last four years, and every time has been struck by how tranquil it is here. Walking into the cemetery always feels like you're stepping out of the busy outside world and into a quieter, more restful one, the atmosphere settling on your skin like soft spring dew.

He follows the wide path between the old and ornate headstones that are closest to the entrance. As the main path curls around, smaller ones begin to lead away to the sides. There's no apparent rhyme or reason to the design; the cemetery is its own little city. Over the years, he has come to think of the paths through it as streets and the plots where people are buried as homes. It's a comforting idea, he supposes. It suggests that your loved ones haven't left you entirely, just moved, and that there will always be an address you can find them at when you want to.

But he is not visiting a loved one today.

After about five minutes, he stops. This particular grave is tucked away down a small side road of the cemetery, and has only a cheap, simple stone marking the plot. No flowers rest on this patch of grass. The ones he brought in July have been removed. He always brings a small bouquet: a meager offering, he knows, but it feels like something.

John puts his hands in his pockets and reads the inscription on the stone before him.

ABIGAIL PALMER

6 MARCH 1970–AUGUST 1998

The breeze sets the leaves rustling in the small grove of trees to his right. He glances over. The grove is empty for the moment, but while he doesn't believe in an afterlife, there have been times standing here in the past when he has imagined a presence there. Brief moments when he has pictured a woman watching him from the shadows between the trees.

It's possible she resents him for keeping her story, and James's, to himself, but he's always hoped that Abigail Palmer, otherwise forgotten by the world, might appreciate that at least one person remembers them.

As he looks at those trees now, though, he can feel a different presence building there. Given everything that has happened—everything he has done, and everything he has learned—a shiver runs through him at the thought of what other ghosts might appear there today.

All the people he has failed.

And he wonders what they might scream at him.

One person a night.

It was fourteen years after he first began his search—four years ago now—when John finally found her. A storm was lashing the island that night. Rain was pelting the windows and wind was rattling in the eaves. And John was sitting in the darkness, dog-tired and thinking he should go to bed.

One person a night, though.

He opened the file and it was Abigail Palmer.

He read the details cautiously. Abigail had been found dead in her flat on August 28, 1998, a few days after neighbors first reported a smell of decomposition gathering in the corridors of the tower block. When police broke down the door, they discovered the body of the young woman lying in bed, the air in the room thick with flies. The coroner's report concluded that Abigail had taken a deliberate overdose of pills, and that she had been dead for over a week before she was found.

Nobody had even realized she was missing.

Abigail's family history was volatile, and she had long been estranged from her parents. Her life had been a difficult one. Periods of employment and stability were brief punctuation marks in much longer and darker passages. Mental illness. Domestic violence. Drug use. Reading about Abigail broke John's heart a little. The file gave the impression of a drowning woman who kept coming up for air, and who might have been saved if someone had noticed her in time. But nobody had seen Abigail. At the time of her death, she was out of work. She had no friends to speak of. None of the other residents on her floor had even known her name.

Only one person vaguely recalled that, when she had first moved into the tower block, there had been a little boy living with her.

It was impossible to be sure of Abigail's motivation for taking her own life, but the coroner remarked upon the close relationship she had previously had with her son, James. By all accounts, she had loved the boy deeply, and he had always been her reason to drag herself back from the blacker places she was drawn to. James had been eleven years old. Like his mother, he was quiet and anonymous. Small for his age, and frequently bullied because he insisted on carrying a stuffed toy lion with him to school. The two of them were each other's best friend.

And then James had died in an accident earlier that year.

To compound the loss, Abigail had blamed herself for his death. The two of them had been on holiday, staying out of season at a cheap campsite on the coast. There were few amenities, but the weather was half decent and they had the place to themselves. The small beach at the site was all shingle and stone, but they played Frisbee there and skimmed stones, enjoying the quiet. Abigail warned James to keep away from the sea, because the currents were strong and he had never learned to swim. But at some point, lulled by the pills she had promised herself she would stop taking, she had fallen asleep on the beach.

When Abigail woke up an hour later, the sun had gone in and the air was cold, and James was nowhere to be seen. Still groggy, she had stood up and called his name. Her feet had crunched in the shingle as she stumbled down toward the edge of the water, and from there along to the next little cove, where she found James's shorts folded up on the rocks by the water.

There was only one phone at the campsite, five minutes back up a footpath. It was over half an hour before the police arrived. A little longer than that before the coastguards began their search.

The next day, James's stuffed toy lion was discovered washed up a short distance along the shore. The coroner's report noted that it was the last evidence of James that was ever found, although that was not unusual for that particular stretch of coastline.

In the meantime, police had looked at Abigail and seen what they wanted to see: a negligent mother, yes, but one who had also been frantically *honest* with them. Consumed by guilt, she had told them exactly what drugs they would find both in her system and in the car. At the time of her death, there were still a number of potential charges hanging over her.

John read the report through several times.

One line in particular resonated with him, although he wasn't quite sure why. Abigail Palmer, the coroner suggested, had been a woman who felt things very deeply.

The file also included the single surviving photograph of James that anyone had been able to find. It had been taken years before his death, when he was still in primary school, but the sight of it took John's breath away. When he compared it with the sketch that Daniel had contributed to, he might have been looking at the same person.

The next weekend, he took the ferry and drove to the campsite where James was believed to have drowned. He walked down to that sad, stony little beach and stood there in the cold wind for a time, looking out over the sea. It was a desolate place. Lonely. Isolated. It *felt* right. And as he walked back, an old camper van drove in down the entrance trail and parked in a dusty bay by the side.

John sat in his car, watching it, and eventually a young family got out.

But the vehicle was the same make and model as the one he remembered from the rest area, and he couldn't help seeing its arrival right then as a sign. A small nod of acknowledgment from the universe that he was right.

That this was the place.

That James Palmer was the boy his son saw that day.

That through sheer force of will, after a decade and a half of bloody-minded searching, John had done what nobody else could.

The weeks afterward were ones of careful consideration. It felt like he should report what he had discovered. And yet for some reason, he found himself hesitating.

What would it achieve, he wondered?

Justice.

That was the obvious answer. Except what did *justice* amount to in this case? The Pied Piper was long dead, and surely so was James Palmer. There were no grieving relatives or friends awaiting a resolution. The world had forgotten Abigail and James almost before they were gone. And knowing the boy's name would not bring the police any closer to identifying who the Pied Piper had been, or where the bodies of his missing victims might be buried.

Validation, then.

For some people, that would have been reason enough to come forward. Assuming John was right, he knew that what he had found would make a mark on the world. He would become known as the police officer who had refused to give up, who had gone the extra mile, who had pulled off what others might have considered impossible. He would get the recognition that had eluded him all his life.

The idea was appealing, but it also left him feeling strangely empty. If you took the bad on the chin without flinching then the same should be true of the good. Whatever anyone else thinks of you, it should be enough for you to know that you're enough.

The final reason, then.

His son.

And in the end, it was Daniel who made the decision for him. It was a few years ago, not long after John identified James Palmer, and Daniel had returned home for a visit. They were sharing a drink outside one evening, and John mentioned his hobby—the research he did into cold cases to keep him occupied—and Daniel asked what he thought he could contribute to the investigations.

John had stared down the garden for a time.

"Brute force," he said.

Daniel had made a joke about it—*you just want to be like the characters in the books you read*—and there had been a moment when John had felt an urge to shake his head and tell his son everything. To *justify* himself.

To make Daniel proud of him.

But he had begun his investigation in the hope of healing his boy and bringing the two of them closer together, and that all seemed so long ago now. They *were* closer. The boy his son had been back then was gone. Daniel was a grown man now, accomplished and impressive. What possible good could it do for him to learn that he had been right all those years ago? The ground had settled, and the idea of John turning that soil over now and unearthing the past seemed selfish and wrong.

So he had forced himself to laugh gently.

The conversation had moved on.

And he had told nobody what he had found.

There was just those twice-yearly visits since, once on Abigail's birthday in March, and once again on James's in July. The very first time he went, he had brought a book with him. His son's tattered old copy of *The Man Made of Smoke*—or his own now, he supposed—and he had left it on the grave with the flowers.

Let that be the end of it, he thought.

Because he had never believed that any of it could possibly matter.

• • •

John stares at the cluster of trees now.

There is nobody there, of course, but he can almost see Abigail Palmer's ghost standing among them. On past occasions, he has imagined James there too. Even if he doesn't believe in an afterlife, he has always liked to believe that, if the boy's ghost were capable of finding its way anywhere, it would have been back to his mother's side.

Because he assumed James was dead.

He can't sense James there today, but it does feel like other ghosts have joined Abigail in the trees. Oliver Hunter and Graham Lloyd; Rose Saunders and Darren Field. He hasn't been able to track down Michael Johnson, but perhaps he is there too. Regardless, the mingled voices John hears in his head are loud enough already.

We might be alive if it wasn't for you.

You fucked up again, didn't you?

You failed us just like you fail at everything.

There's no answer to those accusations. John feels the truth of them in his bones. He'd imagined he could draw a line and move on. That it was all history and wasn't important. But all these people might still be alive if he'd reported what he'd found. He used to think that he and Daniel's encounter with the Pied Piper had poisoned everything, but the reality seems starker than that right now. It's not what happened at the rest area. It's John himself. That afternoon was just another moment in a life spent slipping, falling, and failing.

I'm sorry, he thinks.

But the voices are too angry. There is no possibility of forgiveness there. And how could there be, when the voices are coming from inside him? As they grow in volume and fury, he turns and heads quickly back down the path, moving faster, until, by the time he reaches the car, he is running, his heart pounding hard in his chest. And yet the voices behind him seem to have kept pace, even grown louder with every step.

It's all your fault.

John leans on the side of the vehicle, breathing slowly and steadily, trying to calm himself down. But just as his pulse begins to settle, he registers a buzzing at his hip.

His mobile ringing.

He leans away from the car and takes his phone out of his pocket. The screen shows an unknown number, and he stares down at it for a few seconds before accepting the call and lifting the phone to his ear.

"Hello?" he says.

No reply.

John shifts his body slightly, looking around him. He has the sensation of being watched, even though the world is serene and silent, and there is nobody in sight.

He turns back, pressing the mobile more tightly against his face.

"Hello?" he says again.

Silence.

And then the man speaks.

Twenty-Seven

It was midafternoon when Sarah and I arrived back at the island.

We didn't talk much on the drive home. For most of the journey, I was trying to process the thoughts I'd had back at the rest area, and Sarah either sensed that I wanted some space to do so, or else just needed some of her own.

On the ferry, I kept an eye on the other passengers.

Were we being watched? If so, I couldn't tell.

Nobody sees, I thought. *And nobody cares.*

When the ferry reached the island, I drove us to her mother's home and parked. When she got out, I followed her up the path and waited as she unlocked the front door. Then I went into the front room and rattled the latch on the window.

She looked at me. "What are you—?"

"Making sure the house is secure."

For a second, it seemed like she wanted to argue with me. But then she stared down the dimly lit corridor ahead of us and shrugged.

"Maybe do the kitchen first?" she said. "I need coffee."

"On it."

The kitchen window was locked, the back door bolted. Sarah set the kettle boiling as I headed upstairs, and I heard it rumbling away below me as I did a tour of the other rooms in the house. Everything was locked and safe. The kettle clicked off as I walked back through into the kitchen.

We sat down at the table.

"So," she said. "What are you thinking?"

I warmed my hands on the cup as I told her my theory: that I thought the killer might be driven by a deep sense of self-hatred, and that his crimes now were an attempt to deal with that. That in some ways, he was performing an experiment. If the people who failed him as a child turned a blind eye again now, that meant they were bad people, and that allowed him to accept himself for a while. If they didn't, he exploded into violence.

The coffee was hot enough that my fingers were burning by the time I finished. But I didn't move them.

"Accept himself for what?" Sarah said.

"I don't know exactly. Maybe for things he saw and was made to do. We don't know what his relationship with the Pied Piper was. If he was abducted, we don't even know when. It's possible he ended up playing a part in the murders."

"Jesus."

"The point is, I think he hates himself more than you or I could imagine," I said. "And what do we do when we're angry with ourselves? We lash out. Have you ever done something wrong, but you were so annoyed with yourself that you couldn't admit it?"

"More often than I'd like to say."

"And maybe you took it out on someone else instead?"

"No comment."

"It's a defense mechanism," I said. "It's what the mind does when it feels under attack. Obviously, this is an extreme example of that, but ultimately it's the same thing. Underneath it all, it's a little boy protecting himself."

She was silent for a moment.

"Okay," she said finally. "So does that mean Johnson was right? If he keeps quiet about what happened, that gives the killer what he wants. The end."

I shook my head.

"No, because it's never going to be a permanent solution for him. The source of the anger—the damage—remains unresolved. It's all still there inside him. And I think there's a part of him that enjoys it too. Do you remember what you said yesterday? There's a pleasure in *dwelling*."

"Yeah. But this is—"

"An extreme example," I said again. "But it's the same thing. And Darren Field didn't go to the police, did he? That didn't make him safe. The killer basically sent my father to his front door. Because I think he *wanted* an excuse to do it."

"Which means?"

"That he's escalating. It's a mistake to think of his rules as being absolute. He's not a robot following a program. He's a mess. His rules are there to serve a purpose, but he'll bend them if they don't suit him. And I think he's started to like the killing more than the peace he imagined it would give to him."

She hesitated. And then sighed.

"So what do we do now?"

"I'm not sure."

"I know you're worried that talking to Liam might put Michael Johnson in danger," she said. "But from what you've just told me, he might be in danger whether you talk to the police or not?"

"It's still not my decision to make."

"Okay. So leave him out of it for now. Leave me out of it. Just tell Liam everything else."

She leaned forward and looked at me.

"You can make the police believe it. I *know* you can."

"Maybe."

I wanted what she'd said to be true. I wanted to believe that the insight I'd gleaned at the rest area was useful, and that a concerted police investigation, along with the expertise I could bring to the table, would be able to find him. That I was *good enough*.

But I wasn't sure that I did.

I moved my fingers from the burning hot cup.

"Maybe," I repeated, finally sipping the coffee. "But I need to think."

• • •

Sarah had a shift at the bar in a couple of hours, and we agreed that I'd meet her there later. In the meantime, I drove back to my father's house.

After parking, I stood by the side of the car and looked around. There was no sign of movement on the sun-dappled lane. Even so, I stood there for a few seconds, not just to make sure the street was clear but, if I was being watched right then, to send a signal to whoever was out there that I wasn't afraid.

Then I unlocked the door.

Just as I had done at Sarah's house, I did a thorough search of the property, checking every door and window. There were no signs of disturbance; the building was secure. Whatever else the man might have been doing today, he hadn't attempted to force entry here. That was reassuring on one level, but it was unnerving not to know what he had been doing instead.

I went upstairs to my father's room.

His old leather boxing gloves were still on the floor by the punch bag. I picked them up and turned them over in my hands, looking down at the map of cracked texture that the endless blows had worn into the fabric. It was strange to remember how huge they had seemed to me when I was young. So large that it had been hard to believe my hands would ever be big enough to fill them. When I slipped them on now, they fit me perfectly.

I turned to the bag.

Then started off with left jabs, slow and steady.

Thud.

Thud.

Thud.

One of the first things I'd done when I left the island and arrived at university was join the boxing club there. I never told my father. To begin with, I didn't want to give him the satisfaction. I kept remembering how he'd tried to encourage me, and how I'd pushed back against it because that was *his* way of handling life, not mine. It seemed stupid all these years later, but at the time it had felt important not to admit that he might have had anything to teach me at all.

After I'd warmed up with the jabs, I moved onto combinations, gradually increasing the strength of the blows.

Thud.

Thud, thud.

Thud.

Thud, thud, thud.

But I had soon found a different reason not to discuss training with
my father. It had quickly become obvious that, despite him trying to
teach me to box when I was younger, he had never had any real idea how.
He hit the bag every day, but that was all he was doing. The bag was a
stand-in for all the frustrations and disappointments of his life, and he
spent his evenings pounding it as hard as he could, lashing out with *brute
force* rather than skill or technique. My father knew how to punch, but
not how to box, and in a fight he would always be taking as many blows
as he landed.

When I had understood that, I had felt sorry for him.

That was one the first times that I saw him not simply as *my father*
but as a man in his own right: one who was struggling to deal with
the challenges of life in his own complicated way. There were occasions
when I returned to the island afterward that I considered slipping on the
gloves and showing him what I could do. But I never did. I understood
enough by then to know it would mean showing him yet another thing
that he could not.

Thud.

Thud, thud, thud.

Thud, thud.

As I worked the bag now, I found myself slipping into a kind of gentle trance. I was often at my most relaxed at times like this, with my body
performing movements that ticked thoughtlessly, like clockwork, leaving
my mind free to wander.

There were things I thought I knew about the killer.

He was organized and intelligent, and even if he was escalating and
beginning to change the rules of the game he'd set up, deep down he
would still be motivated by the same underlying mission: to ease the

guilt and pain and self-disgust inside him. But that was all interior. How would he present to the world on the outside? The nature of the murders suggested that he was physically capable and socially adroit. He had the time to research and plan. He traveled freely, where and when he pleased, without attracting attention. Despite the deep-rooted psychological instability inside him, he had managed to integrate into the world and maintain a veneer of acceptability.

How had the boy I had seen back then become this man now?

There were obvious practicalities to consider. He had been roughly my age, perhaps a little older, when I met him at the rest area, and the Pied Piper had died only a couple of weeks later. At that point, he would effectively have been free.

So why had he never come forward?

He had been unable to run from the man when he had the opportunity, which suggested that he had been indoctrinated. As I'd said to Sarah, perhaps he had been involved in the man's murders. An apprentice. In which case, it was possible that he had even been upset when the Pied Piper died and made a conscious decision to stay wherever it was that he was being held, assuming that *held* was even the right word by then.

I hit the bag harder.

That idea suggested a degree of self-sufficiency. If the boy had made it to adulthood without being detected, there had clearly been little need for interaction with the outside world. He had been able to grow into the man he was now in private, presumably living most of his life off-grid, at least when he was younger. Which also fit with the fact that nobody had ever identified the Pied Piper.

I remembered the muddy boots and filthy van.

A working farm of some kind?

Perhaps. I was well aware that I might be overreaching here, and that it was dangerous to make assumptions without evidence. And yet the thoughts were beginning to come as fast as the punches.

Thud, thud, thud.

Thud, thud, THUD.

I held the bag for a second, catching my breath. Then pushed it away and started again.

Thud, thud, THUD.

Why hadn't he reconnected with his real family?

Perhaps they were dead, or there was nobody he *wanted* to return to. It was possible that after everything he'd been through, he no longer felt any connection to the real world. After all, his photograph had been widely circulated and nobody had come forward. No child matching his description had ever been reported missing. And if nobody had cared about him before he was taken, why would he have assumed anyone would do so afterward?

Especially if he had done something terrible.

I stopped again. The bag creaked back and forth on its chain for a second before I stilled it. My arms were shaky, my breath coming hard and fast.

I tried to conjure up a presence behind me.

Who are you? I thought.

No answer.

Where are you?

No answer.

I pushed the bag away again. As I started hitting it now, the punches began to come quicker and harder.

Thud, thud, thud, THUD.

Thud, thud, thud, THUD.

The Zen-like state of a few minutes earlier had deserted me. My subconscious had gone silent, which meant that there must be some detail I wasn't seeing, and that angered me. All the other emotions that had been building up over the last few days were close to the surface too. I could feel them brimming over. And then I lost any sense of technique. I just gritted my teeth and punched the bag with all my force, the blows reverberating through my arms and shoulders. Harder and harder—

THUD THUD THUD THUD THUD THUD.

—until I couldn't hit the bag anymore.

I rested my forearm against the leather, and then my head on my arm, my heart pounding and my whole body trembling. After taking a minute to get my breath back, I opened my eyes. It had been stupid to lose control like that, and I was lucky not to have hurt myself.

I had not been detached. I had not been calm.

Even so, I felt exhilarated.

Feels good, doesn't it, my son?

I held still for a moment. Then I thought: Yes. It does.

You've got pretty good, my father said.

Thank you.

I wish you'd told me. I understand why you didn't. But honestly, it would have been fine. We all have our own ways of coping with things, don't we? And if mine was brute force, then what the hell. It worked for me.

There's no shame in that.

No, I thought.

There isn't.

I undid the straps on the gloves with my teeth and then pulled them off one by one. My hands were still trembling a little, but I could see blood beneath the skin between my knuckles.

It reminded me of the time when I came back at the end of my first year at university: the night when my father had collapsed, and I'd had to help him into bed. That was the moment when I'd realized how much the encounter at the rest area had affected him. That what happened to us all there haunted him too.

Robbie? Was that you?

I'd been staring over at his desk when he said that. The computer had been open on a website; I'd been distracted by the empty bottles beside it, and hadn't bothered to look more closely. But I remembered seeing a box file on the otherwise empty shelves above.

Still holding the gloves, I turned around and looked at the desk.

In the years since, my father had filled the shelves above with his out-of-hours research material. The unsolved murders and disappearances he'd become intrigued by; the cold cases that were far more exciting than the mundane crimes he dealt with every day. I'd diminished his hobby when he'd first mentioned it to me a few years ago. Because what did he

imagine he could bring to the table that all the more experienced investigators who had worked on them could not?

Brute force.

Most of the box files on the shelves were labeled. I even recognized
some of the cases from my father's handwriting on the spines. But that
oldest one was not. And there were another seven old boxes next to it
that had been left blank too.

You know what? I imagined my father saying now.

Sometimes a bit of brute force is exactly *what you need.*

I put the gloves down carefully and walked across the room.

Twenty-Eight

Two hours later, I arrived at the police station.

What I had found shouldn't have surprised me. For all his faults, my father had always been tenacious. A man who, once he started something, kept going.

Brute force.

Having worked through his files, I knew that my father hadn't just gone one step further than everyone else involved in the Pied Piper investigation, he had walked a whole marathon more. Stubborn; persistent; refusing to stop. It was difficult for me to imagine what had compelled him to research the case the way that he had. He had always been so adamant that I forget about it. It had been his disapproval that had led me to accept it was Robbie Garforth I'd seen that day—or at least, that was how it had seemed at the time. But whatever his motivation for pursuing it, his efforts had brought him a name.

And a face.

The shock I'd felt when I'd seen the photograph of James Palmer remained with me now. The boy might have been a few years younger in the image than he'd been when I saw him in the rest area, but there was no doubt in my mind that it was him. He matched the sketch I'd contributed to almost perfectly. More importantly, he fit with my memory. As I'd stared at the photograph, I might as well have been looking back in time.

Why didn't you tell everyone you'd found him, Dad? I thought.

Maybe because I didn't need to.

The voice my subconscious gave him now was stronger than before.

What would it have achieved if I'd gone to the police? he asked me. *I assumed James Palmer was dead. And there was no family left to care about him. I didn't think it would make any difference.*

People would have known how much work you put in, I thought.

Maybe so. But what would it have done to you, my son?

I stared across the darkening street. That made sense, didn't it? How would I have reacted, having moved on from everything, to being told that I'd actually been right all those years ago, and that I'd let James Palmer down not once but twice?

Perhaps I wanted to protect you, my father said.

Perhaps that's all I ever really wanted.

I crossed the road.

Inside the police station, it was the same officer behind the desk as on my first visit. He had been polite enough that time, but his face fell when he looked up and saw me approaching him now.

"Dr. Garvie," he said slowly. "What can I do for you?"

I wasn't Fleming's favorite person on the island, and the officer had the air of a man who took his lead from people he considered more important than him. If something of the school bully remained in Fleming, then this man reminded me of the boys who had stood behind him back then laughing.

"I need to speak to Liam," I said.

He bristled slightly. "You mean *Detective Fleming*?"

"Obviously that's who I mean. You don't have a bunch of other Liams hiding back there, do you? I need to speak to him."

"Detective Fleming is very busy."

"He's about to get a lot busier."

The officer took a deep breath.

"Everybody is working very hard, Dr. Garvie. But there haven't been any developments in the search for your father and—"

"You're wrong." I leaned down on the desk. "There have been. There have also been developments about the body that was recovered from the rocks yesterday. You just don't know about them yet."

Because none of you are as good police as my father was.

I held up the sheaf of paperwork I'd brought with me.

"Trust me," I said. "Liam really wants to see me right now."

That was very far from true, of course.

As I was shown into Fleming's office, it was immediately apparent that the only reasons he might want to see me were ones that neither of us was going to enjoy. After the door closed, and it was just the two of us, he stood up and walked round from behind his desk, stopping a distance away from me that was clearly meant to be intimidating.

"You've got a fucking nerve coming here," he said.

I held my ground.

"Why?" I said.

"Because I know what you've been up to." His face reddened. "I saw your car parked outside Sarah's house yesterday evening. And then a little bird told me the two of you were both at your father's house this morning."

Despite myself, I took a step back now, more out of disbelief than anything else. Given the circumstances of our altercation the other night, I supposed that what he had just said shouldn't surprise me, but it did.

"Jesus Christ," I said. "You've been *following* us?"

"I do what I have to."

The anger in him was obvious. The *indignation*. There would almost have been a childishness to him—like a little boy who'd had a toy taken away—except that he was very much a grown man now. I was aware of both his physical presence and the fact that we were alone together in his office right now.

You are detached, I told myself.

You are calm.

"Sarah's my friend," I said. "Like I told you the other night. There's nothing more to it than that."

"And I'm supposed to believe you?"

"Liam—"

"I ought to beat the living shit out of you."

And at that, he bunched his right hand into a fist down by his side. But if it was meant to scare me, it did the opposite. It was such a clumsy tell that I relaxed the moment I saw him doing it. He wasn't going to be able to put a hand on me.

I imagined my father standing behind me, watching all this unfold.

What would you do right now, Dad? I thought.

Nothing too silly, my son.

Just give a good account of yourself.

"We're not teenagers anymore, Liam," I said. "Why don't you try?"

Fleming looked to one side and snorted quietly. And then, not even deigning to look back, he reached out to grab the front of my shirt. I stepped to the side, turning at the waist so that he grasped at air, and while he was off-balance and still reaching I tapped him with the knuckles of my free hand—once, twice—first in the solar plexus and then up on the chin. I pulled the shots, but made sure there was enough speed and force there for him to understand that it had been my choice not to land them harder.

Before he could react, I stepped past him and slapped the file of paperwork down loudly on the desk.

He turned slightly, staring at me in shock.

"What the fuck? You just assaulted a—"

"No," I said. "I just defended myself very gently against an attempted assault. But I can imagine what you're thinking. Your word against mine, right?"

I gestured around the office.

"But the thing is, Liam, I look at my professional record, and then I look at yours, and I'm happy to take my chances. So if you want to try doing that again, then by all means go for it. But if I were you, I'd make a call to your guy out front first. Because trust me, you're not going to manage it by yourself."

Fleming rubbed his chin. I'd barely made contact, but the real damage had been done to his ego, and it was touch and go right now as to what he was going to do.

I tapped the file on the desk to focus his attention.

"*Or we could talk about this,*" I said. "Which is much more important."

He looked at the file. Then back up at me.

After a couple of seconds, his curiosity got the better of him.

"What's that?" he said.

"Let's start with Darren Field."

"Who the fuck is Darren Field?"

"I think he's the man you fished out of the sea yesterday," I said. "He didn't drown, did he? He'd been badly hurt. He was murdered before his body was dumped in the water."

"How do you—?"

"I *don't,*" I said. "I don't know for sure. But here. Look."

I opened the file and picked out the top sheet—a photograph I'd printed from one of Field's social media accounts—and held it out to Fleming.

"You know I didn't see the body," I said. "But I'm betting I'm right. Does this man look familiar to you?"

Fleming hesitated, still performing a few final mental calculations about what to do next, and whether that involved trying to hurt me. But he understood deep down that might not go well for him, and I thought I'd also done just about enough to pique his interest and offer him an exit ramp.

He took the sheet of paper off me and looked down at it.

I waited.

"Maybe," he said.

But it was obvious he recognized the face on the printout. And yet there was no satisfaction in being right. Unless you counted our encounter at the rest area, I had never met Darren Field, but it was still upsetting to have it confirmed what had happened to him. I thought about his wife—

how she clearly loved him, and was probably still waiting for him to come home even now—and the old guilt began to rise up, threatening to break the surface. There were so many chains of cause and effect at play here, but the truth was that, if I had been better all those years ago, he would still be alive.

"All right," Fleming said. "Who is this guy?"

I shook my head. "That's going to take some explaining."

"So explain."

"I'm going to. But to do that, I need to start at the beginning."

I picked another sheet of paper from the file.

And then I took a deep breath.

"I need to start with a boy named James Palmer."

Twenty-Nine

Hours passed.

Whatever other qualities Fleming might have lacked as a man, he was predictably ambitious. I imagined he was as bored and frustrated with police work on the island as my father had been. Perhaps he liked to think of himself as a king here, but he must have known that his court was a small one. The case I laid carefully out for him was bigger than anything he'd ever encountered. Big enough for him to make a name for himself.

If I had arrived at the station without any evidence then I had no doubt he'd have given me short shrift. Instead, I had provided him with a name for the body found yesterday, and as I walked him through the rest of the case, he became increasingly engaged. I could see it in his eyes. The potential glory of solving the investigation was enough for him to forget how much he hated me.

I explained who James Palmer had been, showing him the photograph and the sketch. I showed him the picture that had been delivered to my father, and explained how it had led me first to Darren Field, and from there to Rose Saunders and the other victims. All the people who had failed to save James that day.

I made sure to flatter him by allowing him to make a few of the connections himself rather than spelling them out. And at the same time,

I didn't give him everything. He didn't need to know about Sarah's involvement for the moment, or about our visit to Michael Johnson's flat today. The former would only inflame him. The latter still wasn't my decision to make. If the investigation led Fleming to discover either thing then I would deal with it then.

He worked at the computer the whole time, looking up details to corroborate what I was telling him, and even making a couple of calls to departments on the mainland. I waited patiently through those, attempting to glean information from the one side of the conversation I could hear. He wasn't being told anything that contradicted the theory I was presenting him with, and he was listening to at least a few details that confirmed it.

Finally, I showed him the last item in the file.

He looked at it and frowned. "What's this?"

"It's a photograph," I said. "Of me. It was taken three days ago, in my father's garden, on the night I came back to the island. I had no idea anyone was there. Whoever took it delivered it to the house yesterday. They wanted me to find it."

It surprised me how calm my voice sounded. The truth was that it took all my resolve to sit there across from Fleming as he stared down at a picture of me at my most exposed and vulnerable. My emotions on display. But it was necessary for him to see it, I thought. Not only was it part of the story, if I hadn't already convinced him then I imagined being this open in front of him would help to clinch it.

He studied the photo for a time then leaned back.

"So," he said. "What's your theory?"

"My theory?"

"Well, you're the serial killer expert." He gestured around the office, as though it was a stage and he was giving me a rare chance to audition. "What do you imagine is going through this guy's head? What makes him tick?"

"Well—"

"Off the record, of course."

Yes, I thought. Of course. I had just delivered Fleming not only a solid lead on an existing serial killer, but the key that might unlock an older mystery too. He had nothing approximating a poker face, and I could see him doing the calculations in his head. *Off the record.* The avarice in his expression was barely hidden; he wouldn't want anyone else taking a cut of the credit.

I imagined my father standing behind me.

Let him have his moment, my son, he said.

Just keep him onside for now. Play the long game.

I will, I thought. But when this is over, you're going to get your due.

I'm going to make sure that everyone knows it was you, Dad.

"*Off the record,*" I repeated carefully, "I've never encountered anyone like this. He's intelligent and organized, and I assume he functions well in society. He moves freely without attracting attention. On the surface, he probably appears relatively normal. But from the ferocity of the murders, there's clearly a deep well of rage and hate inside that's driving him."

"Makes sense."

"But I think it's more complicated than that."

"Really? Go on."

As best I could, I explained my theory: that the killings were a kind of test, an experiment designed to counter the worthlessness the killer felt. Fleming nodded as I was speaking, as though—again—it all made perfect sense. And I was sure I sounded confident and convincing. But even as I was speaking, there was still a wrinkle of doubt in the back of my mind. The picture I was painting was *almost* right, I thought, but it still felt like there was a piece I was missing that might change everything.

What wasn't I seeing?

"But I don't know," I said finally, because it felt important to voice the doubt. "There's still a lot I don't understand. For one thing, I'm not sure how James Palmer could possibly have survived all these years without being discovered. My father must have assumed he was dead, and I would have done too. But there's also just . . . something."

"Like what?"

"I don't know."

Fleming leaned back and folded his arms.

Waited.

I did my best to ignore him. Instead, I thought back to my encounter with James Palmer in the rest area toilets, remembering the fear I'd seen on his face.

Please help me.

Hiding away in the cubicle was the first time I'd failed him. And it turned out that I had failed him for a second time when I gave in and agreed with the police's conclusion that it had been Robbie Garforth.

Was I in danger of doing the same thing again now?

I looked down at the photograph of James Palmer I'd brought with me.

What evidence did I *really* have that he was the individual responsible for these murders? From my father's files, I knew that James had been abducted before the first known victim of the Pied Piper and had still been alive three years later. Which meant I also knew that he had most likely suffered more trauma than I could possibly imagine.

But I also knew that trauma wasn't enough to make someone a killer.

Fleming lost patience with me. "What?"

"I just keep thinking about how he looked that day," I said. "Terrified. Desperate for help. He would have run away if he could have done, but he was too frightened. The one thing he didn't look like was a killer."

I shook my head.

"He looked like a scared little boy."

James

August 2001

James lies awake in the darkness.

The room is pitch black and yet the air seems to be throbbing in his eyes and ears. He's been lying here like this for what feels like hours, his nerves singing the whole time. What is he waiting for? He isn't sure. There's no way to tell what time it is. No way to know how many hours have passed since the man brought him up here earlier.

It had been the same as every other night, except for one small difference. Whenever the man closed the door in the past, James has always heard the sound of the key turning in the lock.

Click.

But not tonight.

He had lain there listening, waiting for it, but the sound never came. Tonight, the man has left the door to James's room unlocked. But then, why wouldn't he? He knows that James has accepted the truth now. The world doesn't want him. It never had. Nobody has ever seen him; nobody has ever cared. And at dawn, the two of them will take the final step together. There was no more need for the man to lock the bedroom door earlier than there had been for him to worry that James would run away from him at the rest area.

Except that the man *doesn't* know that. He only thinks it.

James listens carefully.

The house has been silent for hours now, surely? And if he leaves it much longer then it will be too late. So he slips out from beneath the thin cover and stands up.

Listens again. Hears . . .

Breathing.

He feels a burst of panic—suddenly sure that the man has been standing here in the room the whole time, motionless and invisible in the blackness. But that can't be true. James remembers watching the door close. Later on, he saw the thin line of hallway light at the bottom go out.

It's his own breathing he can hear.

With his palms out in front of him, he walks blindly across the room in what he knows to be the direction of the door. The floorboards are rough against the soles of his bare feet. When he reaches the wall, he takes a step to one side, feeling for the handle.

Finding it.

Then he turns it very gently. A centimeter at a time.

The door opens inward with the quietest of creaks. James listens again carefully. When he hears nothing, he dares to open the door a little wider, his hand trembling the whole time.

Then he steps out into the corridor.

It's dark, illuminated only by a wedge of moonlight from the window at the far end. That's where the stairs are. There are three doors in between. The nearest is the bathroom, but he doesn't know what's behind the other two. He assumes one of them must be the man's bedroom, but he has no idea which one. They're all closed right now.

James wishes that he had Barnaby here to protect him. But the man threw Barnaby into the sea on the day he abducted him, and so he'll have to find the courage inside himself instead. He starts to walk down the hallway, one small step at a time, imagining that his feet are barely touching the ground. That he's lighter than air. And it seems to work. He can feel the soft push of the carpet against his feet as he creeps along, but every footstep is as quiet as snowfall.

He reaches the first door.

If the man were to step suddenly out of nowhere, this is the final spot for him to claim he was just going to the toilet. The temptation to turn back is overwhelming. But he can't do that. He fixes his gaze on that window at the end of the corridor: at the moonlight he can see through the dirty glass. At the outside world. The *real* world.

And he keeps going.

Past the second door.

The third.

And then he is at the top of the stairs. He looks back down the hallway, and all the doors there are still closed. There's no sense of movement. And everything is silent, aside from a faint rush of air he can hear from around the window nailed shut beside him.

The stairs.

He places his weight down gingerly, one step at a time, keeping a gentle grip on the banister for support. The living room below him is lost in darkness at first, but the shapes there begin to resolve the farther he descends. He begins to move a little more quickly—wanting to run—but forces himself to slow down. The danger might be above and behind him now, but he can still feel it, hovering like a knife that will drive itself between his shoulder blades if he makes the slightest mistake.

He steps down into the living room.

Stands still. Listens again carefully.

And the house is no longer silent.

It takes him a second to realize what he's hearing, and when he does, his skin goes cold. He turns his head very slowly. His gaze moves from the wall in front of him to the settee under the window at the far end of the living room, where the man is sitting.

James holds his breath.

As always, he can't see the man's face, but his gnarled hands are resting on his thighs, and an angle of moonlight lies over them like a sheet. They are entirely still.

The soft sound of his snoring drifts over.

James remains frozen in place, and the moment seems to go on forever. There's nowhere for him to hide. All the man has to do is shift slightly and open his eyes, and he'll see James standing there. And then he'll hurt him very badly before killing him for this betrayal. Once again, James feels the urge to go back. It wouldn't be impossible. He could creep up the stairs behind him. Return to his room. The man would be none the wiser, and he would still be alive.

But dawn is coming.

If he takes part in the killing in the morning then the last surviving fragment of him will be dead anyway. And once James realizes that, he feels a sense of resolve, that fluttering hope inside him replaced by a small core of steel.

He breathes out quietly.

Then he turns and moves into the kitchen.

The man has left the door to the cellar unlocked too, and the hinges creak as James opens it. It's so dark that he can only see the very top step below him. Beyond that is just a black hole that seems to go down into the depths of the earth forever. He takes the first step. Then the next. Breathing in slowly as he goes, the air around him beginning to smell of freshly turned soil. Until he feels encased by the ground. *This is what it must be like to be buried,* he thinks. But he isn't buried. He isn't dead. He is alive.

His foot touches the cellar floor.

The darkness down here is absolute, and he doesn't dare pull the cord on the light in case the faint illumination somehow reaches the floor above. But he remembers the layout of the room from when he was down here earlier. He takes four steps forward, moving to the wall where the old filing cabinets are, then reaches out above them in the darkness and begins to feel his way along the row of keys hanging on the metal hooks there. They chitter gently as his hand moves over them.

He finds the one the man used for the main gate when they left today.

It's the only one he needs—that's what a part of him wants to insist—except that it isn't. It's not good enough. So he keeps moving his hand to the left, searching for the other keys he saw earlier. He can't find them. Time stretches out, threatens to snap. Has the man moved them? The voice in his head telling him to run grows impatient and shrill. The silence is singing. But he ignores it all. Focuses as best he can.

And . . .

There they are.

He stands there for a moment with the keys clenched tightly in his fist and his heart beating hard. God—can he really do this? He feels himself faltering. But then he becomes aware of all the invisible things in the room around him: all the souvenirs stored away in the bags and boxes that are lost in darkness against the walls to either side. This little room is a grave. There are ghosts here. And he can sense them in the air now.

You are strong, they tell him. *You are brave.*

You know what you have to do.

Yes, he thinks.

He knows exactly what he has to do.

A few moments later, he turns and starts up the stairs. The doorway to the kitchen is a dark gray rectangle far above, and he keeps his attention focused on that as he climbs, expecting the man to step into view at any moment. But it remains empty.

Back in the kitchen. He listens.

Nothing. The house is entirely silent.

And he's about to start moving when he realizes that's wrong—that it shouldn't be. He edges into the living room. The man remains on the settee under the window, the moonlight still draped over his hands, his face invisible. He doesn't appear to have moved at all.

But the snoring has stopped.

And yet there's no going back now, is there? Not after what he's just done downstairs. James imagines the man staring back at him from the black void where his face should be.

How worthless you are.

No, James thinks. No, I'm not.

The man turns his head in the darkness.

And then the snoring resumes.

There's no reason to hesitate. James walks across the front room. He doesn't need to tell himself that he's lighter than air right now, because it feels like he really is. He walks past the man, into the small porch at the front of the house, opens the door just enough to slip out through and then—his heart giddy now, euphoria coursing through him—closes it quietly behind him.

It's a cold night. The sky is clear and the moon is full, and the farm ahead of him seems so much brighter than the house behind. There's no need for him to be quiet anymore—not out here. He runs as fast as he can across the hard ground, heading all the way down to the wooden pen at the far end by the trees. James hasn't run this quickly in years, perhaps not ever, and he can't remember ever feeling so alive.

The boy chained to the post is awake and alert. Perhaps he's too cold and miserable to sleep, but it feels like he was expecting him. As James skids to his knees in the dust, he can see the boy's bright eyes, and the terror there just makes the resolve in him fold over upon itself, becoming sharper and more defined, like the edge of a blade.

"What are you doing?" the boy whispers.

James takes hold of the padlock on the chain.

"It's time to leave," he says.

He works the first key on the ring into place. It doesn't turn, so he tries the second. He feels untethered from the world now. Triumphant.

"Where are we going?" the boy asks him.

"We're going home," James says.

The second key doesn't turn, so he moves onto the next. Three more to go. Glancing up from the lock, he sees the hope in the boy's eyes now.

"Do you promise?"

"Yes," James says. "I promise."

The boy smiles at him.

And then everything is suddenly brilliantly lit, as though a camera flash has gone off, and the image of the boy's face is burned into James's mind as he winces and closes his eyes.

When he opens them a moment later, the brightness remains.

The whole compound is flooded with light.

"Oh God," the boy whispers.

Still kneeling in the dirt, James turns his head.

The man is standing on the decking at the front of the house.

The two of them stare at each other for what feels like an age, and then the man shakes his head and taps down the steps. James feels the hope die inside him. It was a trap, he realizes. All along, the man was setting him one final test. Just to be certain he had him. Just to be sure he had broken him.

And now there's nowhere to run.

The man walks slowly across the compound toward him, turning the knife in his hand around.

And as he gets closer, he begins to whistle his tune.

Thirty

Fleming walked me back to reception.

"You nervous about this fucker?" he said.

"No."

"Because I'm short-staffed, but I can probably have someone stop by and keep an eye on the house."

I resisted the urge to point out that he'd been doing a good enough job of keeping an eye on the house already. I also didn't like the idea of one of his officers making an unplanned appearance. If I heard a noise in the middle of the night, then I wanted to be alert and on point, not wondering if it might be Fleming or one of his men stumbling around in my father's garden.

"I'll be fine," I said. "Just catch him."

"We will."

I walked down through the streets to the promenade. By now, the moon was low and bright in the night sky. I stood with my back to the sea for a while, shivering a little, the water lapping gently against the stone behind me.

I watched the people walking past.

Nobody was paying me any attention.

But the doubt I'd felt back in the police station wouldn't go away.

I tried to tell myself that talking to Fleming had been the right thing to do, but I also couldn't shake the idea that, without realizing it, I had made a mistake.

Did I do the right thing, Dad?

I imagined my father leaning against the railing beside me. Arms folded. One foot crossed in front of the other. Head down and deep in thought.

I don't know, my son. What do you think?

That I haven't thought things through carefully enough. That there's something I'm missing.

My father didn't reply. I shifted my weight a little.

What if we're wrong? I asked him.

About what?

About it being James Palmer who's behind this.

I imagined him coughing gently. *I just want to be clear that I never suggested that myself.*

Fine, I thought. But it has to be someone connected to that case, doesn't it? So it was natural enough to make that assumption.

And James was the obvious suspect.

Yes, I thought.

But now I wonder if I was jumping to the wrong conclusion—if I wasn't thinking carefully enough. James would have had so many of the markers I expect to find in my patients, but that's not enough to turn someone into a killer. He was just a little boy. When I saw him, it was almost like looking into a mirror. He was *desperate* for help. He wanted to be saved. The most likely explanation is the same as it was all along— that he ended up being another of the Pied Piper's victims.

My father nodded.

That's true, he said. *But you're also right that whoever's doing this has to be someone with a connection to the case. Someone who cares deeply enough about what happened to James for them to take their self-hatred out on the people who were there that day.*

Yes, I thought. But who could that be?

Someone else who feels guilty, my father said.

I glanced to my right. There was nobody there, of course, but for a moment I could almost see my father, and his words echoed in my mind for a second. The doubt I was feeling had become a coil of dread. I *had* missed something—I was sure of it. I had made a mistake. And as I leaned away from the railing, I felt a vibration in my pocket.

My phone was ringing.

I took it out. The number on the screen showed up as unidentified, and that coil of dread inside me grew tighter. I accepted the call and held the phone to my ear.

"Hello?"

For a moment, there was no reply. Just static on the line.

And then a man's voice.

"Hello, Daniel. You've been looking for me."

"Who is this?" I said.

"There's someone here who wants to talk to you."

I waited.

A few seconds later, a different voice came on the line.

"Dan." Sarah was crying. "Please help me."

Thirty-One

The Reach.

Early evening. The sun has been beating down hard on the island all day, but it's cold here. It always is. It's high up and exposed to the elements, but John thinks there's more to it than that. It's the extremity of the place. You're far away from the heart of the island, and whatever warmth circulates back there has faded by the time it gets here. It's a place of last resort. As far as you can go before there's nowhere left to go at all.

He stands a distance back from the edge.

For as long as he can remember, it's been a tradition for kids to approach that and get as close as they dare. Egging each other on. Not wanting to let themselves down and be laughed at. So many rites of passage seem to involve staring death in the face. And maybe that's not so strange, but it also strikes him as a shame that it's what the world expects of children.

It makes him think of James Palmer—bullied for carrying his toy lion to school—and how the world might be a better place if people judged a little less, and understood and cared a little more.

The wind whips around him. Despite the temperature, the sight before him is beautiful. The setting sun is burning the edges of the clouds and bruising the sky behind them. Countless fiery flickers of light are appearing and vanishing on the water, scattered in tiny lines all the way to the horizon.

If this ends up being the last thing he ever sees, it isn't so bad.

Because it isn't just the temperature that's making him shiver. He thinks about the phone call he received at the cemetery. The man told John that his name was Michael Johnson, and that he needed help. John recognized the name: Michael Johnson was the teenager who had been working in the shop at the rest area that day. Johnson couldn't talk about what had happened over the phone, he claimed; it was too much of a risk. Even seeing each other in person might be dangerous. Throughout the call, he had sounded panicked and frightened, and John hadn't needed him to explain why. He had simply suggested the most isolated spot he could think of for the two of them to meet.

Perhaps John really is about to meet Michael Johnson here. But it seems equally possible that it's someone else who is coming for him now. A man who has been manipulating him this whole time. A man made of smoke. Because however convincing he might have sounded on the phone, John isn't sure he believed a word of it.

But it's his responsibility to deal with.

And if he can't? The suicide note he wrote is still there in the glove compartment of his car. *Notify my son.* Before leaving the house to come here, he sat down at the computer, erased almost all of his browsing history, and changed the password. If something happens to him today, there will be just enough information for Daniel to pick up the trail and follow it—but only if he wants to. The trail is oblique enough for Daniel to miss the meaning if he isn't paying attention, or to ignore it if he wants. He can stay out of this; he can remain safe. To John, that feels like the way things have to be.

But it won't come to that. He's going to deal with it himself.

He stands for a while, entranced by the view.

And then—

"John."

He turns around. Craig Aspinall is walking up the footpath from the car park, and the sight of the man gives John's heart a small jolt. *Fuck.* There is nothing strange about Craig being here, of course; he roams around the island every day, acting as an unofficial caretaker of its beauty spots. But this is the worst possible time for him to show up. John has to get rid of him as quickly as he can without making him suspicious.

"Craig," he calls.

Aspinall throws a salute.

"Hey there. You okay?"

"I'm good." John turns and nods at the sea. "Just out here admiring the view."

Craig stops beside him and stares out.

"Ah yeah," he says. "It's always so pretty at this time of the day."

"Isn't it just," John says.

It's already obvious from Craig's body language that he isn't intending to head off straightaway, and John feels a prickle of sweat on his back. He needs the man to leave, but he can't afford to give the impression that anything is wrong. He has to go through the motions as best he can—act as though this is just another day. He's just out here enjoying nature. There isn't a monster somewhere out there in the trees, watching them both right now.

As always, Craig offers him a cup of coffee from his thermos. John sips from it and does his best to engage in the requisite small talk. How are they doing? They're both doing well—or at least, as they ruefully acknowledge to each other, as well as you can be doing when you get to their ages. What have they both been up to? Not much. Craig talks about the daily tours he makes: checking on the land; repairing signs and fences; picking up litter. *People, right?* he says, and John nods. *People indeed.* Craig asks how retirement is treating him, and John tells him that it's better than he expected, that he enjoys a quiet life with a slower pace. And as he says it, it surprises him to realize that it's true. Or that it was, before now.

A moment of silence.

"And how's your boy?" Craig says.

"Not a boy anymore."

"Ha! I guess not. Time, right?"

"It gets away from you."

John thinks about the last time he spoke to Daniel, when he was driving to Darren Field's house. It seems like a lifetime ago. But even then, it had been weeks since their previous conversation. How is Daniel? It's not a question he can answer, and that causes a flower of sadness to bloom in his heart. He knows very little about his son's life.

But he does know one thing at least.

"I'm proud of him, though," he says.

"Really?"

"Yeah." John takes another sip of coffee. "He's doing great."

Despite himself, he glances back at the trail that leads up to here from the car park. There's nobody there. But something strange happens while he's looking: after his head stops moving, the landscape doesn't. The wall of trees behind him continues to rotate for a second. And when he turns back, the same thing happens again. He tries to focus on Craig, but the man keeps being farther to the side than he should be, and his face has too many eyes now.

"I'm sure he'll be glad to hear that," Craig says quietly.

John looks down at the thermos cup he's holding.

He thinks about all the times out here on the trails that he's taken a coffee from Craig: just two old men sharing a drink, shooting the breeze, and putting the world to rights. But he notices that, even though Craig has as many hands right now as he does eyes, all of them are empty.

He's not drinking today.

Damn, John thinks.

"It's all that we want, isn't it?" Craig says. "Our kids to be okay."

John stumbles a little. Drops the cup.

"You . . . have kids, Craig?"

"I did once."

"I didn't—"

Something *pounds* against John's right arm with such force that it knocks the breath out of him and bruises his lungs. There's a moment of disorientation, and then he registers that it was the ground that just hit

him, or vice versa, and that the edge of the Reach ahead has flipped upward into a ragged vertical scar. A second later, the world begins to spin
sickeningly. Craig's muddy boots appear in front of him, but the sight of
them is already lost in the whirling circle that life is becoming.

Damn, John thinks again.

Craig's voice drifts in from a different place.

"I did once," he says again. "But not anymore."

PART FIVE
ACCEPTANCE

Thirty-Two

I drove at a deliberate and steady pace, keeping the speed just a flicker under the limit. The white lights that arced over the motorway swept the inside of the car at regular intervals.

You are detached, I told myself.

You are calm.

That mantra had been with me my entire adult life, ever since I first headed off to university. Being detached and calm had allowed me to put the trauma away and protect me from emotions that had threatened to drown me back then. It had also been a guide for my professional life. When things went wrong in a secure psychiatric facility, you needed to keep yourself under control, and the more dangerous the situation, the calmer you had to be.

But I wasn't calm. I wasn't detached. And while I kept a careful grip on the steering wheel, it was all I could do not to put my foot to the floor and begin to swerve between the other vehicles on the motorway.

You've got half an hour until the last ferry to the mainland. So you'll need to run.

But you're good at running, aren't you?

The man had done his best to sound impassive on the phone, his voice even *detached* and *calm* in its own way. But the anger just below the surface had been obvious; he was barely able to contain the hatred he felt, or control the violence that wanted to erupt out of him. And yet the instructions he gave me had clearly been thought through carefully. Half an hour until the last ferry off the island, and I needed my father's car first. The man had left me with no time to think.

But the calculation was a simple one: there was somewhere I needed to get to, because if I didn't then Sarah was going to die. Even as the man hung up, I was already sprinting up the hill that led toward my father's house. I attempted to call Sarah as I ran, hoping against hope that I had somehow mistaken her voice on the phone. But her mobile was turned off. And of course it was. Whoever the man was, he was organized and efficient. He *had* taken her. And if I didn't get to where he had told me in time then all that violence inside him would be directed at her.

Despite myself, I accelerated a little.

You're good at running, aren't you?

I conjured up a figure in the seat behind me. And even though it would do nothing to change the actions of the man in the real world, I allowed my subconscious to give that figure a voice. To let all the guilt and self-hatred that I'd hidden away for so long spill out into the car now.

It's what you did that day, isn't it? Ran away and hid like the worthless coward you are. You could have saved him. But you were too weak. Too scared.

I concentrated on the road.

What was it you said about me when you were still so sure that I was James Palmer? Underneath my behavior, I was just a little boy protecting himself. Maybe you should analyze yourself, doctor. Because that's all you've ever been. Detached and calm? What a fucking joke you are.

Yes, I thought. You're right.

All to hide the fact that he's dead because of you. Because of all of you.

Yes, I thought again.

But because of you too.

The figure fell silent at that. I could feel the rage beating off it, hot and feverish.

That's true, isn't it? I thought.

You might not be James Palmer, but you're someone who cares that he's dead. And I think I was *almost* right before, wasn't I? Whoever you are, *you* failed James too. And because you can't bear to face up to that, you take your self-hatred out on other people instead. All the people who might also have saved him, and didn't. They're just stand-ins for how much you despise yourself.

You're so fucking clever, aren't you?

I shook my head.

No, I thought. I'm not. Because like I said, you're right. I *have* been running. I've closed myself off from so many things. If I really was clever, I'd have dealt with it all a long time ago.

The truck in front was going too slow, so I indicated and pulled out to overtake. After I'd passed it, I pulled back in and forced myself to slow down to something approaching the speed limit. If I got pulled over then I wouldn't get where I needed to be. I wouldn't be able to save Sarah, assuming I still could.

As the lights washed over me, I registered a noise in the car and glanced down to my side. My mobile phone was on the passenger seat, buzzing softly, the screen illuminated. From the corner of my eye, I registered the incoming details.

[island—police]

I reached down and accepted the call.

"Dan?"

Fleming's voice.

"Yes," I said.

"Where are you, Dan?"

I looked around, trying to keep my hands steady on the wheel. The motorway was disorientating at night. The pulses of light and stretches of darkness had a hypnotic effect, and the empty blackness of the surrounding countryside made the outside world anonymous and indistinguishable. I might have been anywhere right now. Or nowhere.

"I honestly don't know," I said.

He hesitated.

"I've just checked in with the police at Rampton," he said. "They had a call out to a flat there early this afternoon. Resident was a guy named Michael Johnson. That's another one of the people who were at the rest area that day, right?"

"Yes," I said.

"He's dead."

I closed my eyes for a second. When I opened them again, the stretch of motorway and cars around me seemed entirely different.

"How?" I said.

"I don't know yet. It's developing. From what I can gather, they thought it might be a break-in gone wrong at first, but I get the impression that the scene is . . . different."

"Different?"

"Bad."

I tuned Fleming out, trying to think it through. Michael Johnson was the most recent victim in the chain, and he'd believed that if he didn't report what happened to the police then he would be safe. And yet the man had killed him anyway. And from what Fleming had just told me, Johnson hadn't been taken away for a second time like the other victims, with someone else forced to watch him die. He'd just been butchered in his flat.

I could still sense the figure in the back of the car.

The hate there. The *rage*.

"What are you doing?" I asked it.

"Sorry?" Fleming said. "What was that?"

"Nothing. I have to go, Liam."

I hung up and tossed the mobile phone back down on the passenger seat. I needed to concentrate. I had instructions to follow. If I deviated from them, and the man killed Sarah, then that would be my fault. And whatever I had done as a child, I would never forgive myself if I failed Sarah now.

Another wave of light passed through the car.

I could still sense the figure in the seat behind me.

Why did you kill Michael Johnson? I thought. What are you doing?

When the figure answered, it took me a moment to realize it was repeating my own words back to me.

I'm escalating, it said blankly.

It's a mistake to think of my rules as being absolute. All they do is serve a purpose, and I'll bend them if they don't suit me.

And what suits you now?

The figure didn't reply. I looked up and recognized the overhead sign lit up against the night sky ahead. The slip road was coming up.

What suits you now? I asked again

I realized that it's the killing that brings me peace now.

I signaled and took the turning for the rest area.

A part of me expected the place to be as dark and dead as the fields around the motorway behind me, but of course, it wasn't. The hotel to one side and the building ahead were both brightly illuminated, and the car park was swathed in an artificial light that washed the other vehicles of color and painted them all sickly shades of amber.

I drove in slowly, remembering what the man had told me.

You'll know what to do when you get there.

A moment later, I spotted the old camper van. It was parked on its own, far off to one side, in one of the few small pools of darkness the car park offered. A shiver of recognition ran through me as I approached it and then pulled in beside. It was impossible for it to be the same vehicle I had seen here as a child. The Pied Piper's van had been found in a country lane two decades ago, the man dead behind the wheel. When the investigation had run its course, it would have been either locked away or destroyed. It would certainly never have seen a road again.

But the similarities were uncanny. Streaks of mud obscured the license plate. There was the same black window in its side, the same dirt coating the metal. I couldn't see if there were little handprints pressed into the muck below, but I could picture them there. As I drew level with the cab, I had the sensation that the vehicle beside me had passed through time somehow. That it had winked out of a moment in the past and then arrived, intact and unchanged, in this one, here in the present.

I could hear the sound of its engine rumbling softly.

The driver's window was dark, the cab full of shadow. I could just about make out the vague impression of a figure seated motionless behind the wheel.

Thump!

A bright white face appeared suddenly against the glass, and I flinched. The cheeks and forehead were smooth and unlined. A thin line for a mouth. Black hollows where the eyes should have been. It took me a second to realize that I was looking at a mask that the man in the cab was holding up against the window. He tilted it to one side, as though it was turning its head to peer out at me. I could see the tip of his finger in the center of one black eye socket, like the pale smudge of a retina.

I waited, my heart beating hard.

And then my mobile buzzed beside me on the passenger seat.

I read the message he had sent me.

turn off your phone throw it out of the window make sure I see.

I hesitated, unsure what to do. On the one hand, he was *right there*. But the van's engine was running, and I was sure the doors were locked, so there was no guarantee that I'd be able to get to him before he managed to drive away. Even if I did, I couldn't be sure that Sarah was even inside. He could have left her somewhere else. Somewhere that she'd never be found.

I looked up from my phone.

The mask—still tilted—stared implacably at me.

Waiting for my decision.

I switched the phone off. Then I put the window down and threw it out, listening to it clatter away across the tarmac. Perhaps Fleming or Rampton police would trace it eventually; if so—if it came to that—then it seemed right that this would be the last place they could track it to. If I was going to disappear, it was appropriate for it to be from here.

The mask continued to stare blankly at me for what felt like an age.

Then it ducked away out of sight.

The camper van began moving forward. Not racing away, just crawling steadily out of the parking space beside me.

The implication was clear enough.

I released the handbrake and headed after it. Keeping a little distance.
Following it around the perimeter of the car park, toward the exit back
onto the motorway. The van accelerated up the exit that led out of the
rest area, and I matched its pace. And then, a minute later, we were both
part of the traffic there, the taillights ahead of me like a pair of red eyes
staring unblinkingly back from the night.

I had no idea where we were going, and no idea of what was going
to happen when we got there. But as the overhead lights began to wash
over and through the car again, I had a sensation that reminded me of
what happened all those years ago. The feeling that I was leaving the real
world behind and heading toward an entirely different one.

Somewhere out of time where anything might happen.

A place where there would be monsters.

Thirty-Three

Come on, old man, John tells himself.

Keep going.

He rests his shoulder against the wooden post, then drives down with his feet, grits his teeth, and pushes as hard as he can. His shoes skitter in the dust a little, threatening to slip and only just holding.

Is the post shifting a little?

It's hard to tell.

He keeps pushing, staring blankly down at his hands, shackled together at the wrist, and ignoring the pain coursing through his body, and he counts silently to five before finally allowing himself to step back and rest.

Deep breaths.

Shivering in the cold night air.

The wooden pen around him is small and square, three meters to a side by his estimate. The post stands in the very center. A metal plate has been screwed tightly into the side of it, and a short chain connects that to the shackles that bind his hands.

Come on, he tells himself.

He remembers little of the hours after being drugged at the Reach. There is the sensation of having been in an enclosed space, perhaps in the boot of a car, and a dim memory of hearing the horns at the ferry terminal. But the first moment he recalls with any clarity is when he woke up here, however many days ago that was now. He was alone. There was no sign of Aspinall, and when John shouted out the man's name, his calls had gone unanswered, disappearing into the trees. Something about the quality of the silence told him that he was in the middle of nowhere.

Nobody was coming to help him.

The next thing he did was test the limits of his prison. If he could reach the fence, he reasoned, perhaps he could break off a switch of wood to use as a tool or a weapon. But the chain was too short. One by one, he attempted to pry apart the links, but that was no use either. They were much stronger than he was. *Brute force* was not going to help him here. He had then tried to use the little hand movement available to him to pull the post out of the ground. But once again, he had realized very quickly that wouldn't work. The post had been driven in too deep.

Because Aspinall was good at building and fixing things, wasn't he?

The man had spent years now traversing the island, carrying out repairs on the trails and at the beauty spots. The whole time, John had thought of him as being almost part of the landscape. Just a man you saw without seeing, talked to without really listening to. Aspinall was such a reliable part of ordinary, everyday life that it had never occurred to John to imagine he might be building something in a different place, intent on fixing something inside him instead.

For a time, he had succumbed to despair.

But also—shameful to admit—to fear. He was trapped and helpless, subject to whatever Aspinall's whims might be when the man eventually returned. John had remembered the story Darren Field had told him.

He was so angry. He's reds and blacks. He's fucking screaming.

And while he found it hard to square that with the picture he had of Craig Aspinall in his head, he knew now that image had always been wrong. Whatever else Aspinall pretended to be, in his own mind he was James Palmer's father.

He hated himself. And he hated the people who had failed to save his boy that day.

You are going to die here, John had told himself.

But then another idea had occurred to him.

Perhaps *brute force* was not out of the question after all.

Come on, he tells himself again now. And then he edges monotonously around to the opposite side of the post. He gathers his strength and leans into it from the opposite direction, pushing as hard as he can. A minute ago, he wasn't sure, but *this* time he's certain he feels it. The post moved. It's tiny, imperceptible, barely there. But it *is* there. He has to believe that. The post just moved back to correct the minuscule effect he had by pushing from the other side.

He grits his teeth, determined to push the post *ever so slightly* past the point it was at before. Then he'll gather his strength, trudge back around, and repeat the process. Over and over again.

Because that is what you do. You—

Keep going.

He stumbles as he circles back around the post. There's a jolt, confusing him. It takes a second to realize that he's carried on the wrong way this time and taken the chain to its limit.

Stupid. Worthless. Old man.

But that won't do any good.

Deep breaths.

He turns and reverses his course. It's just so hard now though. He keeps trying to gather his strength, but there's so little of it left. For however long now, he has been chained up here, exposed to the elements, without food of any kind. Aspinall left him water, at least, but in a metal dog bowl on the ground, and for the first couple of days John was damned if he was going to lower himself to drinking from that. But eventually the thirst had become too painful, the weakness in his body too profound, and so finally he had succumbed. As he had knelt there in the dust, lapping from the bowl like an animal, he had imagined Aspinall watching from somewhere in the tree line. Laughing at his humiliation.

Perhaps even taking a photograph.

But if so, he hadn't made himself known. Until tonight, in fact, John has been alone. Time has begun to lose meaning. During the hottest parts of the days, he has maneuvered around the post like the minute hand of a clock, trying to catch the thin sliver of shadow it offered. At night, he has lain shivering in the cold, feeling his sunburned skin shining in the dark.

And the rest of the time, he has pushed the post.

Back and forth. Over and over.

There was a period of time—yesterday?—when he had given up. He had put his efforts on hold in the midday sun, and then simply not started again when it cooled. It had felt so easy just to sit there instead. To *stop*. Because the post was implacable. You did your best, he had reasoned, but there came a point when the blows were too hard to pick yourself up from. A moment when you had to accept that you were beaten and there was no use going on.

He had closed his eyes.

No, a voice told him. *Keep going.*

Give a good account of yourself.

And he had opened his eyes again. It was strange, because the voice hadn't sounded like the more familiar one he talked to himself with. It had seemed to come from somewhere away to one side, and it had been so clear that it was almost a surprise to see that he was still alone.

But he had picked himself up again. And he had—

Keep going.

He leans back into the post now, pushing as hard as he can, putting as much of the little strength that remains of his frail body into it. He senses movement again. A little more than last time? He crouches down, resting for a few seconds, then stands up and heads dutifully, robotically back around the post.

Leans into it.

And pushes.

Because there's no time for him to rest now.

Aspinall returned a couple of hours earlier, and he was not alone when he did. John watched—his mind repeating *no, no, no*—as Aspinall dragged Sarah across the clearing toward one of the pens. He pulled desperately against the chain again, and attempted to shout her name, but his throat was too dry and he couldn't make a sound.

A short while later, the silence in the clearing had been interrupted by a sudden humming noise, and then the darkness broken by a series of bright lights blooming into life across the compound. The rows of pens had been transformed into a cat's cradle of wood and dirt and shadow.

And then Aspinall had left.

But he'll be back soon. John is sure of that.

He tries to call out again now.

"Sarah. Can you hear me?"

His voice is raspy, barely. But it must carry a little, because a few seconds later he hears a muffled cry in response.

She is alive, at least.

"It's going to be okay," he tries his best to say. "I promise."

Then he moves around to the other side of the post. He's so weak now though. And angry with himself too. What he wouldn't give to have that handful of lost hours from yesterday back now. They might turn out to have made all the difference, and that's a horrible thought. That after being a failure all his life, he has carried on being one to the very end.

It's another spur. He leans into the post. Plants his feet against the ground. Pushes as hard as he can.

Come on, old man, he tells himself.

Keep going.

Thirty-Four

The longer I followed the camper van along the motorway, the more the real world seemed to be falling away around me. The darkness of the countryside and rhythmic sweep of the overhead lights had the effect of a slowly swinging pendulum. The intermittent signage above began to lose coherence. The place names listed there meant nothing to me, the words appearing to be written in an alien language. While I should have been able to keep at least a vague grip on where we were, I was disorientated and lost, divorced from geography and adrift in time.

All the while, the red lights ahead stared back at me.

I kept a steady distance.

After however many miles, the van indicated and took a turning off the motorway. I followed. Within minutes, we were driving down country lanes. At first, the roads were wider, surrounded by dark fields, but soon they began to narrow, with trees pressing in on both sides. The man was taking us into woodland, and it was far thicker even than that on the island. The trees here were so tall that, looking up through the windscreen, only a thin stretch of night sky was visible overhead. It created the strange sensation that I was seeing a black road inverted up there. That a vast distance above there were two tiny vehicles making a mirror journey.

The red eyes of the camper van rounded a corner ahead.

And when I rounded it a few seconds later, they were gone.

I slowed down immediately, a flare of panic cutting through the wooziness. If I lost the van, what would happen to Sarah? The road ahead stretched out into the distance, and there was no way the van had been traveling fast enough to disappear from view so quickly. So where had it gone? I glanced to my left and caught a glimpse of red light flickering between the trees there, and I pulled my father's car to a stop just as I passed a break in the tree line. A dirt trail led away into the forest there. The entrance was thin and overgrown, and the angle was so tight that I had to reverse back and round slightly before driving awkwardly in. The wheels undulated on the ground, and the branches of the trees to either side began thwacking and scratching at the sides of the car.

The camper van's red eyes were lost ahead of me now, but the trail snaked along without any turnoffs the vehicle could have taken. I drove carefully, my headlights occasionally picking out the sharp tips of branches where they had been cut away. At some point, the killer had widened this route to make it more accessible. Perhaps he had even carved the whole trail out by hand. It was hard to imagine the act of willpower that must have taken, but this man had willpower, didn't he?

I might not know everything about him, but I knew that much—

The back of the camper van appeared out of nowhere. I pressed down hard on the brakes, bringing my father's car to a stop only just behind it. My headlights illuminated the dirty metal door in the back of the vehicle. Its engine was silent and all the lights were off.

Dust from the trail swirled gently in my headlights.

I waited for thirty seconds.

Nothing.

Okay, I thought. I opened the glove compartment and took out the knife I had picked up from my father's house before leaving. When I turned off the engine, the world fell dark for a moment. But then, as my eyes adjusted, I realized it wasn't as pitch black as it should have been. A faint glow was coming from somewhere beyond the camper van.

Little dots of light flickered on the trees there.

I stepped out of the car, holding the knife casually down by my side, slightly behind my leg. The place we had come to a stop in was a little wider than the trail directly behind me, the tree line a short distance away on both sides. I stood still, listening for a moment. The forest was silent. But the man had brought me here and must have known exactly where I was right now, so there was no point in being quiet.

"Sarah?" I called loudly.

No response.

I moved quickly down the passenger side of the camper van, banging on the side once as I went.

"Sarah?"

Nothing.

When I reached the cab, I peered into the window. There was nobody inside. Through the dirty glass, I could see the flickering lights from ahead playing over smudges of leather and plastic. As I moved to the front of the vehicle, the source of the illumination became apparent. The trail continued ahead of the camper van, and the path there was lit by strings of white fairy lights that had been draped between the trees on either side.

It's the lights in the trees I remember most, Michael Johnson had said.

They seemed so out of place—like a fairy tale.

I watched as the tiny bulbs flicked on and off in a steady, repeating pattern. Perhaps they were supposed to create the impression of a magical path in a forest, but there was nothing enchanting about them. They looked more like the kind of decorations a child might encounter at some cheap outdoor Christmas grotto.

I turned the knife in my hand.

Regardless, the lights created a corridor of sorts, one that it was obvious the man intended for me to follow. But I didn't have to do what he wanted me to. I could get back in my car and reverse out of here; try to find a phone and lead the police to this place. But there was no guarantee that the man would be here when they arrived, or that Sarah would still be alive by then either.

The man's voice in my head again:

You're good at running, aren't you?

I moved forward cautiously.

Once I was on the path, the lights around me seemed almost viciously bright, the woods behind them deep and black. As the flashes alternated, the lights danced over the trees and the leafy ground. My footsteps crunched softly in the silence. I felt scared: exposed and vulnerable. And yet something told me that the man wasn't waiting in the trees to ambush me.

That he was ahead of me right now in every sense.

Thirty seconds later, the trail widened out into a more open space.

I stopped at the edge.

It was a clearing, illuminated by a number of larger bulbs embedded in the tops of wooden posts. The light from them cast elongated, cross-shaped shadows onto the land. Cables were spooled everywhere on the ground. I looked to my right, and saw the remains of an old, broken-down building that had been almost overtaken by the trees around it. The stonework had collapsed in places, and the panes in the downstairs windows were mostly gone: just a few jagged teeth of glass all but lost in the tangles of grass that were growing out over the sills.

The sight of it made me shiver.

And when I looked to my left, the feeling got worse.

It took a moment for the sight there to resolve itself and make sense. From what I could tell, there was a series of wooden pens and metal cages, and my gaze was drawn to the pen closest to the house. There was somebody in there: a shape on the ground that looked like a human being, lying on their side. Light was glinting on what appeared to be a chain tethering whoever was in there to a wooden post in the earth.

I took a faltering step in that direction, glancing around.

Speaking more quietly now.

"Sarah?"

The shape on the ground responded to the sound of my voice. A head lifted up in the shadows. Even in the darkness, I could tell it was her from the way her hair hung down. She didn't reply, but I didn't know if that was because she was gagged in some way or too badly injured to talk.

The thought of that made me want to head across to her, but that was exactly what the man would be expecting me to do, so I fought it down and forced myself to remain where I was.

And he was here somewhere.

"Dan."

The voice came from right behind me, and I turned quickly, raising the knife as I did. I didn't know what I was expecting to see. A monster, perhaps. A man in a mask. But it was just Craig Aspinall, and for a split second that didn't make any sense to me at all.

Why was he here?

What was that in his hand?

And then the side of my head exploded.

Thirty-Five

"Dan."

John has been drifting—almost unconscious—but hearing his son's name causes him to jerk awake. Where is he? It takes a second to realize that he's crouched in a pen, weak and trembling, his body braced awkwardly against the post. He looks up the farm in time to see Daniel crumple, like a chimney collapsing, one moment upright, the next gone entirely.

Dust puffs up into the bleary, crisscross streams of light when his body hits the ground.

And then he lies still.

John tries to call out—*Daniel!*—but he doesn't have the strength left to speak. All he can do is cling to the post and watch as Craig Aspinall stands over Daniel for a moment, looking down at him. John can see enough of the man's face to recognize the rage burning there. Aspinall crouches down beside his son, the blackjack in his hand, and John visualizes him bringing that weapon down on Daniel, again and again and—

Do something!

But he can't.

He has nothing left.

All he can do is watch. Aspinall reaches out with his free hand and turns Daniel's head, then peers down into his face. It looks like he says something. But even though John can't make out the words, he has the impression that Aspinall is checking Daniel isn't dead.

Please, he thinks.

Please, please, please . . .

Aspinall nods to himself.

He discards the blackjack and picks up something from the ground beside him. John squints, trying to make out what it is—and feels a lurch of horror when he does: a knife, glinting briefly in the light for a second. Then Aspinall stands up, his free hand gripping Daniel's wrist, and he begins pulling his body down the compound.

Down toward where John is crouching.

Three empty pens between them.

John watches helplessly as Aspinall passes the first, dragging Daniel behind him. Coming closer. He seems so strong, so effortless. It's horrifying to see his son's body being pulled across the ground like dead weight, but there's a deeper sense of horror too—

Past the second pen.

—because John knows that the three of them—Sarah, him, Daniel— are the last remaining victims in Aspinall's chain. And there's only one possible reason why Aspinall needs Daniel to be alive. When he kills John and Sarah, he wants Daniel to be aware of what's happening. He wants him to see and feel every second of it, and—

Past the third pen.

Brace yourself, John tells himself.

You'll only have one chance.

Aspinall reaches the entrance to his pen. John wants to hold his breath but knows that he'll faint if he does. All he can do is hope. And Aspinall doesn't turn his head. He doesn't care; he doesn't see. He just keeps going, dragging Daniel behind him, focused on the next pen along. John knows there will only be a second before the man sees the ragged hole in the ground where the post once was. Before he realizes the pen is empty.

He forces himself to his feet.

He only managed to move a little way from his prison before collapsing, and he's so much weaker now, but he tries to gather some last trace of strength inside himself. Stumbles out of the pen, his vision blurry, the farm off-kilter and turning around him. Aspinall is still holding both the knife and Daniel's wrist, staring into the next enclosure, caught in that split second between seeing and understanding that offers John his only chance.

Come on, old man. Keep going.

Aspinall starts to turn—

And John launches himself at him.

Thirty-Six

I opened my eyes.

All I could see was darkness and dusty ground and shadows that stretched out at odd angles. What had happened? Everything was blurry and strange. It reminded me of ducking my head beneath the surface of a swimming pool on sports day. The cheering from the stands suddenly muted and dulled; my heartbeat in my ears; and then all that noise returning, incomprehensible for a second, as I broke back up into the air to take a breath.

I rolled onto all fours and vomited into the dirt.

Broken fragments of memory slotted together in my mind.

The farm.

Aspinall.

Sarah.

Panic flared as I remembered where I was and what I was doing here. My right hand was pressed to the ground. I noticed there were shadows playing over it, and then I heard the sound of fighting from beside me to the right.

I turned my head.

Two people were wrestling on the ground a bare couple of meters away. At first, that was all I could make out, because their bodies were only half illuminated by the lights, and they were rolling this way and that. Puffs of dust were rising from the ground, and the shadows spilled out like fingers opening and closing against the dirt. One of the men suddenly shouted out in pain, and a moment later the light caught Craig Aspinall's face, now sitting astride the other figure.

Aspinall pulled the knife out of wherever it had been stuck in the man beneath him, then raised it and brought it down with a thud into the front of his shoulder. The impact caused the other man to lift his head, and when his face caught the light too, I realized it was my father.

Aspinall pulled the knife out and raised it again, his free hand gripping hold of my father's hair, turning his head to hold the target steady.

And somehow I moved.

It was as much a stumble as anything else—a desperate half fall across the short distance between us—but I managed to loop my left arm under Aspinall's, and my right behind his back, joining my hands at the far side of his head, and the momentum took him off my father and sent us both sprawling into the dust on our sides. With my chest against Aspinall's back, I kept my hands gripped tightly together as best I could, then tried to hook my foot over to pin him at the ankles. As we wrestled, the shattered lights of the compound whirled around us. The ground was at my back, and then against my elbows with Aspinall underneath me, but then the two of us were rolling, his weight on top of me again. I lost track of where the knife was, or if he even still had it.

You do not let go, I imagined my father saying.

You do not give up.

But Aspinall was much stronger than I had expected, fueled by that burning rage inside him, and my own body seemed watery and weak in comparison. I caught a flash of light on the knife, and slackened my grip and reached out to grab his wrist. But he moved as I did, squirming out of the loosened hold and catching me hard in the face with an elbow. The world filled with stars again. And then Aspinall was on top of me, lifting the knife up into the night air.

There was no time to avoid the blow.

But then there was a sickening thud as my father swung the wooden post into Aspinall's head. The strength of the blow knocked Aspinall off me and into the shadows to my side. I rolled over, my father stepping across me, and I watched as he raised the post again before bringing it down in an overhead strike that landed where Aspinall's face must have been.

The force of the collision took my father off-balance. He stumbled back toward me. I thought he was going to trip, but somehow he gathered himself, corrected the half fall, and ended up kneeling down in the dust next to me.

We looked at each other.

Silence for a moment.

And then I realized that, from off to the side, I could hear Aspinall attempting to breathe through the remains of his face. It was a horrible, sickening noise.

And it sounded for all the world like someone was whistling.

James

James stands up.

The man is walking toward him across the compound, approaching him slowly and steadily. There's no need for him to rush, because he knows there's nowhere for James to escape to. There never has been.

Perhaps it's strange, but James realizes he's not afraid anymore. Until this moment, the man has been a monolith, a demon, a monster. But as he walks toward James now, the lights of the compound are bringing him into sharp relief, and it's clear that he's only ever been a man. Average height and build. His face is finally visible now, and the features that James can see there are unremarkable. While he's still whistling his tune, it sounds small and silly now.

He might even look pathetic if he wasn't holding the knife.

James glances down. All he has are the keys he took from the cellar. They won't save him, but he clenches them between his knuckles anyway.

Just give a good account of yourself, he thinks.

He's not sure where the voice comes from, but it's right. That's all he can do. Because he *is* going to die—he understands that clearly. It should have been obvious from the very first moment he was taken on the beach that there wasn't going to be a happy ending. And perhaps a part of him had recognized that all along, and that's why he held on to that little flame inside him.

He was always going to lose.

But that doesn't mean the man has to win.

He is only a few meters away now, but he has his back to the house, which means James can see something that he can't.

You know what you have to do.

He remembers the old kerosene lamp on the shelf in the cellar.

The crumpled box of matches beside it.

The man has left the front door open and, over his shoulder, James can see a faint glow coming from inside the house. The first few tendrils of smoke from the fire he started in the basement are already beginning to emerge out into the air above the porch. The man doesn't know it yet, but his storeroom full of dark magic is burning: all his power turning to ash and smoke. And by the time he does realize, it will be too late to rescue any of it.

James glances down at the boy beside him.

I'm sorry I didn't manage to save us, he thinks.

But I tried my best.

And as the man finally reaches them, James looks away from him entirely: past the pen and into the woods beyond. His mother is standing between the trees again now, half illuminated by the floodlights, half illuminated by something else.

She smiles at him.

"Are you proud of me?" he says.

Her smile broadens.

More than you could ever know, she says. *I love you so much.*

Now close your eyes and come here.

ISLAND RESIDENT PLEADS GUILTY
TO MAINLAND MURDERS

Craig Aspinall has today admitted his role in the murders of five people. The local handyman, well known in the community, pleaded guilty to the murders of Oliver Hunter, Graham Lloyd, Rose Saunders, Darren Field, and Michael Johnson. All five killings occurred between June and September this year.

Aspinall, 72, appeared by video link, having previously admitted to additional counts of assault and abduction at an earlier hearing. Sentencing was adjourned until next week, with the judge warning him that he faces a mandatory whole life term.

DCI Frank Smith said, "These were brutal crimes, showing a high degree of sophistication and planning. Craig Aspinall is an exceptionally dangerous man, and I hope that today's events can begin to bring some degree of closure to the families and friends of his victims. Our thoughts are with them."

He said, "I would like to thank the large team of officers who have worked tirelessly on what has been a complex and challenging investigation. Special credit is due to former officer John Garvie, whose efforts in helping to solve this case cannot be overstated."

DCI Smith declined to comment on reports that further remains had been discovered following Aspinall's arrest, stating only that the investigation remains open.

John Garvie was unavailable for comment.

Thirty-Seven

A knuckle rapped on the car window.

I looked up quickly from the newspaper clipping. The glass was dappled with rain. Beyond that, one of the security guards at the prison was leaning down next to the car, sheltering under an umbrella.

I put the window down.

"Hi, Eric."

"Hey there, Dr. Garvie." He gestured behind him with his thumb. "I buzzed you in at the gate, but I wanted to check. You're not listed on the rota I was given as being at work today. Did someone make a mistake?"

I looked ahead, out through the windscreen. With its old brick walls and blocky towers, the prison was a forbidding sight at the best of times. Today, the weather made the building look even more washed-out and forlorn. A hopeless place. One that was perhaps best left obscured by the rain, assuming you couldn't avoid it altogether. And today, I couldn't.

"No," I said. "I'm not on call. I'm here to see someone."

He smiled. "Just can't stay away, right?"

I did my best to smile back.

"Not a patient," I said. "Not today."

I walked around the perimeter and saw the queue of people waiting at the main entrance. They were all here to visit husbands, friends, loved ones. I'd seen them hundreds of times before in the past, and had always been oddly touched by the everyday sense of humanity their presence here suggested. Whatever the prisoners inside here might have done, they were just human beings. They had connections to ordinary lives that continued outside the prison's walls. And maybe one day they would rejoin them.

My own appointment today was very different.

After I signed in, I was searched, and then a guard led me down an endless series of corridors, buzzing us through one door after another as he went. Eventually, we stopped outside one without a handle.

"You ready?" he said.

"Yes."

He scanned his card. The door opened.

I stepped inside.

Craig Aspinall had been brought in before me. He was handcuffed and dressed in prison overalls, seated on the far side of a table in the middle of the room. There was a chair across from him, and I walked over and sat down.

The door closed behind me.

Silence for a moment as we stared at each other.

Despite everything he had done, I found it almost painful to look at him. I still remembered how he had seemed on the island: sun-worn and strong; a man who walked the trails and fixed things that other people had broken. But that man was gone now. His skin was pale, and the operations he'd undergone while awaiting trial had only been half successful. The surgeons had managed to reattach his lower jaw, but it remained misaligned, and his face below the nose was a mess of angry scar tissue. As a consequence of his injuries, it had been difficult for him to eat solid food, and his body appeared thin and weak beneath the overalls.

But appearances could be deceptive.

Because the rage that I knew consumed him inside was still burning softly in his eyes. If anything, he probably hated me even more now than he had before. And perhaps I should have hated him in return, but I didn't. I was detached; I was calm. There was no such thing as monsters.

Aspinall was only a man. He was the product of his environment and experiences: the focal point of the damage done to him, and the damage he had passed onto others because of it.

And I knew a lot more about that damage now.

I knew about the abusive childhood he had suffered while growing up on the island—common to many men his age there—and I knew that the demons he'd acquired had followed him when he escaped in his early twenties. I knew about his history of drug use and petty criminality after he moved to the mainland. The violence. The periods of incarceration as his offenses gathered momentum and became more serious.

I knew a lot less about his relationship with Abigail Palmer, but enough to understand that it had been a fractured and volatile one. My father told me that, when he first found Abigail's file, it had given him the impression of a drowning woman who kept coming up for air. Having read it since, I agreed with him. And while I imagined Craig Aspinall believed he had loved her in his own way, I was equally sure that he had been one of the things that kept emerging from the depths to pull her down again.

Had he been James's father? That wasn't clear—no father's name was recorded on the birth certificate—but I suspected so. Regardless, he had been an intermittent presence in the boy's early life: sometimes there; more often not. At the time of James's disappearance, Aspinall had been estranged from both of them, beginning a five-year sentence for robbery and assault.

By all accounts, he had been determined to turn his life around. Perhaps he had even imagined there might be a family waiting for him outside when he did. But given he had no official connection to Abigail and James, he hadn't been contacted when James drowned, or when Abigail took her life later that year. He only learned of both events upon his release. By which point, the media coverage of the Pied Piper was long over.

In the meantime, his father had died. Aspinall inherited a ramshackle house on the island. His childhood home probably had monsters in every room, ghosts in all the shadows, but there was nowhere else for him to go by then.

I remembered the look of bitterness on his face when I'd spoken to him while collecting my father's car.

That's the thing about this island, right?

You think you've got away, but the place keeps dragging you back.

"Did you bring it?" he asked me now.

The injuries made it as difficult for him to speak as they did for him to eat. But even though I had to concentrate, I would have understood what he was asking regardless. The need in his body language was clear. He was like an addict. As much as he hated me, he was willing to endure my presence here in order to get what he wanted.

Did you bring it?

I glanced down at the folder in my lap.

"We'll get to that, Craig. But there are a couple of questions I want to ask you first. And then maybe I can help you."

I took the first item out of my folder.

My old, battered copy of *The Man Made of Smoke*, by Terrence O'Hare.

It felt strange to touch it again after all these years. I ran my fingers down the edge of its weathered and faded pages, and then across a cover that was now only barely attached. The book was secondhand in every way. I had spent so much time reading it when I was younger: lost for a while in the trauma it contained. When I left it behind me, I had passed it on to my father without realizing.

I thumbed through it now, recognizing the passages I had underlined and the notes I had made in the margins. My father had added his own annotations and asterisks too. A different hand and a different pen. And then finally—and again, without realizing—he had passed it on to someone else.

"That's mine," Aspinall said.

"Where did you get it?"

"You know where."

I supposed that was answer enough. My father had pursued his investigation over the years—as obsessed, in his own way, as I had been—and when he finally solved it, he had made a choice. The world had moved on, he decided, and there was nothing to be gained from unearthing the past. It was better to draw a line and move on. His first visit to Abigail Palmer's grave had been on what would have been James's birthday, and he had left the book there.

Where Aspinall must have found it upon his own yearly visit.

"Did you see him at the grave?" I asked. "My father?"

He nodded. "Every year. I watched him."

I flicked through the book to the photographs in the middle. Past the pictures of Sean Loughlin, Paul Deacon, and Charlie French, to the pages dedicated to Robbie Garforth. The portrait that had been taken at his school. The photograph I had found at the rest area.

And the sketch I had helped the police to draw. Which because of my persistence back then, had turned out to be an almost perfect likeness of James Palmer.

"And is this when you realized?" I said.

He nodded again.

"I'm sorry," I said quietly.

"Don't you fucking dare apologize."

Before I had a chance to react, Aspinall was out of his seat. He smashed his hands down on the table and stared across at me, the hatred and rage burning brightly in his eyes now.

"It's your fault that he's dead."

Equally quickly, the door opened behind me, and I sensed a guard stepping into the room. But I didn't turn around. I just stared back at Aspinall, and held up my hand as a signal to the man behind me.

It's okay.

After a moment, Aspinall settled back down in his chair, breathing heavily as much as he could manage. Then I heard the sound of the guard retreating, and the door closing again.

I looked down at the book.

It's your fault that he's dead.

I had spent so long believing that. At first, I had allowed the guilt to consume and suffocate me. And then, in the years afterward, I had forced myself to feel far too little of anything. It wasn't that I had locked what happened away behind a door. It was more like it had been in the room with me ever since, filling the air around me, and I had spent my whole life too afraid to breathe in.

What a waste.

Because looking back now, I realized how much compassion I felt for the boy I had been. The encounter with the Pied Piper had happened at the worst possible time for me: no longer a child, allowed to be scared of monsters; not yet a man, capable of taking responsibility. I remembered thinking of the rest area as a liminal space—a crossing-over spot between different worlds—but the truth is that I had been in one of those that entire summer.

And I could forgive myself for that.

"I'm not apologizing, Craig," I said. "Because it's not my fault. I said that I was sorry, and that's not the same thing."

He stared at me for a few seconds, still breathing heavily.

"But you *are* right," I told him. "This belongs to you now."

I put the book on the table and slid it across to him. He picked it up quickly and began thumbing through its pages as best he could. But I knew that it wasn't the book he was interested in so much as what he had kept in it, and when he didn't find it, he looked up at me.

"Where is it?"

"Maybe we'll get to that. There's something else I want to know first." I leaned forward.

"I know that you worked on your farm for months," I said. "It was important to you to duplicate what you imagined in your mind's eye."

"Yes. Because it had to be right."

"But what interests me more," I said, "is how you found that location to begin with. In your statement, you said you spent a lot of your free time driving along country roads, searching for somewhere. You'd stop in a place and check, and it wouldn't feel right, so you'd move on again. Over and over again. Three years of this?"

He nodded.

I thought about the newspaper article I'd read in the car.

DCI Smith declined to comment on reports that further remains
had been discovered following Aspinall's arrest.

When the police arrived at the compound that night, the whole area
had been immediately cordoned off. The searches they made were thorough and comprehensive. And on the third day, while investigating a
patch of land in one of the pens, they found four sets of human remains
buried in the ground there. Initial examination of the bones recovered
suggested that they belonged to males between the ages of five and fif-
teen, and that the bodies had been there for a long time, possibly decades.
The information had yet to be released to the public, but I knew that
recent DNA tests had finally established the identities of all four boys.

Sean Loughlin. Paul Deacon. Charlie French.

And James Palmer.

The farm had obviously been abandoned and derelict for years before Aspinall chanced upon it, and the precise chain of ownership was
murky and unclear. The most recent entry on the land registry suggested
it belonged to a man named William MacGuire, who had inherited it
from his father. But that had been many years ago, and there were no
other surviving records of MacGuire. There were no photographs of the
man. No available DNA. Beyond the farm, and the bodies left there,
he appeared to have left no trace on the world at all. It might never be
proved beyond doubt that he was the Pied Piper, but it seemed likely to
me. Never a monster at all. Just a man.

But none of that explained what had led Aspinall there.

"Years of searching," I said. "What happened on the day you found it?"

He didn't reply.

"Craig?" I prompted.

Nothing.

I stood up, making it clear I was going to leave—

"I heard him."

—and then I sat back down again slowly.

"Heard who?" I said.

"My boy."

I waited.

"It was like I was lost that day," he said. "I was driving down all these roads and had no idea where I was. It was the middle of nowhere, everything overgrown. I was looking for him, but I was ready to give up. And then I heard him calling out to me. It was only for a second, but his voice was clear as day. He was shouting out for help. That's when I saw the path in the trees."

"Which you followed."

"I did."

Aspinall nodded.

"And when I got there, it felt like I was home."

As I looked at him now, I saw that the rage had faded from his eyes. He seemed helpless, haunted, and for a moment, I could see the little boy in him. His expression reminded me of James Palmer's that day at the rest area.

"Did you bring it?" he said quietly.

"Yes."

I reached into my file and produced a piece of paper. The best I could offer Aspinall was a color photocopy. The original had been discovered in his house, tucked away inside *The Man Made of Smoke*, but it was something that Aspinall had kept and lived with for far longer than he'd had the book.

I slid it over the table to him.

It was a letter that he had received many years ago, during that final spell in prison. As he rested his hands on it now, they obscured most of the page, but I could see the awkward handwriting at the top.

To Dad.

The picture that James Palmer had drawn for his father was visible at the bottom. Three stick figures standing side by side. The smallest one was holding what looked like an orange smudge. And beside the three of them, a Christmas tree, with little colored fairy lights dotted everywhere in the branches.

Thirty-Eight

Despite my best intentions, I was late.

I parked outside the gates of the cemetery, and then walked quickly through its streets, following the directions my father had given to me. In an ideal world, I would have met him at the entrance, and we would have walked in together, but in some ways, it was comforting to arrive after the fact. Because as I reached the grave and saw my father standing there alone, it was possible to imagine that a throng of people had been here a few minutes ago, and had dispersed and drifted away after the short ceremony was over. In reality, it would just have been my father. But it was nice to be able to pretend that there had been a crowd.

As he heard my footsteps, he turned a little awkwardly, holding his arm against his body. He was still recovering from the wounds Aspinall inflicted on him that night—to the extent that he ever would. His arm had been out of the sling for a few months now, but he hadn't regained anything close to full movement, and the doctors had warned him that he might not.

The past few months had aged him more than it felt like they should have. Part of that was down to an inability to exercise, which I knew had frustrated him beyond words. Certainly, he hadn't been able to hit anything all this time. But it was also difficult to escape the feeling that his whole life had been spent fighting, enduring, *carrying on*, and that now—finally—he was allowing himself to relax a little.

While he appeared older, he also looked happier.

"I'm sorry I'm late," I said.

"That's okay." He smiled. "You got here in the end."

I looked down at the grave in front of us.

Most of the plots in this part of the cemetery were old, the grass bedraggled and barely tended, the headstones simple and cheap. For many years, this grave had been identical to its neighbors. But today, it was a rectangle of freshly turned brown earth. The plain headstone that marked the plot previously had been replaced by a new one, commissioned and paid for by my father and me, made of white marble that glinted in the winter sun.

I read the inscription there now.

ABIGAIL PALMER

6 MARCH 1970–AUGUST 1998

JAMES PALMER

9 JUNE 1986–AUGUST 2001

WE SEE. WE CARE.

"Was the ceremony suitably delightful?" I said.

"No. The priest said far too many words."

I detected a familiar grumble of disapproval in his voice. My father had never had much time for the trappings of organized religion.

But his tone mellowed slightly when he spoke again.

"But yes, it was nice," he said. "Have you brought it?"

"Of course I have."

I walked around the side of the grave and put the stuffed toy lion down in front of the headstone. It wasn't the same one that was found at the beach after James Palmer went missing, but there was a photograph of that in the coroner's file, and I'd done my best to source the closest possible substitute I could find.

After a moment, my father looked at me.

"Are you still coming back to the island tonight?"

"Yes." I frowned slightly. "I mean—as long as that's okay?"

He turned away again.

"Of course it is. I was just checking."

"Then yes," I said. "Of course I am."

We stood there in silence for a time, both of us absorbed by our own memories and feelings. But the breeze was cold, and after a while my father began shivering. I was about to suggest that we leave when I realized that he was waiting me out without wanting to say so. That he wanted a moment here by himself for reasons of his own.

"See you back at the car?" I suggested.

"You will."

I headed off. But I turned back as I reached the corner, and I saw that my father was still standing there, lost in thought. But rather than looking at the grave like I expected, he was staring at a small copse of trees in the distance. And because it was still so unpredictable what he could do with his arm, what happened next might have been my imagination.

But I thought he raised his hand slightly.

When we get back home, my father makes us dinner, and we share a bottle of red wine while we eat. Then I go up to the attic to get changed. As I'm putting on a jumper, I hear his footsteps on the stairs, and then he knocks on the door.

"It's open," I say.

He pokes his head round.

"Want to sit out back for a bit?" he says. "I can put the heater on."

I brush the front of my jumper down.

"Normally I would say yes," I tell him. "But I think I might actually head out for a few hours, if that's okay?"

"Of course. Just don't wake me up if you get back late."

"I won't."

"And say hello for me."

I resist the instinct to look at him.

"I've no idea what you're talking about," I say. "Old man."

It's a cold, clear night, with no clouds to hide the prickling of stars in the sky. My breath steams in front of me beneath the amber streetlights as I walk. The seafront by the ferry terminal is brightly lit and busy for out of season, but the world grows quieter and darker as I follow the coastal road around. I see the bar up ahead and hear her voice at the same time.

The place is almost empty—just the same handful of elderly regulars as the first time I came in. I grab a beer, and then sit quietly at the back, watching as Sarah finishes up the song. She's lost in the moment, pitch-perfect, the disco ball turning slowly above her.

She looks like a star.

There's a little applause at the end, which I join in with as she gives an ostentatious bow. A moment later, she looks down the bar and notices me sitting there. We hold each other's gaze for a couple of seconds, and then she walks over.

In the time it takes her to reach my table, a number of things go through my head. The most immediate is that I can't remember the last time I was as nervous as I am right now. When I've ever felt this vulnerable and exposed, or when my heart was beating quite so hard.

"Hey there, stranger," she says.

"Hey there."

And then I release a breath I've been holding for so very long.

"I was thinking about that duet," I say.

Acknowledgments

Thank you so much to Joel Richardson and Ryan Doherty for their patience, expertise, and support. As always, this book is so much better because of your editorial advice and encouragement. And a massive thank-you—for all those things—to my wonderful agent, Sandra Sawicka, and to Leah Middleton and everyone else at Marjacq.

I also have to thank a number of other people who have helped in various ways along this book's long road to publication: Susie Brustin, Rachel Chou, Lucy Beresford-Knox, Riana Dixon, Anna Belle Hindenlang, Grace Long, Jaime Noven, Emily Radell, Rebecca Ritchey, Frances Sayers, and Faith Tomlin. Thank you to Will Staehle for a beautiful US cover, and also to Lauren Wakefield for an equally gorgeous UK cover. Thank you to Sarah Day and Justine Gardner; after so many drafts, it becomes hard to see the forest for the trees, and I'm indebted to you both for pointing out the tangles in the undergrowth. And I'm painfully aware that this list is incomplete. As with every novel, there will be people who contributed without my knowing, and I am grateful to every single one of you.

The crime fiction community is famous for being open and welcoming, and I've been lucky to have the friendship and support of so many writers along the way. Thank you all for the advice and the laughter, with a special mention to Colin Scott on both counts. Thanks are also due to all the booksellers, librarians, book groups, event organizers, podcasters, and reviewers who have been so kind to me over the years. And perhaps most important of all, thank you to the readers who have enjoyed the previous novels. I really hope you like this one too.

Finally, a huge thank-you to my family. Lynn and Zack, thank you putting up with me. This one is dedicated to you both with gratitude and love. They all are.

About the Author

Alex North is the internationally bestselling author of *The Angel Maker*, *The Shadows*, and *The Whisper Man*. He lives in Leeds, England, with his wife and son, and is a British crime writer who has previously published under another name.